'A remarkable achievement that expertly blends pathos and humor ... comparisons to *One Flew Over the Cuckoo's Nest* are obvious and warranted, but Kirshenbaum's dazzling novel stands on its own as a crushing work of immense heart.'
Publishers Weekly

'Kirshenbaum has excelled at capturing one woman's disturbing mental illness and the daily struggles to cope with survival even in a setting that supposedly offers support and rehabilitation.' *Library Journal*

'Kirshenbaum is a remarkable writer of fiercely observed fiction and a bleak, stark wit; her latest novel is as moving as it is funny, and that – truly – is saying something.' *Kirkus Reviews*

'In her first novel in a decade, Kirshenbaum reclaims her scepter as a shrewdly lacerating comedic writer, joining Sylvia Plath, Ken Kesey, Will Self, Ned Vizzini, Siri Hustvedt and others in writing darkly funny and incisive fiction about life in a psychiatric hospital ward.' *Booklist*

BINNIE KI... ...llection
History on a P... ...*ermaid*
Avenue, ... and
The Scenic Route. Her novels have been chosen as Notable Books of the Year by the *Chicago Tribune*, *NPR*, *TIME*, the *San Francisco Chronicle* and *Washington Post*. Her work has been translated into seven languages.

Rabbits for Food **was a** *New York Times* **Notable Book for 2019 and an** *NPR* **Best Book of the Year**

'Binnie Kirshenbaum is an unflinching teller of truths. She's also sublimely funny. *Rabbits for Food* shows this immensely gifted writer at the height of her powers.' Jenny Offill

'Binnie Kirshenbaum has hit her considerable stride in *Rabbits for Food*. This novel is compulsive reading; it's wonderfully paced, explosively funny and witty and very, very wise about many grave things – but mostly about merely being human.' Richard Ford

'Kirshenbaum doesn't trivialize mental breakdown. She makes Bunny's debilitation raw and worrying, and not without its insights.' Lucy Ellmann, author of *Ducks, Newburyport*

'A joy-giving and hilarious letter from the realm of despair. Also, somehow, a gentle love story. Marvelous and beautiful.' Rivka Galchen

'Kirshenbaum's portrait of intractable depression is acerbic, heartbreaking and improbably hilarious.' *People*

Rabbits for Food

Binnie Kirshenbaum

This paperback edition published in 2020

First published in Great Britain in 2019 by Serpent's Tail,
an imprint of Profile Books Ltd
29 Cloth Fair
London EC1A 7JQ
www.serpentstail.com

First published in the United States of America in 2019 by Soho Press, Inc.

Interior design by Janine Agro, Soho Press, Inc.

1 3 5 7 9 10 8 6 4 2

Printed and bound in Great Britain by
CPI Group (UK) Ltd, Croydon CR0 4YY

A CIP catalogue record for this book is available from the British Library.

ISBN 978 1 78816 466 5
eISBN 978 1 78283 664 3

Anthony, Ferne, Isaac, Lucie, Newton, and Susan

Carorum meus, ego te requiro

Rabbits for Food

Part 1

Waiting for the Dog

THE DOG IS LATE, AND I'm wearing pajamas made from the same material as Handi Wipes, which is reason enough for me to wish I were dead. I'm expecting this dog to be a beagle, a beagle dressed in an orange dayglow vest the same as the orange dayglow vests worn by suitcase-sniffing beagles at the airport. To expect that the do-gooder dog will be the same breed of dog wearing the same outfit worn by narco-dogs no doubt reveals the limitations of my imagination.

On the opposite wall from where I sit is the Schedule of Activities board. The board is white, and the Activities are written in black marker across a seven-day grid. Seven days, just in case I want to plan ahead, map out my week. Next to the board is the clock, one of those schoolroom-type clocks, which moves time as if through sludge. That's it. There's nothing else to look at other than the blue slipper-socks on my feet. Shoes with laces are *Not Allowed*. Other shoes *Not Allowed* are shoes with high heels or even kitten heels, as if a kitten heel could do damage, which is why I'm wearing the blue slipper-socks. Slipper-socks with rubber chevrons on the soles. Chevrons are *V*-shaped, but the *V* is upside-down. The slipper-socks also come in dung-colored brown.

A partial list of other things *Not Allowed* includes: pencils, nail clippers, laptops, cell phones, vitamins, mouthwash, and mascara.

It doesn't take long to grow bored by my slipper-socks, and I turn my attention back to the clock. The second hand stutters, fffffffifty-one, fffffffifty-two. *A watched pot never boils.* My mother used to say that, that a watched pot never boils. Also, *every cloud has a silver lining, tomorrow is another day*, and *time heals all wounds*. Words of comfort that invariably resulted in a spontaneous combustion of rabid adolescent rage. One of the nurses, the tall one, tall and skinny, gangly not graceful—Ella, her name is Ella—walks by, and then as if she'd forgotten something, she pauses, pivots and retraces her steps. "Mind if I join you?" she asks. To sit on the bench, Ella has to fold herself as if her arms and legs were laundry.

In stark contrast to the rest of her, Ella's head is round like a ball; bigger than a baseball and smaller than a basketball, but that's the shape. Exactly like a ball. She's like a stick figure come to life, having stepped out from that ubiquitous Crayola crayon-on-paper drawing, the one with the three stick figures and a tree and a square house with a triangular roof set like a hat at a jaunty angle. From the upper left-hand corner, a giant yellow sun warms this lopsided two-dimensional world. No doubt it's some standard developmental thing, that most children draw the same crap picture at the same crap-picture stage of life. Except for the prodigies and the children who are already fucked up. With the fucked-up ones you get a different picture, something along the same lines, but with the house on fire or the stick figures missing their heads. The prodigy, as young as the age of four, will draw a split-level house with gray shingles, and in the foreground, beneath a maple tree in autumn, a dog frolics in a pile of leaves. I know this for a fact because my sister, the older one, Nicole, was a prodigy in art although later she did not live up to her potential, assuming there was potential and her talent was not one of those things kids simply outgrow, the way my younger sister, the third of us three girls, was born with allergies to milk and wool among other things, which she outgrew at puberty.

Ella and I sit here on the bench as if the two of us are in this together, as if we are both waiting for the dog, but then Ella says, "You know what, hon? I don't think the dog is coming today." Ella calls everyone "hon." I'm not special, which is one of the things that about kills me from the hurt of it, that I'm not special.

And worse than the hurt of not being someone special is the shame of it, the shame of how much I want that, to be someone special.

The dog is supposed to be here. It says so on the Activities Board. Mondays and Thursdays from 10 A.M. to noon: Pet Therapy (Dog).

"He didn't come on Monday, either," I say, and the sorrow I experience about the dog not showing up is way out of proportion to the fact of it, but that is why I'm here, isn't it? Because the sorrow I feel about everything is bigger than the thing itself?

At home, Albie and I have a cat who is almost, but not quite, two years old. A rescue. Literally. A man found him in a brown paper bag in a trash can on Third Avenue and Sixty-First Street. A kitten tossed into the garbage as if a kitten were a banana peel. We named him Jeffrey, and on his first day in his new home, he trailed after me the way a duckling follows its mother, or the way a puppy would've trotted at my heels. "I know he looks like a cat," I said, "but I think he might be a dog."

The following morning after Albie left for work, I got out of bed, as it was my habit to start my day alone. Here, now, in this place, there is no such thing as alone, which would drive me out of my mind, if I weren't already out of my mind. Jeffrey raced to follow me to the kitchen where I put fresh food in his dish and clean water in his bowl. Down on one knee alongside him, I gave him a scratch behind the ears and kissed him on the top of his soft little head before getting up to take a shower.

It was only after I'd rinsed the shampoo from my hair, when I opened my eyes, that I found Jeffrey there, at my feet, in the shower, looking up at me as if mildly confused: Why are we getting ourselves wet on purpose? I scooped him up into my arms and turned away from the shower spray to cuddle him, to shelter him from the storm raging at my back. In the telling and re-telling of this episode, I would leave out the last part and let the story be about nothing other than a goofy kitten's extreme cuteness.

Ella suggests that we give up on the dog for now, that I join some other Activity. "So, what do you think, hon? How about Arts and Crafts?"

On Monday when the dog didn't show up, I went to Arts and Crafts.

Activities are not exactly mandatory but, as Dr. Fitzgerald made clear from the get-go, the road to mental health is paved with Activities such as Painting with Watercolors, Board Games, Origami, Spirituality, Yoga, or even worse—Sing-along, for example.

"Positive interaction within a group is a strong indication of mental health." Dr. Fitzgerald could not stress enough the importance of social engagement with the other lunatics.

Even at my mental-healthy best, I'm not one for Activities. Positive interaction within a group has never been much part of my social experience. "It's not just now," I tried to explain. "Please," I said. Please, the *please* subverted an assertion into a request, as if I were asking a favor, as if I were begging.

I do not want to go to Arts and Crafts again. The Arts and Crafts therapist clearly believes that a troubled mind is a simple mind, that to be clinically depressed is the same thing as to be a congenital idiot. In Arts and Crafts on Monday, we glued mosaic tiles to a square piece of wood to make the exact same whatever-the-fuck-it-was that I made in arts and crafts class in the third grade. Even in the third grade, I knew that this was something only a demented person would want, and sure enough, the obese loon sitting next to me asked if she could have mine. That night after dinner, when Albie came to visit, I told him, "I made something for you in Arts and Crafts, but one of the crazy people stole it."

As if perhaps there is something she's overlooked, Ella concentrates on the Activities Board. She has overlooked nothing. She knows what choices remain: Creative Writing or Jigsaw Puzzles.

Granted, I am clinically depressed but I'm not *that* depressed, so low as to go with Jigsaw Puzzles, and Creative Writing—you've got to be kidding me.

Prompt: An Introduction (300 words or less)

Bunny

Funny Bunny

Bugs Bunny

Bunny Wabbit

Honey Bunny

Easter Bunny

Fucks like a Bunny

Bunny Bunny Punkinhead

Voyage to the Bunny Planet

Playboy Bunny

Ski Bunny

Beach Bunny

Dumb Bunny

Dust Bunny

Energizer Bunny

Echo and the Bunnymen

Bunny Lake is Missing

Bunny Hop

Fluff Bunny

Bunny

Where to Begin

DECEMBER 31, 2008. ALL TOO often paper hats are involved. Other things about New Year's Eve that mortify Bunny are false gaiety, mandatory fun and that song, the one that's like the summer camp song. Not "Kumbaya," but that other summer camp song, the secular one, where everyone links arms and they sway as they sing, "Friends, friends, friends, we will always be." It's not that song either, but the New Year's Eve song also requires arm linking and swaying and it sentimentalizes friendship with an excessive sweetness that is something like the grotesquerie of baby chicks dyed pink for Easter. The overplayed enthusiasm for the passing of time, the hooting and hugging at the stroke of midnight baffles her, as does the spastic rejoicing to be that much closer to old or dead, as if old or dead were something to be won, like a three-legged race or *American Idol*. The only way Bunny knows to keep safe from the countdown New Year's Eve is to lock herself in the bathroom and wait for the fanfare to fizzle out like the silvery sparks of a Catherine wheel.

But there is time yet.

It's still morning, and although her eyes are closed they might as well be open, the way she knows Albie is there at the foot of the couch, looking down at her, just as she knows that he is wearing blue jeans, a pair faded from wear—never pre–faded or stone-washed or anything but 505 Levi's—and a light blue button-down oxford shirt, one of the same Brooks Brothers button-down oxford shirts he's been wearing since he turned twelve. For thirty-three years he's been wearing the same make and style shirt, although there has been variation in the color. That is, if you consider white to be a color. On his feet are rubber beach slippers. Not flip-flops, but rubber slippers with two wide straps that crisscross; rubber slippers that are generally worn at the beach by skinny old men in plaid swim trunks whose perfectly round bellies protrude as if they'd swallowed a honeydew melon whole, the way a snake swallows a rodent whole, and you can see, all too clearly, the shape of the mouse until it is digested. When a python swallows an alligator or a person, such as that fourteen-year-old boy in Indonesia, the shape of the meal is sharply defined for days or weeks. This is one of those things she wouldn't have minded not knowing, and it's not an easy thing to forget. Even now, when there is much that she forgets, she remembers that if an anaconda eats your dog, the outline of your dog will be visible for far too long. Although Albie's belly does not protrude like a honeydew melon, he has developed a hint of a paunch, just a hint but, coupled with the rubber slippers, it is enough to distress her. Then again, what doesn't distress her? Well aware that when she opens her eyes, she will find him dressed exactly as pre-dicted, and for the duration of a flashbulb popping, she will hate him for his predictability, and for the forlorn irrevocability that accompanies a solid marriage, a marriage that requires no effort, which is meaningful disappointment only if you stop to give it some real thought, if you stop to give it, like the rubber slippers, more attention than it deserves.

"I'm awake," Bunny says.

To sit beside her, Albie needs to sidestep one of the five or six stacks of books on the floor. Books stacked without a plan, just as the books in the floor-to-ceiling bookshelves are arranged carelessly. His books. Her books. The books she reads, as opposed to *her* books, as in books she has written. Those, the many remaindered copies of them, are in boxes and, like all bogeymen, they are hidden under the bed.

Albie doesn't write books. He publishes articles and papers in magazines like the *Journal of Natural History* and *Animal Ecology* but, for him, public recognition has no bearing on the pleasure he derives from his work. He is freakishly well-adjusted. The books that are his, those he reads, are an eclectic and, unless you know Albie, an irrational lot. Aside from zoology and its related fields, his interests include cartography, game theory, phila-telic history, ancient Greek poetry, and magic tricks, among other super-nerd subject matter, although—the rubber slippers excepted—Albie is not a super-nerd person. Not even when he was a teenager, but that could be because he went to Stuyvesant High School where geeky boys are considered dreamy.

Bunny's range of interests is also varied: history, politics, antiques, animal rights, psychology, fashion, and literature, *serious* literature, although now she is interested in nothing.

Seating himself on the edge of the couch parallel to her hip, Albie keeps some inches of distance between them, the way you'd keep a few inches back from the edge of a cliff, and he asks, "Did you get any sleep?"

Sleep has never come easily to her, but until recently the drugs worked well enough. But now, two or even three times the prescribed dose brings her no closer to drifting off at night like a normal person. Often, she doesn't fall asleep until dawn, and from there, she'll sleep away the day, the entire day. You'd think that ten, twelve, thirteen hours of sleep would be restorative, but hers is sleep that keeps to the surface, as if she were floating on a rubber raft in a pool. However relaxing that might sound, to sleep, to really sleep, is not to float on the surface, but to be deep down near the ocean's floor.

On other nights, nights like last night, when she does manage to fall asleep before the sun comes up, the sleep is fragmented, interrupted by spates of waking and restlessness. It was the waking, the restlessness, and weeping in distress that had cut into Albie's sleep, too. Despite that weeping wants an audience, it was never her intention to wake him. To cry when no one can hear you could well belong in the category Bunny calls "Wow Thoughts for Stupid People," like the sound of one hand clapping. But unintentional or not, there came a night when Albie woke yet again to the ugly noises of his wife's despair, and he snapped, "Shut up. Will you please just shut the hell up," at which point Bunny took her pillow and went to sleep, or went to try to sleep, on the couch where a few hours later she put the same pillow over her face to block out the relentless morning sunlight. There she stayed until late afternoon when the sun was less aggressive. On her way to the bathroom, she cut through the kitchen where she found a pot of coffee kept warm but gone stale, and a blueberry muffin from Carol Anne's, her favorite bakery, on a plate next to a note that wasn't really a note. It was a lopsided heart and *xoxo Albie* scribbled on a torn-off corner of a brown paper bag. She wasn't hungry, but because it was there and because Albie meant well, she broke off a piece of the muffin. In her mouth it tasted like an apple going bad, without flavor and mealy.

What Time Is It

BUNNY SITS UP, BUT NOT *up* up. Her feet are not on the floor, but her back is resting against the arm of the couch, which is camel-backed, olive green velvet. What had passed for shabby chic at the time of purchase is now the furniture equivalent of a dog with mange. The upholstery is shredded, puffs of stuffing stick out like Albert Einstein's hair. When Jeffrey had commandeered the couch as his scratching post, neither Albie nor Bunny had it in them to chastise the little idiot for what he couldn't possibly understand. Also, Bunny's been occupying much of her time pulling at the fabric's loose threads. Her legs are stretched out and covered by the blanket as if they were useless, and she says, "Some. I slept some."

It's been over a week since Bunny last showered or changed the T-shirt she is wearing, which reeks of sweat and fear and emits a vapor which Bunny pictures as a visible fume of noxious gas, like the way a bad smell is depicted in cartoons. But her unpleasant odor is not why Albie chooses to sit more or less parallel to her hip with the three or four inches of couch cushion between them. It's because sometimes when he touches her, even accidentally, she flinches. It's not him in particular. She'd flinch no matter who touched her, but Albie is the only one with opportunity. It's been many weeks, maybe months since she's seen anyone other than Albie. And Jeffrey. Because it's incomprehensible to their goofy cat that a snuggle might not be welcome, he jumps onto the couch where he winds his way into the unoccupied inches of space between Albie and Bunny, as if that space were there purposefully, intended for him. Albie strokes the cat's ears and asks, "How much is some?"

"I don't know," Bunny says. "What time is it now?"

Albie checks his watch. "It's nine twenty-one." He cannot help but to be exact. Bunny, however, is an approximator. Piecing together the segments, the snippets of sleep, she calculates, "Four hours. Give or take," she says.

Albie leans in closer to his wife seeming like he is going to lift a few stray strands of hair away from her face, except he's about to do no such thing. "About tonight," he says. "You know we can cancel. It's no big deal."

"I know," Bunny says, which brings them to a lull in the conversation, such as it is a conversation. Jeffrey's purring fills the void. His purr is unusually loud for a house cat, more like the purr you'd expect from a tiger, but Jeffrey is decidedly not a tiger. He is more like a battery-operated toy. His purr hums warm against Bunny's hip, the sound waves ripple. His whole body vibrates, including his tail.

"Four hours is hardly a good night's sleep," Albie says.

"Maybe we should stay home. Get some rest. Because if you'd rather not go, I'll call Julian. No big deal."

"What time is it?" Bunny asks.

"Nine twenty-three." Albie does not point out that she'd asked the same question when it was nine twenty-one because, as if the previous two minutes never happened, he too, although not word for word, repeats himself. "I'd be just as happy to stay home."

It's true. As far as he's concerned, New Year's Eve is no big whoop, which might seem out of character if you knew the incident about the odometer flip; about how as a small boy sitting in the passenger's seat of his father's infrequently used Volvo while driving to Far Rockaway, the odometer turned from 9,999 miles to 10,000, and Albie nearly passed out from the thrill of it. His father had to pull off to the side of the road for Albie to breathe in and out of a paper bag. But the flipping of the calendar page from one year to the next does not elicit even a remotely similar effect. But neither does New Year's Eve disturb him the way it disturbs Bunny.

Second to New Year's Eve, Bunny's most loathed holiday is Thanksgiving. She used to loathe Christmas, too, but that changed after she and Albie got married. Although Albie is Jewish, they celebrate Christmas, albeit in their own, irreligious, somewhat screwy way, which has to do with gifts, pancakes, *Santa Baby*, and old Japanese horror movies. But the only holiday Bunny will claim any real affection for is Arbor Day because it has a purpose, which has value. Also, it's free of

tradition and not burdened with memories. It's not even cel-
ebrated, really.

Last year, last New Year's Eve, she'd said to him, "You know,
I'd really rather stay at home and drink Clorox." But that was
last year. This year, she would say no such thing. This year, to
indulge in the kick of a joke or the pleasure of hyperbole is to risk
being taken at her word.

Yet, despite knowing that she will experience only despair
and regret, every year she forges ahead with the New Year's Eve
celebrations as planned. The plans for tonight are the same as
they were last year and the same as 2006, 2005, and 2004, too: a
vaguely unpleasant dinner with Trudy, Elliot, Julian and Lydia
before heading off to the Frankenhoffs' after-party to watch the
ball drop, which is the worst part of the night.

Dinner out with friends is something they do frequently,
which does not mean that it's easy. First, there is the *when* of
it. They are busy people, their friends, with many dinners on
their dance cards. A good amount of back-and-forth is required
before they can locate a night mutually free of prior engage-
ments and other obligations. Then, where to go? *Where* they
have dinner is important, important the way a matter of life and
death is important because at the next dinner out the previous
dinner will be a significant topic of conversation. The dinner
itself, the food, will have been either exquisite or overrated and
the wine list excellent, although sometimes insufficient, but,
always, the conversation is smart and warm and delightful, and
what could be bad about that?

But, still. One night, nearly a year ago, they had dinner with Nathan and Philip. They are very fond of Nathan and Philip, though they were far from keen on the restaurant. *Aviary*, it was called, because the menu was all about freshly killed birds. The bird Philip ate was served with its feet and head, with the beak attached. On their way home Bunny said, "A fucking beak, and he ate it." Even Albie, a zoologist at the Museum of Natural History, and therefore no stranger to dead birds with their parts intact, had to admit, "That was a little rough." After that, nothing, not one word, passed between them until they got home. Then, while hanging up her coat, Bunny said, "If I have one more delightful dinner with delightful people engaging in delightful conversation, I am going to scream. I am going to scream and scream and never stop. I will die screaming."

Albie sat on the edge of the bed to take off his shoes. "What's wrong with a lovely dinner with lovely people?"

Either there was no explanation or not one that she could articulate. At a loss, she said, "*Delightful*. I said *delightful*. Not *lovely*. *Delightful*."

"And the difference," Albie asked, "is what?"

Prompt: A Favorite Song (300 words or less)

From the kitchen window I could see only an opaque apparition of myself backlit by an unsettling yellow halo from the overhead light. It was like déjà vu. I could not remember when or where I'd encountered this same apparition of myself in a kitchen window before, except that it was now familiar and unsettling, like a memory from a past life. Except I don't believe in past lives, or after lives, either. I believe that this is it. This is my only life. During the day, from that window there is a view of a courtyard where the trash bins are kept, and there is a bicycle rack, too. I do not have a bicycle. In the summer months, wispy bits of grass and weeds sprout from the cracks in the concrete, but never enough to be inspiring, and it isn't summer anyway. The trash bins are earmarked: Garbage, Bottles & Cans, and Paper like laundry sorted into Whites, Darks, and Delicates, each to be washed separately. Sorting the trash makes me feel good about myself, as if I were to be lauded for doing my bit to combat global warming, and never mind that sorting the trash is city mandated, nor is global warming the accurate term, or even the preferred

term, for climate change. Nonetheless, I call it global
warming because I picture it in images of polar bears
set adrift on melting ice floes, or birds nesting in
the wrong season and then waiting in vain for their
eggs to hatch, or migrating butterflies that wind up
freezing to death. Global warming is one of the world's
wrongs that I care about deeply, except for times like
this when all I care about is sleep, and also there are
those times when I care about nothing, nothing at all.

It could've been that I woke up because I had to cry,
the same way people wake up when they have to pee.

Two amber-colored vials from the pharmacy were
paired on the kitchen counter like salt and pepper
shakers. Lunesta 'n' Ambien. With the help of one or
the other or both, I might've dropped off to sleep—not
drifted off, but dropped off like a drunk passing out. But
I wouldn't have slept for long. Two or three hours, tops.
The Lunesta tablets were blue, and the Ambien were
white. I alternated. Two Lunesta on one night; Ambien
on the next. I did this to prevent building up tolerance to
one or the other of them, but I need not have bothered.
Neither of them worked for shit. I decided to take one and
a half of each, which made me think of that song, that
one about *Alice in Wonderland*, or maybe it was *Through
the Looking Glass*, whichever, it was about Alice popping pills. It's not a song from my generation, but I know
it was Jefferson Airplane. Grace Slick and Jefferson

Airplane. Gracie Slick. Imagine having a name like
Gracie Slick.

In the kitchen drawer where we kept scissors,
Band-Aids and kitchen matches, we also kept the
gizmo for cutting pills down the middle. The gizmo
worked like a guillotine.

And the Red Queen's off with her head.

What Is Known

TONIGHT, NEW YEAR'S EVE 2008, they are going to the Red Monkey for dinner. The same as every year, it was Julian who chose the restaurant, made the reservations, arranged that they get a decent table. A freelance food critic, Julian writes for some reasonably popular magazines, although his reviews are most often sidebars, and he doesn't always get a byline. Nonetheless, he is afforded what *he* calls a personal relationship with hotshot chefs and gatekeeping maître d's. That he gets paid in pennies for his efforts is irrelevant because Lydia, his wife, is rich. No one in Lydia's family, going back three generations, ever had a job. Instead, they sat on boards for ballet companies and small museums and they studied things like Chinese brush painting and Sanskrit, and Lydia, holding fast to family tradition, is on the board of an off-Broadway theater that does interpretations of plays by Chekov and Ibsen, and she does a lot of Pilates.

The Red Monkey, Julian had reminded them, is a known restaurant, which left Bunny no choice, as far as she could help it, but to put the word in air quotes. "Known." A relic from the era when like-minded uber-snooty restaurants were, for all intents and purposes, closed to the public, until without warning or explanation, poof! over, *so* over, but the Red Monkey held on. Although hardly what it was in its '80s heyday—for example, the phone number is now listed—*The* Monkey, as Julian calls it, remains sufficiently attitudinarian that to score a reservation for New Year's Eve means that you are famous, in the New York way of famous, which means you're not necessarily someone recognized on the street, but in certain circles, your name is "known." That, or else you know the chef.

Albie can't imagine this dinner being anything but difficult. At best, difficult. At worst, a scene. A scene. He tries to reason with his wife. "Four hours of sleep? How could you possibly enjoy yourself on four hours of sleep? You're going to be exhausted."

"I want to go." Bunny enunciates each word emphatically. I. Want. To. Go.

"But why?" Albie asks. "Why do you want to go?"

"Because they are our friends, and dinner with them is a New Year's Eve tradition." She, who mocks tradition, scoffs at family rituals, hides away in closets from time-honored practices—such a statement is practically aphasic in its incomprehensibility. Even Bunny knows it is a crackpot response. "And I'm trying to be normal."

Albie wishes he could tease her, tell her to give it up because she'll never be normal. He wishes he could say that he loves her just as she is, but he's not sure if it's true; not as she is, not as she is now. Instead, he suggests, "Maybe later you can take a nap."

Last year, midway through their New Year's Eve dinner, Bunny, impatient and desperate for a cigarette, got up from the table saying, "Excuse me. I need my fix." With Albie's sports jacket draped over her shoulders, she braved the cold for a Camel Light. In the relative quiet of the out-of-doors, relative to the clamor and clatter of the restaurant, it was with the clarity and intensity of hyperrealism that she was struck by a thought: *I cannot stomach those people*. It was an uncomfortable thought because, except for Stella—Stella who was like a sister had she been able to choose a sister, a sister she loved—*those people* were her closest friends. It did not feel good to acknowledge that her closest friends were people she could not stomach. But that wasn't quite right. She *did* like them. She *did*. It was only that she wished she liked them more. She wished she liked them a lot. Done with her cigarette, she ground out the remains with the heel of her shoe, and readied herself to return to the restaurant to rejoin her husband and their closest friends for dinner on New Year's Eve.

The Embarrassments of Suffering

THE CAT STRETCHES HIS NECK, and Albie scratches him under the chin. If only Bunny were more like Jeffrey. Or even a little bit like Jeffrey. "How about some breakfast?" Albie asks. "There are bagels in the freezer. I can scrape the mold off the cream cheese." He hardly expects Bunny to laugh at what is a pale attempt at humor under any circumstances, yet he has hopes for a droll ha-ha or even a half smile, but Bunny only says, "I'm not hungry."

"Coffee, then? What about a cup of coffee?"

"No," she says. "Not now. Maybe later."

Every day Albie tells her it would be a good thing if she were to get dressed and go out for a walk, and every day she says, "Not now. Maybe tomorrow."

Now, seemingly apropos of nothing unless you're privy to her state of mind, Bunny wants to know, "What's that animal? The one that curls itself into a ball?" At that, on cue, Jeffrey gets up and does that cat thing, the walking in tight circles, counterclockwise, a ritualistic three times around, as if taking part in a druid divorce, before he settles down and curls into a ball.

Bunny shakes her head. "No, I mean as a defense mechanism. Against predators," she adds, unnecessarily. Her attempt to remember what surely she knows blinks like a light bulb loose in the socket, and her effort to recollect comes to her in an unrealized image that breaks into particles of dust before it can take form. She is certain that there *is* such an animal, but she can't come up with what it's called or what it looks like except she's pretty sure it has a tail.

Intermittent and short-term memory loss is symptomatic of her affliction: facts and dates elude her. She frequently drops the thread that pulls a thought through from beginning to conclusion, and words—not all words, but deeply desired words—vanish in a flash like lantern fish at the bottom of the ocean. She finds she can describe a scene, but the connective tissue needed to tell a story becomes white space, like lines skipped on the page.

Her affliction. Bunny does not know how else to phrase it, how to articulate what is wrong with her. Not what is wrong with her in the big picture, insofar as what is wrong with her personality. *That* she knows how to articulate; like a line memorized for the stage, Bunny will often say, "Generally speaking, I am a headache of a person who is not easy to like." It's true. Bunny is not easy to like, but it's possible to love her.

Although there is no chill in the room, Bunny pulls the blanket up to her chin. The blanket—Adirondack pine-tree green wool, coarse in texture similar to a hair shirt—is a blanket that she associates with the Girl Scouts. Not that Bunny ever *was* a Girl Scout or a Campfire Girl or a member of any other fascist or neo-fascist organization that requires wearing a uniform with a sash to display medals, ribbons, and badges. Lack of firsthand experience, however, plays no part in her formation of intractable ideas, one of which is that the Girl Scouts, a socially regimented youth group ripe for totalitarian indoctrination, spend their weekends goose-stepping along mountain trails. But, even for Bunny, to connect the Brownies to the Brown Shirts was pushing it, although it's never stopped her from mentioning—just mentioning, mind you—that brown is a curious choice of color for a uniform for little girls because, as far as children's tastes are concerned, well, there's a reason there are no brown balloons.

Pronouncements such as these are emblematic of problems with her personality. But contrarian disagreeability is irrelevant to this particular iteration of what is wrong with Bunny. Although she cannot bring herself to say so in these words, Bunny is suffering from depression. In reference to herself the inherent theatricality of the verb *to suffer* embarrasses her. In this context, *to suffer*, she believes, would be melodramatic and self-aggrandizing, not to mention rendering her a person empathetically stunted when you consider real suffering like starving to death or stage four colon cancer or a baby rhesus monkey given a wire coat hanger to cling to instead of a mother. To refer to herself as suffering would mean that, on top of everything else, she'd also be an asshole.

Of all the things that can go wrong with your mind, of all of the Oliver Sacks-ian mistaking your husband for a pair of mittens kinds of things, depression, even major depressive disorder, isn't likely to elicit much more than a yawn or a roll of the eyes. In fact, it could be said that there is nothing wrong with Bunny other than her indulging a penchant for self-pity. But if there isn't anything *really* wrong, then what *is* wrong with Bunny?

No matter what is wrong with Bunny, whatever you want to call it, one thing is certain—to be sick in the head is not at all the same as being normal sick. If you are normal sick, people will at least pretend to care. If you are normal sick, people will call or even stop by for a visit. They will offer to run errands for you, pick up orange juice and NyQuil; they will offer to bring you soup and banana smoothies; they will offer to walk your dog. They will say, "Please, let me know if there's anything I can do. Anything at all." Of course they are counting on you to take them up on none of it, but at least they go through the motions. Sometimes they send flowers. But no one has come to visit Bunny. No one has offered to bring her hot soup; no one has sent her so much as a Get Well card or a balloon, one of those Mylar balloons with a yellow happy face, and you can forget about a basket of fruit.

In all fairness, the bit about no one sending her a card, that is not entirely accurate. Although it wasn't exactly a Get Well card, less than two weeks ago, Lizzie Frank sent her an email:

Dear Bunny,

We all have bad days. You're not special. Pull up your pants and get over it.

XO Lizzie

PS Don't forget. New Year's Eve. We're expecting you.

Also to be fair, people do call Albie to ask how Bunny is feeling; what they won't do is call when Albie isn't home. No one wants to talk to Bunny. They are afraid to ask Bunny how she is feeling.

As to be expected in light of his profession, Albie knows about the ways of animals, their habits and habitats, their mating rituals, what they eat, and which ones have tails. He knows about their defense mechanisms, those that hide, those that run with the wind, and those that curl into a ball as a means of defense. In answer to Bunny's question he says, "The armored millipede, the hedgehog, the armadillo." Then, unable to resist, he gets carried away with himself about the armor of the armadillo. Overly effusive in his description of the plates of the dermal bone, he is waxing on about the horn-covered epidermal scales when Bunny cuts him off. "No," she says. "Not the armadillo."

Although Bunny has always been enthused, fascinated even, by what he knows, by what excites him in his field of study, her evident lack of interest now in dermal bones is to be expected. Expected, which doesn't mean there's not a nettle-like sting to it. But the sting subsides quickly, and Albie says, "Maybe you're thinking of the hedgehog. The hedgehog has quills that look like the quills of a porcupine, but they are hollow and don't easily detach." Before Albie can explain how the hedgehog curls into a tight ball, the quills, or spines, projecting outward, Bunny asks, "Would you make some coffee?"

Relief comes like the release of a coil. Albie springs up from the couch. "Colombian?" he offers her a choice. "Or French Mocha Java? We might still have some of that Sumatran blend left."

"I don't care," Bunny says, and when Albie is out of earshot, she says it again. "I don't care." And then softer, "I don't care," and softer still, *I don't care. I don't care. I don't care. I don't care. I don't care. Idon'tcareIdon'tcareIdon'tcare.* The words take on a perpetual motion of their own like Newton's pendulum, or the flow of a river, or the *om* of some pretend-Buddhist yahoo fraud. Bunny lacks the decency of tolerance when it comes to converts to Buddhism because her older sister is a pretend-Buddhist yahoo fraud. Bunny doesn't much care for her older sister, and she doesn't much care for her younger sister either, and the lack of affection is returned in kind.

Coffee Mugs

I DON'T CARE, AND THEN without any warning or preamble, no lump in her throat, no twitch of her lip, not the single sob that heralds the onset of a good cry, Bunny is weeping in the curious way she's been weeping as of late. Without sound, without so much as a sniffle, her face is impassive, her eyes open and her stare as blank as that of a glass-eyed doll. The tears come, not in teardrops that roll down her cheeks like raindrops on a windowpane, but like water when a faucet is turned on all the way. The copiousness of her tears is remarkable, and equally remarkable is how, snap! just like that, the tears stop. By the time Albie returns from the kitchen with two mugs of coffee, it's all over, as if there had been a sun shower, except without any sun.

"You made coffee?" Bunny says.

"You said you wanted coffee. Three minutes ago, you said you wanted coffee."

"I did? What time is it?"

Before he can check his watch, Albie sets the two coffee mugs on the coffee table, which isn't really a coffee table. It's an old steamer trunk that serves as a coffee table. "It's nine minutes past ten," he says, and he slides the ashtray, filled with tar-stained filters and ash and one cigarette that is broken in half, to the far end of the trunk. One of the mugs, the one Albie sets closest to Bunny, is a souvenir mug from St. Thomas, white industrial ceramic adorned with a blue sailboat. As if she were about to reach for it, which she is not, Albie says, "Be careful. It's hot."

Instead of seating himself again on the edge of the couch, Albie sits on the other side of the coffee table in one of two mismatched chairs that are arranged for easy conversation; not that he harbors any illusions of engaging in easy conversation. Hanging on the wall to his left is a professionally framed black-and-white photograph of children in ballet costumes that is, in fact, quite brilliant. Bunny got the photograph at the same thrift store as the pair of paint-by-numbers—swans on a lake—that hang vertically alongside the photograph. Also hanging on that wall are the two paintings—both bright swirls of textured colors—they bought years ago at a small gallery because the artist is a friend, which is to say they don't like the paintings, but they don't hate them, either. They also own a cuckoo-looking collage—a chicken drawn with crayon on a torn sheet of old newspaper, bits of fabric and string for feathers—which hangs in her office. Her office is the second bedroom in their two-bedroom, fourth-floor apartment. The other walls in the living room, floor to ceiling, are lined with bookshelves. Behind the chair where Albie is seated are three windows. The sheer white

curtains are no longer bright white. They never bought anything like a bedroom set or a dining room table with matching
chairs. All of their furniture and household goods—dishes and
silverware—were things picked up piecemeal at flea markets
and junk shops or low-end antique stores. Except for the fact
that it's a co-op, which they now own outright, having long
since paid off the mortgage, their apartment is emblematic of
the lack of maturity in the way that Bunny and Albie live their
lives. Bunny is forty-three years old; Albie is forty-five, but
there is little to indicate that adults live here, and not graduate
students. They don't own a car or a summerhouse or have
children. These deprivations, such as they are deprivations,
are by choice, and not the result of frugality. So what, then,
do they do with their money? They pay their bills; they make
monthly charitable donations; and after that, they pretty much
just piss it away.

Although she makes no move to reach for the coffee mug
emblazoned with the blue sailboat, Bunny eyeballs it with sus-
picion, hostility even, as if to say, "What is *that* doing on our
coffee table?" Neither she nor Albie—neither together nor
apart—have ever been to St. Thomas. For starters, Bunny has a
thing, a big thing, against sand, and Albie prefers not to go anywhere if *to go* includes staying overnight or flying. When Bunny
travels, sometimes for work, to give readings, to sit on panels,
or for pleasure because Bunny likes to see the world, she would
go with Stella or alone. Albie has always encouraged Bunny to
travel because he likes her to do whatever she wants to do, and

because he doesn't at all mind time to himself. Now, she asks about the coffee mug. "Where did that come from?"

In yet another attempt, needless to say in vain, to get Bunny to lighten up, Albie says, "St. Thomas." As if there were any light left in her, which there's not. Or, at least none in evidence.

"I meant here. Where was it?"

"I don't know," Albie says. "It was in the cabinet."

"Which cabinet?"

"The cabinet with all the other coffee mugs."

"Have we had it a long time?"

"I don't know." Albie is good man, but he is not a saint. He gets exasperated the same as anyone would. "It's a coffee mug. Who cares?"

It's a coffee mug. Who cares? There's no need to reply to what is a rhetorical question, but for the record—*he* cares, to the degree that his coffee mug is *his* coffee mug. Albie's coffee mug was a gift from Bunny, a Valentine's Day gift, a Valentine's Day gift from so long ago that the bright red hearts have faded to a pale pink, but he's been known to wander around the kitchen asking, "Where's my coffee mug? Did you see my coffee mug?" When Bunny would then take it from the dishwasher, Albie would be visibly relieved as if it were a critical document or something of great value that he thought he'd lost. Albie has no disdain for cheap sentiment when it's sincere.

Albie's a little nuts in his own right. But isn't everyone?

Bunny used to have her own coffee mug, one that was hers alone. One of those personalized ones, with your name on it.

Wildflowers against an all-black background except for the block of white where *Francine* was written in calligraphy with red glaze.

The *Francine* mug had been a birthday gift from her friend Stella. It came with a card that read: *You put the fun in dysfunctional.* Stella gave her this gift at least eight or nine years ago. Maybe even more. It broke one day in August. This past August, it broke.

To try to read the look on Bunny's face is like trying to figure out what a napkin is thinking.

"Dawn," Bunny says. "It was Dawn."

"What was Dawn? What about her?" Albie asks. Dawn is Bunny's sister. The younger one.

"They go to places like that, places with sand," Bunny says. "Family resorts," she emphasizes.

Although Bunny cannot remember what time it was six seconds ago, or what she had for lunch yesterday or the word "parachute" or the difference between a simile and a metaphor or her wedding anniversary or what year she graduated from high school or how old she was when her father died or who wrote *Of Time and the River* or the title of that Martin Amis novel that she adores, she somehow has managed to remember that it was Dawn who gave her the coffee mug from St. Thomas. Dawn and her husband have two children, a boy and a girl. Her husband owns a small surgical supply company, which is like a gift to Bunny who never tires of saying, "My sister's husband sells bedpans."

"Dawn gave me that coffee mug," Bunny says, and Albie responds, "It's the French Mocha Java."

Gift Giving

IN THE DINKY ST. THOMAS airport, not all that long ago, but when her children were still young enough to be excited by family vacations, it hit Dawn like a conk on the head: Although she remembered, as she always did, to get Nicole a gift, as sometimes happened, she clear forgot to get one for Bunny.

"Fuck Bunny," her husband said.

"Fuck Bunny, fuck Bunny," the kids chanted, rocking in their seats as if Fuck Bunny had an irrepressible beat to it.

The gift Dawn bought for Nicole, selected in deference to Nicole's worship of Planet Earth, was a bracelet made of sea glass. Chances were good that neither Dawn nor Nicole knew that sea glass is the by-product of littering. For Nicole's wife, Dawn bought a pair of sea glass earrings, and a sand dollar for their kid who was gravely disappointed to discover it was not a cookie, which was totally understandable because only twice in what, at that time, had been all of four years of life, had their kid ever had a cookie, both times at birthday parties not his own. At his birthday party, the kids got pita chips and hummus, which elicited, from Bunny, a surge of pity for the little boy. Nicole is a devoted mother, but she is similarly devoted to the folly that all things derived from the soil and the sea are healthy, exuberant with nutrients. Provided it was organically farmed, Nicole would drink a hemlock smoothie.

Bunny once let it drop that the lesbian couple who live next door to her also have a little boy, and that little boy is allowed to eat cookies. "I once saw the kid eating ice cream," Bunny said, and Nicole shook her head. "Not *all* lesbians are good mothers."

"You're missing the point," Bunny had said. "What I'm trying to say is that it's unlikely their kid will develop an eating disorder."

Bunny might've been lacking in sensitivity in the way she put it, but she did have evidence, clinical studies, to support the point she was trying to get across.

"Let it go," Albie had advised. "Science can't convert a true believer."

And Nicole is a true believer, as well as, according to Bunny, a true hypocrite, one who doesn't have time or money to spare for the Environmental Defense Fund or Greenpeace, to actively engage with the same issues that she will rail on about, because, according to Nicole, she is busy raising a child and climbing the ladder to Personal Enlightenment, which, as she describes it, sounds no different from a Scientologist reaching OT Level VIII. Nicole's claim is that her own spiritual growth, and that of her son and her Wiccan princess wife, will result in a better world for everyone.

"Right," Bunny had said. "You'll be in Nirvana and the rest of us will be munching on Soylent Green."

"Soylent Green?" Nicole didn't know about Soylent Green, and Bunny told her, "Kale. It's a kind of kale."

Because Dawn is a mother of *two* children, she's done with her contributions to society. Moreover, she has a lesbian sister whom she loves and whose approval she seeks, and isn't that proof enough that she is a good person?

The St. Thomas airport gift shop was bountiful with an array of trinkets that no one could possibly want: St. Thomas–embossed shot glasses, pencil boxes, souvenir spoons and thimbles. Dawn did think the Christmas tree ornaments—swordfish and dolphins wearing Santa hats—were kind of cute, but Bunny could get very snide when it comes to things that are cute. Dawn shelled out $14.98 for a two-dollar coffee mug, and fuck Bunny if she doesn't like it.

On those odd occasions when one or the other of her sisters would come to the city, Bunny would disrupt her day, an irritation unto itself, to meet Nicole at the Tea Retreat or to have coffee with Dawn at whichever Starbucks was most handy to where Dawn had parked her car. To sit down long enough to have a meal with either of her sisters would be to push the boundaries of tolerance, on both sides of the table. At the Starbucks on Sixth Avenue at Seventeenth Street, when Dawn was nearly done with her skim-milk latte and Bunny was swirling the dregs of her black coffee in the paper cup, the conversation running on fumes, both sisters eagerly anticipating their goodbyes, Dawn fished a cube-shaped box from her tote bag. "We got you a little something when we were in St. Thomas."

"When were you in St. Thomas?"

"Right after Christmas. I told you we were going. Don't you remember?"

"Apparently not." Bunny opened the white box. "A coffee mug," she said.

Other gifts from Dawn and her bedpan salesman husband included a set of wine glasses with a note *To Dawn and Michael, Happy Anniversary, Love, Melissa and Stephan* tucked inside the box. There were mezcal-flavored lollipops from Mexico. Last Christmas they gave Albie two books: *Secrets from the Egyptian Tombs,* and *Dangerous Dan: Memoirs of a Snake Trainer.* Bunny also got two books: *Fifty Strategies for Creating Characters* and *So, You Want to Write a Novel?*

"She meant well." Albie made excuses for her sister. "It's not malicious."

But what did Albie know? He was an only child and he was loved.

Bunny took the St. Thomas coffee mug from the box and said, "How thoughtful of you."

Dawn's smile was brittle, as if you could snap it in half, like a dry twig or a chicken bone. "I remembered that you drink coffee," she said.

"Yes," Bunny said. "We're in Starbucks. I do drink coffee." She turned the mug over in her hands, holding it out for her sister to see the sticker on the bottom. "Look at that. You bought it in St. Thomas, but it's made in China."

Dawn wasn't looking at the coffee mug; she was looking straight on at Bunny when she said, "And you wonder why we don't like you."

"Actually," Bunny said, "I don't wonder. Not at all."

Dawn grabbed her coat off the back of her chair, leaving Bunny alone at the table where, tearing off bits of her Starbucks paper cup, she stayed long enough for the sting to subside, and the need for Albie's comfort to pass. On those occasions when the last thing Bunny wants to hear is the truth, Albie does not equivocate. Bunny knew perfectly well what he'd say. He'd say, "Come on, Bunny. You asked for it."

No shit. Obviously she asked for it. That much she could admit. What she did not want to hear from Albie was why, *why* did she ask for it?

At home, the St. Thomas mug went in the cabinet with all the other coffee mugs, and until now, it had been forgotten. *And you wonder why we don't like you.*

Prompt: A Shoebox (300 words or less)

Erma Bombeck or Ann Landers, Dear Abby, Miss Manners, Garfield, Madame Blavatsky, Charlie Brown—one of those purveyors of wisdom in a can—whichever of them wrote this treacle in print, my mother clipped the column from the newspaper and left it on my bed, as if a newspaper clipping were a piece of foil-wrapped chocolate.

It was not unusual for my mother to cut columns from the newspaper or an article from some idiotic magazine to leave on my bed. Articles or pamphlets about Girl Scouting or quilting bees for teens, but I was not one for group activities. Then there was that spate of straight-from-the-heart-of-Hallmark greeting cards left there for no occasion other than *Just Because I Love You* or *I Love You Thiiiiiiisss Much*. I never knew what to say about those cards, and so I said nothing.

The title of this newspaper clipping read "*To the Middle Child.*"

Although titled "*To the Middle Child,*" it opened with the part *To the Firstborn*:

To the Firstborn—I've always loved you best because you were our first miracle. You were the fulfillment of young love. With you, we became a family. Nothing was ever as thrilling as your first smile and your first words. We cheered your first steps but we were afraid to let go of your hand. Your Baby Book was an encyclopedia, fully illustrated and annotated. You had more clothes than a Barbie doll.

There was more, but it was more of the same.

To the Middle Child—I've always loved you best because you drew the dumb spot in the family, and it made you stronger for it. You cried less. You had more patience. You wore faded clothes that were hand-me-downs. You were forgiving. You never in your life did anything "first" but it only made you more special. The world would not come to an end if you went to bed with dirty feet.

To the Baby—I've always loved you best because you will always be my sweetest baby, even when you're all grown up with children of your own. You are the joy that gives . . .

I read and I re-read: *the first miracle, the dumb spot,*

the sweetest baby, the sweetest baby, the first miracle,
the dumb spot, the dumb spot.

I read this again and again until the words melted into
each other, like a spill on the floor. Then, I flushed the
newspaper clipping down the toilet, and stayed in the
bathroom until it—whatever it was—went away.

There was another clipping also dedicated to the
plight of the middle child that my mother left on
my bed. This one was a poem that had to have been
transcendent, something I could not yet comprehend, but, over time, with the wisdom I was sure I'd
acquire—because, fundamentally, I was sure that I was
deep—it would become clear. In light of the anticipated
epiphany, I put the poem in the shoebox where I'd
kept ticket stubs, postcards, notes passed in class, a
dried flower, all of which, I imagined, would someday
be a box filled with memories; ones I'd actually *want*
to remember. Lots of people keep that sort of box. The
difference being that, even at the time, I knew that my
box contained pretty much nothing but evidence of my
desperation. Nevertheless, for quite a few years, I kept
the box of good times that never happened with the
hope that posterity could be duped. In whatever way
I'd wished my life might be imagined after my death,
I was unable to deceive myself on such a grand scale. I

had no desire to sift through my scraps of humilia-
tion. Other than the poem that my mother had left for
me on my bed, I never took a second look at anything
secreted away in that particular shoebox of memories.
The poem I returned to many, many times.

The Middle Child

Even though your [sic] not the oldest,
Or the youngest, you're the middle.
With a sandwich of ham and cheese
It's good to have a pickle.
And in the middle of your body,
You will find your belly.
The belly is like the engine
that runs a good machine;
your family wouldn't be the same
without you in between.

There had to be a code, a way to reveal the secret,
the mystery behind these words, and although I was
unable to grasp it, to *know* it, I never ceased to marvel
at its otherworldliness, how the words were strung
together to create nothing. Nothing. The creation of
nothing is mind-bogglingly beautiful. Like how infinity
is beautiful, and how stars have long before burned
out by the time we see them, that where we see a star,

there is, in fact, nothing. The poem belonged with
those elements of the natural world like the speed of
light and quarks and that there is so much shit packed
into one nucleus, things I knew to be true, but still,
I could not make them real. The poem was there, on
paper, in my hands, but I could not grab hold of it any
more than I could grab hold of the nothingness before
the Big Bang.

It's good to have a pickle.

*Middle Child Syndrome is sometimes referred to as
Middle Child Personality, and it's not much of a good
personality. A quick Google search yields yards of
postings of negativity: resentful, attention-seeking,
withdrawn, lonely, and often voted most likely to fail.

This Historic Year

IT SHOULD BE NOTED THAT this year, 2008, this year when our nation elected the first African-American president and did us proud, Bunny's sister Dawn did not go to the polls to vote. What with tending to the needs of two children nearing adolescence, it slipped her mind. Nicole, also, did not vote. She was too busy with the harvest. And Bunny? Because she couldn't bring herself to get out of bed that day, because she could not stop crying, Bunny did not vote, either.

When Albie got in that night, he told her that the line at the polls was wrapped around the block. "I was there for over an hour." Then he asked, "How was it when you went?"

"Not bad," she lied. She didn't *have* to lie to Albie. He wouldn't have passed judgment on her. But, as a person prone to sanctimony when it comes to civic responsibilities, Bunny had already placed the great weight of judgment on herself. A heavier burden of guilt, even, than when she furtively ripped up the periodic summons for jury duty, flushing it down the toilet; and therein is the difference between her sisters not voting and Bunny not voting: Bunny was sick with the shame of it.

Other People's Children

MUFFLED SOUNDS—NOW FAMILIAR—EMANATE from the adjacent apartment. Rocky is at that age—late twos, early threes—when, like a pint-sized King Lear, he rages and bellows over nothing, which, you could note, puts him on a par with Bunny, except you can assume Rocky will outgrow it. When it first started, his mothers apologized for the disturbance, which was thoughtful of them but unnecessary. "It doesn't bother us at all," Albie had said, which wasn't consistently true. The sounds of the kid going ballistic did, on occasion, set Bunny's teeth on edge, but she never would've complained because Rachel and Kelly never complained about her cigarette smoke, as opposed to the crank who lives one floor below who slid notes under the door: *I can smell your smoke!!! It's disgusting!!! If it doesn't stop, I am going to report you!!!*, which prompted Bunny to slide a note under his door: *To whom are you going to report me? The American Cancer Society? The Health Police? Your mother????* Preferring, in the end, to rise above the squabble, Bunny bought one of those expensive air purifiers to absorb the smell of cigarette smoke. He no longer slides notes under the door, although he scowls whenever he sees her. When you consider all the litigious crackpots out there, or even worse, such as the neighbor who wants to be your best friend, Bunny and Albie lucked out with the lesbians next door. Any disruption resulting from their kid throwing a tantrum is piffle.

When Bunny first learned that Rachel and Kelly were pregnant, Albie wanted to know, "Which one?"

Bunny shrugged. "I didn't ask." When her sister Nicole had announced that she and the Wiccan princess were pregnant, Bunny did ask, "You? Or the Princess?" and Nicole repeated, "*We're* having a baby."

"You might not know this," Bunny said, "but only one of you is going to grow fat and lactate."

"Do you have to ruin everything?" Nicole asked.

And you wonder why no one likes you.

Rachel, it turned out, was the pregnant one. On a stultifying July afternoon, she and Bunny met up at the mail bank in the lobby. As if over a matter of a mere few days, Rachel's stomach went from relatively flat to freakishly huge, like one of those monster squashes, and Bunny couldn't help but stare. Rachel placed the palm of her hand on her belly, and said, "He's kicking. Do you want to feel?"

"What?" Bunny asked.

"Do you want to feel him kick?"

The pause that followed was suffocating, as inescapable as a stench in the air, until Bunny managed to scramble together an excuse; something about bacteria, the kitchen counter and a sponge. "My hands." She held them up as if they were evidence.

One night, a year or so after Rocky was born, Albie, home from work, burst into the kitchen where Bunny was slicing tomatoes for a salad, and he said, "You're not going to believe this. Rocky is walking. He's in the hall with Kelly. Walking!"

"Yeah? So?" Bunny did not look up from the task at hand. "They do that. They learn to walk."

"But don't you think it's exciting?"

"I'd be excited if he were flying. But walking? No."

"Do you have to be that way about everything?"

"Yes," Bunny said. "I *do* have to be that way," and Albie asked, "Did the paper come?"

The delivery of the daily *Times* was, as of the last few weeks, erratic; it often came late and sometimes not at all.

"No. I'll call tomorrow." Bunny had been promising to call tomorrow for a few weeks already. "But the *New York Review* came. It's on the coffee table."

Bunny dumped the sliced tomatoes from the cutting board into the salad bowl where they landed on top of the packaged, pre-washed mixed baby lettuces. She shook the bottle of salad dressing—Newman's Own—but paused before pouring it. Bunny was never unaware of her own limitations.

Soon after Albie and Bunny were married, her mother asked, "Should I be looking forward to a grandchild?"

Second on the list of things Bunny feared having was a baby.

Third on the list was facial hair. Whatever was first, she never mentioned it.

Bunny shook her head. "Albie has no sperm. None," she said and, as was Bunny's intent, that was the end of that conversation.

Except it's a conversation that never really ends because *everyone* wants children. A woman who doesn't want children? Something must be very wrong with her.

In the apartment above, one flight up, lives a family with two children. Twins, a boy and a girl. When they moved in, Bunny claimed to smell sulfur coming through the air ducts in the bathroom. She swore to Albie that those children had cloven hooves like pickled pig's feet instead of feet with toes. You might then imagine Bunny's displeasure at finding herself in the laundry room with them and their mother who acted as if their opening and slamming shut the dryer door, as if determined to snap it from its hinges, were the same sort of wholesome activity as drawing stick figures on paper.

"It's even better than I imagined it," she said to Bunny who, although she did not look up from sorting her laundry, did ask, "What's better?"

As if it were objectively obvious, the mother said, "Having children. Don't wait too long," she advised. While she was recounting her Herculean efforts with *in vitro* fertilization, Bunny cut her off. "I don't want children," Bunny said.

"You say that now, but just you wait until you have your own."

"I don't want children," Bunny repeated, but some people can't let go.

"You'll change your mind," their mother said, "and you'll see. It'll be the best thing you ever did."

"Let me ask you something," Bunny fished around in her bag for her cigarettes. "If I said I didn't want a dog, would you urge me to get one nonetheless?" To which the mother of those two little shits said, "You can't smoke in here."

It has, as of late, crossed Albie's mind that perhaps he should be the one apologizing to Rachel and Kelly for Bunny's tantrums.

Rocky kicks at, or throws something at the shared wall. The sound is soft, but clear and it reverberates. "My little echo," Bunny says.

Is it safe to laugh or not? Albie waits for a clue.

You've Got to Start Somewhere

YET, WHEN SHE WAS IN her early thirties, it happened, suddenly, seemingly out of nowhere the way a fever sets in, that Bunny was beset with the irrepressible urge to cradle a baby in her arms. "I do not want a baby," Bunny was adamant, and it wasn't simply a matter of her being stubborn, in that way that her mother referred to as "cutting off your nose to spite your face." She liked her life as it was, and she did not like babies and her interest in children had limitations quickly reached. Nonetheless, there she was, staring into the window at Peanut Butter & Jane's, melting at the sight of teeny-tiny Converse All Stars and pink overalls that would fit a cat.

"The biological imperative is telling you to reproduce," Albie explained. "Your genes are crying out for expression."

As far as children were concerned, Albie had no strong feelings either way, which could be read as a contradiction in his personality considering the way he once yearned for a baby sister, for the concept of a family of four or five. And, he would've made for a good and loving father, but Bunny, so often delightfully childlike—wide-eyed at the sight of a butterfly; or slayed-dead over the toot of a fart; who needed him, without being clingy—brought him something like paternal joy. And when, distinct from child*like*, she behaved like a child, like a fucking little brat, she provided all the rationale necessary to opt out of parenthood. And, like Bunny, he too had an appreciation for fewer responsibilities and no overwhelming desire for change. He liked his life as it was.

"And how do I get my genes to pipe down?" Bunny asked.

Albie suggested they get a pet.

A kitten, a Siamese kitten, with a crick in her tail, the cross-eyed runt of the litter, the kitten that no one wanted, except for Bunny and Albie. They wanted her desperately. They named her Angela, their little angel. "Angela. My baby," Bunny said. Always, Bunny said, "My furry little baby," and she cradled the cat in her arms.

At night, Angela slept snuggled up with Bunny, her head resting on Bunny's shoulder as if it were a pillow, and Bunny would look at her and her world would go soft. That's how it was, so let's not argue about it. A kitten might not be the same as a baby, a human baby, but love is what it is. Bunny loved that cat in a way that she'd never loved before, and who is to measure?

Anyone who knows cats, knows how they can be about food: picky, fickle, perverse; cats will go hungry rather than eat what they suddenly and inexplicably deem to be slop not fit for a dog. Angela was no exception. On nothing more than a whim, she'd turn up her precious, pink nose at the Flaked Tuna, which would set Bunny rushing to open the Beef Morsels in Gravy, and sometimes a third can and even a fourth, until hitting upon one the cat would eat. It was a regular habit of Albie's to bring home a filet of smoked salmon or a rotisserie chicken, which he would cut up into little pieces to feed to her, by hand, bit by bit as if a morsel of salmon were a grape.

And so the years passed, the happiest of families: Albie, Bunny and baby Angela, who was forever their baby.

The same as every morning, Bunny put up a fresh pot of coffee and opened a can of Seafood Stew, a sure-fire favorite. Or, at least it *was* a sure-fire favorite. "Cats in India would kill for Seafood Stew," Bunny said, and she opened a can of Mideast Feast. But, little fussbudget Angela was not in the mood for Mideast Feast or Minced Duck, either, and that evening, when Angela refused the bits of rotisserie chicken that Albie picked up at D'Agostino's, he said, "I'm not sure those D'Agostino's chickens are always fresh." He got his coat from the closet and went to get a rotisserie chicken from Gristedes.

Evidently, something was awry with the Gristedes chicken, too. It was also possible, unthinkable, but possible, that Angela picked up one of those stomach things that go around. Not about to take chances where their baby was concerned, they put Angela in the cat carrier, which Bunny carried, not by the strap, but in both arms, pressed against her chest, and Albie hailed a cab.

At Animal Medical Center, in the waiting room, while Angela underwent tests, Bunny flipped through the pages of *Cat Fancy* magazine, neither reading it nor looking at the pictures, and Albie said, "She's going to be fine. It's probably just a parasite. A stomach bug. Maybe something she ate."

"I know," Bunny said. "I'm not worried."

But Albie knew that Bunny was worried, just as she knew he didn't think it was a stomach bug.

There was nothing to be done. The veterinarian said, "I'm sorry. She's not in pain now, but it's only a matter of days before she will be." He wrote down the name and number of a vet who makes house calls. "At home," he said, "she'll be comfortable and not afraid."

At home, Albie set Angela down on two pillows alongside the radiator because she was one of those cats who basked in heat, tracking patches of sunlight, burrowing in blankets, or curling up under the lamp on Bunny's desk. All that night Bunny stayed on the floor beside Angela, watching over her. "I'm here," she whispered. "My sweet furry baby, don't be afraid. I'm here. I'm here."

In the morning, the veterinarian who makes house calls put Angela's body in a box and took her away.

In a frenzy of grief all his own, Albie gathered up Angela's toys—the crinkle balls, the cat dancer, the pink mouse filled with catnip—her food dish, her water bowl, her litter box, the pillows alongside the radiator, and took them out of the house, while Bunny got into bed and stroked her chest as if she could quiet a howling heart.

There is no way of knowing for sure, but this might well have been the marble that dropped to set the Rube Goldberg contraption in motion.

Is She Getting Any Help?

YOU MIGHT ASK: IS SHE getting professional help? Does she see someone?

Someone? Some*one*? How about: two psychologists, six psychiatrists and one psychopharmacologist for a grand total of nine mental health professionals for well over half her lifetime, and it's fair to say, "Fat lot of good it's done her."

When Bunny turned sixteen she told her parents that she wanted to go to a psychiatrist, but her parents said no. "Those people," her mother said, "they blame the mother for everything." Later this anecdote was to become part of Bunny's canon of therapy fodder.

Although the incident in her freshman year of college that required her to go to Student Mental Health Services was a regrettable one, she was elated at the prospect of seeing a psychologist. She imagined it to be something like undergoing psychoanalysis in old Vienna, but to be a staff psychologist at Student Mental Health Services is more like being a physician for the prison system, insofar as it doesn't necessarily attract the top tier of the graduating class. But at the time, how was

Bunny to know such a thing? However, halfway through her first session with Dr. Browning, Bunny came to the obvious and accurate conclusion: Dr. Browning was no Otto Rank.

Next was Dr. Itsy, which was not her real name. Bunny can't remember her real name, but she was the height and weight of an average ten-year-old girl. Each week, Dr. Itsy went on and on about how Bunny had to embrace her pain, as if Bunny's pain didn't already have her in a chokehold. "Embracing your pain is the only way you can move on," Dr. Itsy said, while Bunny, sitting in the opposite chair, marveled at how Dr. Itsy's feet did not reach the floor.

Bunny, in her way, took the doctor's advice and moved on.

Dr. Sellers, a burly man with a beard, who wore Birkenstock sandals, put great store in hugging. A hug when you arrived, a hug when you departed. Dr. Sellers's hugging was more like tree-hugging than inappropriate hugging. Inappropriate hugging at least would've been interesting. Dr. Sellers *did* blame Bunny's mother for everything, which, oddly, didn't please her quite as much as she thought it would, but in the end she quit seeing Dr. Sellers because, as she told Albie, "You know how I feel about facial hair. I can't get past the beard."

Bunny would've given up on mental health professionals entirely but for the medication. The meds—not those that came with side effects, such as loss of libido and narcolepsy, because, given *that* choice, who wouldn't rather be depressed—were effective, which is not the same as being happy. But as she put it, "All my life I had a headache, and now the headache is gone."

The headache was gone until it came back.

Dr. Stine prescribed a cocktail, adding Effexor to the Zoloft. Dr. Stine wore velvet shawls and wrote papers for professional journals in which she psychoanalyzed artists and writers. They were all dead, the artists and writers, but still, she should've changed their names. A year or so in with Dr. Stine, Bunny related an exquisite example of the systematic erosion of her confidence, how when it was time for Bunny to apply to college, her mother left on her bed a brochure and application for dental hygienist training.

"Read this." Dr. Stine gave Bunny a copy of a paper she'd written called "Too Much Mother Too Close to Home," one she just happened to have on hand, in which, based on his story "So Much Water So Close to Home," she psychoanalyzed Raymond Carver as if his story and his life were one and the same. Goodbye Dr. Stine.

The Effexor/Zoloft cocktail wore thin.

Unlike the others, Dr. Lowenstein neither gave her advice nor spoke in platitudes. Mostly, he said nothing, which might've provoked Bunny to ask, "What am I paying you for? I can talk to myself for free," except it seemed that he rarely spoke because he was listening. Moreover, he was the one who found the best mix of drugs for her to date and the only side effect was a dry mouth. In mid-November, at the onset of the holiday season and after approximately eight months of weekly sessions with Dr. Lowenstein, at the end of their hour, which, as with all psychologists, was fifty minutes, Dr. Lowenstein took a moment, and then he clasped his hands together and leaned forward. "Bunny," he said, "this is something important for you to know. So listen carefully to what I am saying." He waited for her to nod, and then, his Bronx accent as thick and dark as history, he continued. "In the eyes of the world, Bunny, people such as yourself are the same as the mentally retarded. You're both at the far ends of the spectrum. You're not the norm. People in the norm, they can't relate to what's at either end. There's nothing you can do to change that. Do you understand what I am saying?"

When Bunny was six years old, her grandfather, a world-class misanthrope who loved only his wife and one of his grand-daughters, came and sat beside Bunny under the willow tree in his backyard. "You're smarter than all of them put together," he said. "And I'm including your parents in that. They're not even smart enough to know how smart you are." When Bunny was seven, he died.

All that prevented Bunny from staying on with Dr. Lowenstein from then until forever was a massive stroke that forced him to retire, for which Bunny has yet to forgive him. He's probably dead by now.

The woman who took over Dr. Lowenstein's practice had elephantine ankles, and she responded to Bunny's stories by scrunching her face. When, for the fourth time in three months, she analogized Bunny's profound lack of confidence to some boring story about her kid learning to brush his teeth, Bunny moved on to Dr. Rodgers.

Dr. Rodgers upped her dosage of Wellbutrin to 450 mg. Dr. Rodgers was massively empathetic. He felt Bunny's pain far more than she did, which she thought to be unfair.

Dr. Manfrid, the psychiatrist who followed Dr. Rodgers, was the one she disliked most of all, and for good reason. Yet, she stayed with him for more years than any of the others because, as she said to him, "It's sort of like a hostage situation here."

"Do you want to explain what you mean by that?" he asked.

"This," she gestured, her hand moving like a flipper, "this, me, you, here, this is a waste of time. But if I don't come here, then you won't write me the prescription."

"That's right," he said.

"So, that's what I meant. It's like you're holding me hostage."

As if he were issuing her a challenge or a dare, he said, "You're free to leave any time you want."

"You've got a point," Bunny said, and then, neglecting to close the door behind her, she left. You could read into her neglecting to close the door behind her, something about wanting to keep the door between them open. But you'd be wrong. It was only Bunny being rude.

Hence, the psychopharmacologist. Once every three months, he took her blood pressure, asked how she was feeling and wrote out her prescription. Over time he raised the 450 mg of Wellbutrin XL to 600 mg, which is the maximum dose. Eventually, he threw in some Lexapro.

When it was becoming evident to Albie that the drugs were

failing, and Bunny was slipping, he suggested she might want to go back into therapy.

"I've been talking to those people for more than half my life," she said. "And what good has it done me? What? I'm going to start in with someone new, and they'll ask about my childhood, and I'll tell them those same stories I told all the others? There's only so many times you can tell the same stories."

Albie suggested that perhaps she tell some different stories, some other stories, but Bunny said, "I don't have any other stories."

The People, They Come and Go

EVEN MORE THAN HE WORRIES over what could go wrong at dinner, Albie fears what could go wrong at the Frankenhoffs' after-party. The Frankenhoffs are Lizzie Frank and Jack Hoffman. Yes, the same Lizzie Frank who sent Bunny the Get-Well-Quit-Sniveling email. Everyone calls them the Frankenhoffs. The origin of the portmanteau is long forgotten, except Bunny remembers because she was the one who coined it. But to make mention of that, no matter how off the cuff, would be embarrassing, like bragging about a big nothing, and she might not even be believed, like when Al Gore said he invented the Internet, and everyone laughed at him.

"If we do go to the dinner," Albie ventures, "let's at least skip the party."

"What party?" Bunny asks.

"The Fankenhoffs' party," he reminds her.

The Frankenhoffs live on the forty-fourth floor of a vacuous building in an apartment with walls that are mostly windows. It was the sunlight and the view that the windows offered that convinced the Frankenhoffs to buy an apartment too easily mistaken for a suite in the Park Lane Hotel. The bedroom windows look out over the river, which is nice enough, but from the wall-to-wall living room window, although a dozen blocks uptown and two avenues west, they have a panoramic view of the eyesore that is Times Square, which is why every year beginning in 1998, when they first moved into their over-priced Trump Dump, the Frankenhoffs have hosted an after-party. What better place for all their friends to gather together to watch the ball drop?

Their friends. Again, Bunny would make quotation marks with her fingers. Their "friends." Bunny is a fan of air quotes. Air kisses, too.

Bunny and Albie go to the Frankenhoffs' after-party because Elliot and Trudy and Julian and Lydia go, and they feel obligated to go with them; a reason which is sufficiently inane and made worse by the insufferable tedium of being there. The Frankenhoffs' party mixes their old friends with their new friends, which means an interminable hour or two of making small talk with exclusive people who are, and will remain, strangers, and catching up with people they've not seen since the New Year's Eve before because who would want to see these people by choice? Catching up boils down to verbal updates of *curricula vitae*. The Frankenhoffs' friends, old and new, are people who define themselves by their professions: film producers, editors, architects, professors in theory-dominated English departments, neuroscientists, museum curators, something-in-the-theater, and administrators for non-profit organizations, none of which get Bunny's charitable contributions because she tends to give to organizations dedicated to the reduction of suffering.

This year, Bunny defines herself as nothing.

The Frankenhoffs' new friends are people with whom they became acquainted throughout the year, people they cultivate like winter annuals in the hope that a friendship will bloom, people whom Bunny refers to as ornamental cabbage. Ornamental cabbage cycles, from germination to death, in a mere eight weeks of the growing season.

"Not always," Albie had told her. "Mostly it does. But often, the ornamental cabbage winds up as a biennial."

Bunny shrugged. It is the same with the Frankenhoffs' new friends. With particularly rich fertilizer, some of them will hang in there for another year, which is why they fuss and fawn over their new friends, compliment their clothes or hair color or the brilliance of their accomplishments, while keeping a watchful eye, taking care that their glasses are full, and have they tried the pastries? Lizzie baked them herself. Lizzie bakes pastries that span the globe. Tacked to her kitchen wall is a map of the world. Each year she bakes pastries of a different nation, noted with a push-pin. The pastries of some nations taste like Silly Putty.

Because what's to be gained by gushing over friends you've had for years? Friends you've had for years are practically losers. Inevitably, Bunny was to be found standing alone in a corner of the Frankenhoffs' minimalistically furnished living room, sipping her wine, her pastry wrapped in a napkin until she could locate a trash can. Eventually someone would approach her, someone like that filmmaker who had a mustache, one that arched like an eyebrow, which was sufficiently disturbing. He wanted to know *what* she had written, had she written something he might've read, or something he might've heard about.

"Probably not," Bunny said.

"Are you someone I should know?" he asked.

"Probably not," Bunny said, to which he said, "Well, good luck to you."

Good luck to you.

Equally predetermined would be the conversation about her name, such as it was a conversation and not a prosecutorial inquiry: *On your birth certificate, it says Bunny? For real, your parents named you Bunny?* As if, if the question were reworded and asked often enough, she'd be tricked into confessing that her real name is Amanda or Jeanne. "Why would they name you Bunny?"

"Because," Bunny would say, "they raised rabbits. For food."

An irritating but harmless exchange, except for last year's after-party when Bunny was approached by a professor of Gender Studies at Yale—"at Yale," she emphasized. "Bunny?" she asked. "That can't be your real name. What is your given name?"

"Bunny is my *given* name. It's on my birth certificate. Any other questions?"

The professor wore black-framed eyeglasses to announce

her fierce intelligence, and her haircut was as sharp and ugly as her tone of voice. "Bunny is a pet name for a child. How can you expect anyone to take you seriously when you have a child's name? I strongly urge you to change it," she said.

Bunny thanked the professor of Gender Studies at Yale for her advice, and then offered up some of her own. "A mint. Or a piece of gum. Something. Because it's bad. Offensive, really."

The professor of Gender Studies at Yale recoiled as if Bunny were the one in need of a mint, and asked, "What exactly is your problem?" Then, she brushed at her shoulder as if she thought she might have dandruff, too, as if bad breath and dandruff go hand in hand. "Because something *is* wrong with you," she said. "Very wrong."

Now, Albie again urges they don't go to the party. "Let's do ourselves a favor and skip it. It's not as if we want to watch the ball drop." In fact, Bunny has never seen the ball drop. Not on television, and she'd have scooped out an eyeball rather than go, in person, on the ground, to Times Square on New Year's Eve. And in previous years at the Frankenhoffs' parties, in those few minutes before midnight, when everyone crowded by the window, the anticipation gathering like static electricity, rising in preparation to assuredly fall, just the same as the ball will drop in its sixty calibrated seconds, Bunny would slip away and lock herself in the bathroom, where she'd sit on the edge of the tub, light a cigarette, and wait for it to be over.

Prompt: A Movie (300 words or less)

To dismiss the traditions and rituals and holidays is to mock what is sacred to others, to insult their beliefs, and to ruin the pleasure for everyone else because you are a difficult and disagreeable person.

"I'm not *mocking* Thanksgiving," I said. "I just don't want to go."

Why? Why wouldn't I want to spend a day with family. Extended family. Uncles and aunts and cousins, and last year there was an infant, a cheesy-stinking font of spit-up, and everyone carrying on as if the parents had actually done something extraordinary like publish a book or win the lottery, until I broke in and said, "The earthworm is impressive because it impregnates itself." After that, they all gave me the cold shoulder except Natalie, my nine-year-old nose-picking booger-wiping-on-walls cousin with the mouse ears: circular ears set nearer to the top of her head than where you'd expect to find human ears; ears I could only hope were genetically recessive.

"You want to stay home," my mother gave up the argument, "then stay home. Alone," she added with emphasis, as if alone were a state of being that I'd come to deeply regret soon enough.

Positioned at the living room window, I watched the car pull out of the driveway and down the road until it went beyond my range of vision, and then I went to the kitchen to make a feast of my own. In the refrigerator was a packet of Oscar Mayer bologna and another of sliced ham, which had a pig for a logo. A cartoon pig wearing a chef's hat, which was cruelty all on its own. I made myself a cheese sandwich. Three individually wrapped slices of Kraft American cheese on Arnold's Bakery White garnished with two slices of a grainy-textured tomato, grainy-textured like wet sand, and topped off with dollop of mayonnaise. For side dishes I chose a can of Diet Dr. Pepper and a stack of Oreo cookies, and I carried the tray to the family room, where I sat, cross-legged, on the floor in front of the television and ate my Thanksgiving dinner while watching *Miracle on 34th Street*, a movie I'd seen a trillion and a half times before. Yet, still I was not prepared for how nearly unbearable it was to watch the movie to its very end, to that last scene when young Natalie Wood's wish comes true, when we see the ordinary house with a backyard swing under a patch of sunlight, an image that foreshadowed the inevitability of the excruciating ache of wistful regret that comes with a perfectly nice life.

Already, it was dark outside. The kitchen light

glowed with a yellow halo, and I caught sight of my
reflection in the window, faint and opaque; there, but
not there. I contemplated giving myself the finger, but
didn't bother. Taking the box of Oreos with however
many cookies were left, I went to the living room where
I cozied up in one of the two matching armchairs to read
Peyton Place, yet again. *Peyton Place* was one of the
half-dozen books in our house, all hardcover, navy-blue
cloth bound, a shade of navy blue that was a near-
enough match to the navy-blue upholstery of the couch,
which matched the armchairs. The books filled the
small shelf built into a corner table where my mother
would've preferred to put geranium plants, but this
shelf was not positioned for sunlight. I'd read the other
five books a bunch of times too; they stunk even worse
than *Peyton Place*. The one about the cattle drive in the
Old West was the one that stunk the most.

As if an Oreo were a Communion wafer or a tab of
acid, I popped a cookie into my mouth, whole, where
it was ablated, creamy on my tongue. I opened *Peyton
Place* at random. Despite having it practically memorized
word for word, I was sufficiently engaged with *Peyton
Place* not to hear the car pull into the driveway. Instead,
I heard the absence, the absence of sound of the motor
turned off. Then came the muffled basso click of the car
doors opening followed by the satisfied clap when shut.

The four of them—my parents and my sisters—like

the four cups of milk to a quart, the four quarters to a
dollar, the four seasons in a year, four people to make
a family—were in the foyer unwinding scarves, taking
off their coats—the *faw-yay*, my mother called it, to
which I'd said *right, the faw-yay because we live in
France*—when Dawn, the youngest of us and already
showing signs of the twat she would become, made a
beeline for the living room to where I pretended to be
deeply engrossed in my reading, as if I were oblivious
to Dawn who was right there in front of me doing the
little bouncy-dance of someone who really has to pee;
really, really has to pee but, for whatever reason, is
holding it in. Except Dawn didn't have to pee. She
was holding in words, words that she was desperate
to utter, restraining herself only to sweeten the
release, until she could contain it no longer. "Bunny,
you won't believe it, but I swear to you," Dawn said,
"the entire day, and no one, not one person, not even
Natalie, asked where you were. It was like, Bunny
who?"

On that first Thanksgiving without me there, my
extended family regenerated seamlessly, a Darwinian
adaptation of evolution that, among other improve-
ments, allowed for more elbow room around the table.

Even now, looking back, in retrospect, that was my
happiest Thanksgiving ever.

There Has to Be a Reason

THE RING OF THE PHONE comes at Bunny like a bomb gone off and, as if debris were about to fall, she grips the edge of the blanket, ready to pull it over her head. When the phone rings for a second time, Albie gets up to answer it, and Bunny has recovered well enough to say, "If it's one of my sisters, I'm not here."

"I'll say you're out shopping. For confetti," he adds and instantly regrets it. You never know what will set her off, but Bunny smiles. A sad little smile, nostalgic, almost, for the time when "for confetti" would've genuinely amused her. Still, it's a smile and not a crying jag or an enraged fit, which it could've been because how she responds to jokes, quips, expressions of love or the last drop of patience—there's no way to predict.

As of late, her sisters call often. Or rather, they call often compared to how rarely they called before, and despite Albie's periodic urging, Bunny never calls her sisters. Albie puts value on family, on the idea of family, but, as Bunny has pointed out, as an only child, he has no practical experience in the field.

Albie's childhood was a good one; happy, if you believe there is such a thing. He'd wanted for nothing except an older brother to pal around with, or even better, a baby sister to care for, to keep from harm. If he'd grown up anywhere other than New York City, Albie would've been the kind of kid who'd bring home a squirrel with a broken jaw or a baby sparrow fallen from its nest; a creature to rescue and protect, which is, not inconceivably, what drew him to Bunny in the first place.

As far as Bunny is concerned, at least in theory, family amounts to no more than shared DNA; as random and meaningless as the collision of two electrons before they are off again, each in its own orbit. Albie and Jeffrey are the whole of her family. Stella had been family, too, like a sister to Bunny except that the filial devotion, the love, was genuine and not foisted upon them by indiscriminate protoplasmic whimsy. Bunny misses Stella. So much, she misses Stella. Some people might say it's too much, which is like saying that there is too much water in the ocean. The way she misses Stella is different from the way she misses Angela, but it's the same insofar as that there is no consolation to be had. The loss of Angela and Stella both, feels to Bunny like longing that is endless. But it's not endless. It's longing that is limitless.

Bunny's sisters call because, they say, they are concerned about her. Perhaps there's something to that, but the real reason they call is for an answer to the question: *How did this happen? Have they found the cause?* Dawn wants it to be something like food poisoning. She wants Albie to say, "It was the mayonnaise," although really any explanation will suffice provided it rules out the possibility of the hereditary factor. She needs to be reassured that it's not one of those genetic mutations that can cause breast cancer or bad teeth. "So it's definitely not genetic, right?" Dawn has asked Albie this question more than once.

Although it was never Albie's intention to provoke hysteria in Dawn, he answered her question as best he could, which was to say, "I'm not an expert on these things."

"Maybe, but still," Dawn said, "you know more than I do."

Dawn is desperate for certainty, and she seeks comfort in the fact that her children bear no physical resemblance to Bunny. If they don't have her eyes or her mouth, then it's not likely that they got her sick-o gene, either. Right? "Right?" she asked Albie. "They probably don't have any of her genes. They don't look anything like my side of the family. You've seen them. They look just like Michael. So even if it is genetic, they wouldn't have that gene, right?"

"I can't answer that," Albie said. "I *really* don't know."

Dawn might be a wishful thinker, but Nicole has managed to believe that there's direct causal link between Bunny's crack-up and her use of aerosol deodorant. If Bunny's meltdown can be attributed to her lifestyle—face it, she *smokes*—Nicole can rest easy. Twice-daily meditation, a raw food diet and a weekly colon cleanse is practically a guarantee that she will not die, that she will never die. However, Nicole can't quite rid herself of the lingering concern that it might've been the bits of Bac-Os that did this to Bunny, the Bac-Os that their mother sprinkled liberally on salads and baked potatoes when the girls were in their formative years.

Nicole's fixation on a squeaky-clean colon interests Bunny, in a general interest sort of way, a curiosity to occasionally ponder the way she'll occasionally ponder who killed JonBenét Ramsey.

It's not only her sisters who ask, "What happened?" People who barely know Bunny from Bonnie, they too want an explanation, a reason they can identify, identify and thereby avoid as if it were a matter of using a condom, or something they can control the way they can control their intake of salt. They want to know what it takes to keep a tight lid on your mind. They say, "We never saw this coming." If no one saw this coming, it was because no one was paying attention; a lack of attention that might well have been a contributing factor. *A* contributing factor. One. One of many. Because it's never just one thing. Still, they ask, "How did this happen?" Because they need to be sure that people don't fall apart without a solid reason, they sift through her life panning for gold: she spends too much time alone; she's got a negative attitude; she never had children; she smokes *cigarettes*; not having children messes with a woman's hormones; all day working alone, that can't be good; she eats processed food; she is a middle child; she's never even *been* to a gym; she's not very likable; she's always been moody, difficult, dark, *overly* sensitive and easy to anger; even as a child, she wasn't likable; she should've had children; she wears perfume; she drinks too much coffee; she smokes *cigarettes*.

Whatever the reason, they want to be assured that it was her own damn fault.

Predicting Snow

WITH AN ACUTE DOG-TYPE OF sensitivity to tone, Bunny detects the catch in Albie's throat when he says to whomever is on the phone, "Not at the moment." The catch gives way to artificial buoyancy. "She's right here. Hold on. I'll ask her."

"It's Trudy." Albie covers the mouthpiece with his hand. "She wants to know about tonight."

It's like a muscle contraction, the way Bunny pulls in on herself, tight, like a pair of pursed lips. She is intent on control, on refraining from the desperate need to hurl the coffee mug across the room or to bite off a hunk of her pillow. When the flash of rage has passed, she asks, as if she did not know, "What about tonight?"

"If we're still on. She wants to know what our plans are. Because, you know, we're not sure."

"Yes, we are sure," Bunny says. "We'll be there."

Again, with the calculated and calibrated enthusiasm of a pep squad captain, Albie tells Trudy, "We're on. We will see you at eight." Then, after a pause, he says. "I have no idea." He returns the phone to the cradle, taking care that it is perfectly aligned the way you would take care when hanging a painting on the wall, and Bunny asks, "No idea about what?"

"Oh." The word come out like a gulp. "If it's going to snow." Albie knows that he's a lousy liar—he has little experience with the art of prevarication—but he forges on. "Because they're predicting snow, and Trudy asked what I thought. If it was going to snow or not."

Bunny pulls at the blanket, wrapping it tighter around her shoulders, and she asks, "What is it you think I am going to do?"

Albie doesn't respond, which is the worst answer possible. Bunny rolls over, facing the back of the couch, and as if the sky were falling, she presses her hands flat to the top of her head, tucks her chin, and brings her knees to her chest. *What's that animal, the one that curls up into a ball?* Jeffrey also repositions himself, cozies into the nest made by the curve of her legs. She wishes she could bring herself to push him off the couch, kick him away from her as if that stupid, sweet cat were an empty soda can.

The Shattering Clarity of the Irreplaceable, Yet Again

THE DAY BEFORE THE MOMENTOUS Election Day of 2008, in that lull of time when it's no longer afternoon but not yet evening, the sky was washed in opaque indigo blue and, standing at the living room window, Bunny was overcome by an emotion she could not identify. Whatever it was, she thought she might drown in it. She put the palm of her hand, her left hand, flat against the cold glass. An early arctic chill was blowing in from Canada, and just like that, Bunny got inspired. Ice-skating, to go ice-skating, to have fun.

Fun not shared is not fun. You can derive great pleasure alone, enjoy yourself enormously, experience bliss, but fun requires someone else, like a friend or a dog. Jeffrey is not a dog, and Stella is gone.

When she called Lydia, to ask if Lydia wanted to go ice-skating, the phone went straight to voicemail, but Trudy picked up her phone on the third ring.

"Ice-skate?" Trudy asked. "Since when do you ice-skate?"

"I don't," Bunny said. "But I did once. I mean, one time."

At that age, nine or ten years old, girls had ice-skating parties, bowling parties, or played twelve holes of miniature golf; activities followed by a hot dog, a Coke, and a slice of Carvel ice cream cake. At one of the bowling parties, Bunny bowled a zero. She pretended to do it on purpose. Better the girls on her team be mad at her for deliberately failing than for all the girls to goof on her for being a spaz.

In the days leading up to the skating party, Bunny imagined gleaming white skates with pom-poms dangling from the aglets of the laces like a pair of fuzzy dice from the rearview mirror of a car. But the rental skates were the same shade of white as pee-stained sheets. There were no pom-poms, and when she stood up, her ankles turned inward, as if to kiss each other on the nose. While everyone else whizzed past her like they were Hans Brinker and his sisters, Bunny clung to the rail, inching her way around the rinky-dink rink. When she dared to let go, she fell. A fish out of water, Bunny on ice.

"It's not about *ice-skating* ice-skating," she told Trudy. "It's about falling down." Bunny effused on the fun of foolishness, the fun to be had flopping and falling on the ice at Rockefeller Center. Her voice sounded as if her eyes were glittering.

"Hardly my idea of a good time," Trudy said. "And at Rockefeller Center, no less? Where do you get such ideas?" Rockefeller Center is for tourists and adolescents who over-identify with Holden Caulfield. Moreover, there was a documentary about Stockhausen on at seven that she really wanted to see.

"Who?" Bunny asked.

"Stockhausen," Trudy said. "Karlheinz Stockhausen."

"Right. Right. Stockhausen."

To replace lost love, the way you can replace your broken computer with a new one or replace the battery in your watch, is not an option.

Bunny hung up the phone and googled "Karlheinz Stockhausen," whom, she learned, was a pioneer in aleatory music. Then she googled "aleatory music," and after that she sat there staring at the computer screen as late afternoon turned into night.

When Albie got home, he wanted to know why was she sitting there in the dark staring at the computer screen.

"For fun," she said. "I'm having fun," and then she said nothing.

Bunny doesn't talk about Stella.

Prompt: An Imaginary World (300 words or less)

The same way *Miracle on 34th Street* was a movie with an ending that promised disillusionment and a future of amorphic discontent, *The Wizard of Oz* was another movie from which I could find no hope to salvage. For eighth-grade English class, I wrote an end-of-term paper comparing the film version of *The Wizard of Oz* to the book version of *The Diary of Anne Frank*, positing that although the stories and their circumstances were entirely different, both were tragedies born of a pitiably naïve optimism which afflicted both protagonists.

After years of hiding from the Nazis in an attic where there was no such thing as privacy, although there was plenty of stress and raw nerves, along with the fear of knowing perfectly well what would happen if they were discovered, Anne Frank wrote in her diary that, in spite of everything, she still believed that people were truly good at heart; this from the girl whose doom was sealed behind the closed door of a cattle car, whose mortal remains were turned to ash in the incinerator that was Auschwitz* because—yoo-hoo, Anne, get real—what about the people who, in spite of everything, are, at heart, truly sociopathic?

And Dorothy? Liberator of the Munchkins? Rightful owner of the ruby slippers? The darling of the Emerald City? What did she have to say for herself? *There's no place like home.* Dorothy wanted to go home. *Home*, as if home carried with it the implications and assumptions of a place where you are loved and cared for and kept safe; where you have a family, all of whom wear reindeer sweaters during the holiday season because home is a place where it snows in winter and winter is followed by the green of spring as opposed to some miserable scrap of hardscrabble earth where dyspeptic Miss Gulch snatched your dog, bent on snuffing out his little life, all the while Auntie fucking Em just stood there with her thumb up her ass. *That* was home, Dorothy. And yet, three times she clicked the heels of the ruby slippers as, three times, she said, "There's no place like home," which was the magic spell to transport her from the Emerald City to the dustbowl that was Kansas, where dreams shrivel and die like the crops, where Toto would be thrown to the wolves, where the rest of Dorothy's days would be bleak and lonely because—oh, poor naïve dum-dum Dorothy—"There's no place like home."

Under the big red F, which was circled three times,

my teacher wrote, "There is something very wrong with you."

*For the record, Anne Frank did not die in the gas chambers at Auschwitz. She died from typhus at Bergen-Belsen where her body was tossed into a mass grave and buried like toxic waste. And she died six weeks, not two weeks, before the camp was liberated.

But Auschwitz and the gas chamber and the irony generated by two weeks rather than six, make for a better story.

Except it wasn't a story.

The Point is the Pain

"SO, IT IS OKAY WITH you," Albie asks, "if we skip it?"

"If we skip what?"

A deep breath, Albie sucks back his aggravation. "The party," he says. "The Frankenhoffs' party. I really don't want to go."

To which Bunny responds, "The windows are hermetically sealed."

"What windows? What are you talking about?"

"The Frankenhoffs' windows don't open. So if you're thinking I might jump, don't worry. It's not possible."

"Jesus. No. Cut it out, Bunny. Not even as a joke. But really, what is the point of going? To come home and complain about having been bored out of our minds?"

"We don't have to decide this minute, do we?" Bunny asks.

"No. Of course not. We'll wait and see. We'll see how we feel. Later."

As far as taking a header out the Frankenhoffs' window, which would be less like a swan dive and more like the Flying Nun, limbs going gawky every which way until the sails of her wimple that looked like folded tablecloth would catch the winds like a kite, even if the Frankenhoffs' windows did open, it would never happen. People are not kites. With people, gravity kicks in, and Bunny has no calling to splat onto the sidewalk on New Year's Eve as the ball drops at Times Square.

Never would she make such a spectacle of herself.

Never would she give some fraud at the Frankenhoffs' party cause to say, "Frankly, I'm not surprised. Did you know that her parents named her Bunny because they raised rabbits? *For food*."

Taking note that Bunny has not touched her coffee, that it must be cold by now, Albie asks, "Do you want a fresh cup?"

"What did you say?" She blinks her eyes as if she were just waking up, and not quite sure of her surroundings. "Did you ask me a question?"

Albie repeats his offer to make her a fresh cup of coffee, and Bunny says, "Yes. Thank you."

"No problem." He kisses her forehead and then leaves, taking the St. Thomas coffee cup with him.

To fling herself out a window, whether it be the Frankenhoffs' window or any window, is not Bunny's idea of the way to relieve what is killing her. Falling or jumping from up high is not of her ideation. Ideation is the way we imagine doing away with ourselves. Even people who would never, ever, kill themselves, they too, although less frequently, indulge in suicidal ideation, imagine their own funerals, relishing the grief, the guilt, the remorse resultant from their self-inflicted death. Ideation, when we get into the specifics of it, when we get down into orchestrated details, is as particular to the individual as are their sexual predilections.

In the kitchen, Albie pours the cold coffee down the sink and drops the mug in the trash, where it lands sailboat-side up. After filling the pot with water, Albie calls out asking if Bunny would like something to eat.

"Not now," Bunny says.

"I can't hear you." Albie raises his voice, "What did you say?"

The pressure of irrationality rises up in Bunny the way atmospheric pressure rises, and under the cover of the blanket, she wraps her right hand around the middle finger of her left hand. It's similar to warm-up exercises for the piano or the attempt to alleviate writer's cramp, the way Bunny bends her middle finger back toward her wrist. Because, anatomically speaking, a finger doesn't bend backward of its own accord, Bunny ought to be showing signs of discomfort, some indication that she's gone beyond the point of stretching and nearer to the point of tearing a ligament, but to look at her face you'd think, "Here is someone who is at peace with herself."

It's plain white, the cup Albie sets down on the coffee table. Bunny thanks him for the coffee, as if coffee were exactly what she'd wanted, and wasn't he sweet to know. "It smells good," she says, acting; acting like a normal person, but she makes no move toward the cup, and a normal person wouldn't be trying her best to snap off her own finger. Because this particular self-inflicted Torquemadian punishment draws no attention to itself—no howling or wild gesticulations or limbs flailing—and her hands are hidden from view, Bunny is like a junkie shooting up between her toes or one of those teenage girls who cuts herself where no one will see, which was something Bunny never understood. Why bother cutting yourself if not for the attention? But Bunny has newfound insight into these girls. She gets it now, how the release of the pressure, like air escaping from a balloon, can defuse what would otherwise explode.

Albie, again, sits on the edge of the couch, alongside her, and puts his hands over hers, her hands covered by the blanket, and gently pries them apart.

More than the weeping, more than the lethargy, more than the utter battiness of it all, it's the self-inflicted trauma that disturbs Albie most.

Her thighs are a bleed of bruises, like a pansy, purple- and yellow-tinged with the green of the sky before a storm. Whenever she pummels herself or smacks her head, hard, with the palm of her hand, Jeffrey flees to a safe spot under the bed, and Albie wraps his arms around her as if his arms were a straitjacket, and in that same way, she struggles to break free of him. To be held tight like that is suffocating, and she gulps for air. These episodes cross the line of that with which he can cope, and that which is simply too damn much for him. "Please," he says. "Please don't hurt yourself."

It is counterintuitive to inflict pain, tangible pain, as a way of relieving pain, but pain you can point to, pain that has a place, is pain that can be relieved. Bunny's pain has no place. She hurts everywhere. She hurts nowhere. Everywhere and nowhere, hers is a ghostly pain, like that of a phantom limb. Where there is nothing, there can be no relief. To bring the pain to a place, like leaves gathered into a pile, to a nexus, no matter how much it hurts, to know that it hurts *here*, is to bring clarity. Only when she hits herself or pulls her hair or bends her finger back or bites the inside of her mouth can she experience the pleasure of pain found and pain released. It is the only way to be rid of the pain that is Bunny. She is the point of the pain.

Eating Disorders

HAVING PUT ON HIS SOCKS and shoes, and therefore now fully dressed, Albie returns to the living room to find Bunny unfurled from her curled-up-in-a-ball position. "Did you sleep?" he asks her.

"I don't know. What time is it?"

"It's getting close to one. How about some lunch?"

"Not now. Soon."

Albie glances at the coffee cup, the second cup of coffee, also untouched. "You didn't have any breakfast. You've got to eat something."

It's not an eating disorder like anorexia, and you can forget bulimia, and it's not like Angela's stomach cancer, either. People who are clinically depressed have their own disturbances with food. For some, it's as if hand to mouth were an involuntary reflex, as if food could fill the abyss. Which it can't, and they grow fat, which does nothing good for their state of mind. The others are rarely hungry or else they are never hungry. They emaciate, become insubstantial, a manifestation of the wish to disappear. Bunny is one of the thin ones.

She was always thin, but now you could rest a teacup on her clavicle.

No, she wasn't *always* thin, but she was mostly always thin.

Now, she appears gaunt. Not just undernourished, but malnourished. Her lips are chapped and cracked. Her skin has a gray tint and her hair is flat, lifeless. It could be that she needs a good scrubbing even more than a good meal, but Albie prefers to approach her disturbances one at a time. "I really wish you'd eat something," he says. "You haven't had anything since yesterday afternoon."

"I didn't have dinner? I thought I'd had dinner."

"You had a late lunch," Albie says. "You need to eat. There's some nice cheese in the refrigerator. A fontina and a Morbier. From Murray's. And there's an Amy's sourdough in the freezer."

"Really," Bunny says. "I'm not hungry. But you go ahead."

"I have a lunch date with Muriel," Albie tells her. "That is, if you don't mind my going out for a while."

The holidays have resulted in an abundance of togetherness, and Albie is desperate to escape, even if only for a few hours. The air is stifling, thick and dank from Bunny's misery and neglect of her personal hygiene. Her linen—sheets and pillowcase—are squirrel gray with grime.

"I don't mind. Really, it's fine," she assures him.

And it is fine. Even if Albie's presence didn't feel like a plastic bag over her head, it would've been fine. One example of their compatibility is that neither of them believed that to be married was to be conjoined at the hip. Trust is, and has always been, solid and their loyalty to each other is complete. Trust and loyalty in the ways that matter most.

When Bunny and Muriel met for the first time, Bunny later said to Albie, "You should tell her to lighten up on the mascara." Then, to put her remark in perspective, Bunny added, "But I really liked her." About Bunny, Muriel had said, "She's quite fabulous." Yet, neither Bunny nor Muriel made any effort toward a friendship of their own because Muriel was Albie's friend, *his* friend from work. A friend from work should be a compartmentalized and exclusive friendship; that is, *my* friend from work, as opposed to *our* friend from *my* work. Everyone should be free to go to lunch or dinner with a good friend from work without your significant other sitting there at the table letting go with bull-snort exhales of boredom laced with rising irritation while you and your friend are having what amounts to a private conversation about office intrigue.

Bunny knows that no matter what, you've got to have a friend all your own. Albie and Stella got along famously, but Bunny and Stella had a history together, one that was pre-Albie, one that didn't include him. Stella was Bunny's friend. Muriel is Albie's friend, and Bunny is glad he has her.

To hurry him out the door, Bunny tells Albie to have a good time, and Albie asks her, "Do you want me to bring anything back for you?"

"A pack of cigarettes," Bunny says.

"That's it?" Albie asks.

That's it. Bunny doesn't want anything else except for Albie to go out and to leave her alone. *Alone, as if it were something she'd come to regret.*

Holding On

THE MECHANISM OF A LOCK turning makes a definitive, finite sound, and Bunny listens for the final reckoning of the tumbler as it falls into place. When she hears the elevator doors as they open and close, sounds less vivid but still audible, Bunny sits up, and pivots so that her feet are on the floor. Something under her skin, but deeper near to bone, throbs like an infection, pulsates the way a heart beats, something that cannot be quieted or contained, but it can, and does, expand. Bunny grabs her pillow, hugs it, squeezing the life out of it, and this, whatever it is that feels like love but is not love, definitely not love, pushes from the inside to get out.

The impact of a plate or a book, when hurled across a room, is declarative, but the pillow proves to be a disappointment similar to the disappointment of a hurricane that changes course and blows out to sea.

Because there are some thoughts, certain kinds of thoughts, that need to be said aloud, Bunny needs to articulate the words to make them tangible and undeniable. Even if no one is listening, the words are there, like a pet rock on your night table, just there, doing nothing, but over time stone does turn to sand, and out loud Bunny says, to no one, not even Jeffrey, "I do not want to be in this world."

To see her when she stands up is to know that the grimy white T-shirt reaches just below her hipbone. Her black panties sag at her butt. Not that she cares, although she does remember her mother's admonition about the importance of clean underwear because what if you got hit by a car.

"I'm pretty sure if I were hit by a car," Bunny had said, "I wouldn't be thinking about my underwear. I'd be thinking about other things. Like am I going to lose a leg."

No one need be concerned that Bunny will be wearing dirty panties when she walks in front of a bus because she would never walk in front of a bus, just as she'd never jump from a window or a cliff. Bunny believes, she has always believed, that life, all life, is sacred. You don't just snuff out a life on a whim. She is a person who apologizes when she kills a bug, despite being well aware of the fat lot of good her apology does for the spider whose guts are squashed on the kitchen wall.

Bunny does not *want* to kill herself. She does not *want* to die. It's that she no longer wants to live. To not want to be alive is not the same thing as wanting to be dead. Bunny would prefer to die of natural causes, but she's not sure she can wait it out.

Imagine it this way: imagine being on the twelfth floor of a burning building and your options are to be consumed by the fire or jump from the window to a certain death. Can you cling to the hope of being rescued, saved from being burned to a crisp by two brave firemen? Can you bear the intense heat for just a little bit longer? But to feel the heat of the fire, to hear the snap and pop of the flames, to be overcome by the smoke, to be unable to breathe, to imagine melting like wax, melting like the Wicked Witch of the West, and then comes the moment when you know that no one is going to rescue you; when you know that you will either die by fire or jump from the window and die by falling. Neither choice is a good one, but still, you'll have to decide which way you are going to die, which will hurt most.

A Brief Return to the Subject of Coffee Mugs

WHEN THE *FRANCINE* MUG BROKE, Bunny tried to gather up the pieces, hoping to glue them together, but there were too many pieces, too many chips and shards; bits the size of motes of dust.

Means of Escape

WITH JEFFREY TROTTING ALONGSIDE HER, Bunny walks to the bathroom, where she stops at the threshold. With one hand on either side of the open door, she grips the molding as if to bar exit or entry. Her thoughts, along with her gaze, are fixed on the bathtub. Rectangular shaped, flat to the floor but with early twentieth-century fixtures. White porcelain faucets, *Hot* and *Cold* enameled in Dutch-blue script on round caps set into brass findings. The spigot, too, is brass. Solid brass, bought when Bunny had ideas to remodel the bathroom with a freestanding sink and a claw foot bathtub. Soon after buying the faucets and spigot at a boldly overpriced salvage warehouse, Bunny's attention drifted, redirected, away from remodeling the bathroom. To where or to what is irrelevant. What matters here is her lifelong lack of stick-to-itiveness: oil painting, sewing, piano, guitar, graduate school for applied linguistics, archery, chemistry, refurbishing furniture, or when she was fifteen and signed on for volunteer work at the Simms Home for Mentally Retarded Children, an altruism which lasted less than an hour when she discovered that these mentally retarded children were not preternaturally wise children who happened to speak in simple sentences, but in fact were overweight adolescents who grabbed at her breasts. Whatever she started, Bunny quit.

Except for writing, writing fiction. With that she persevered.

She should have stuck with archery.

All she wanted was to be taken seriously. Was that too much to ask for?

How can you expect anyone to take you seriously when, as one astute critic put it, your book jacket looks like an ad for a feminine hygiene product? The cover that her editor explained was intended to appeal to the widest common denominator.

The widest common denominator is also the lowest common denominator.

How can you expect anyone to take you seriously when you have a child's name?

Aside from the porcelain faucets and brass spigot, the bathtub itself is nothing special, although it is deeper than the average bathtub, thereby it's a tub conducive to long, relaxing baths, with bubbles.

Nerve Endings

*H*OW COULD SHE DO THIS *to Albie?*

What is difficult, if not impossible, to understand, unless you're in the thick of it yourself, is that she would not be doing this *to* him. Albie has no place, not so much as a cameo shot, in this picture, in the video that plays in her head. Pain, fixed with laser beam focus on itself, is self-centered, allowing for thoughts only of alleviation. Even the pain of something as common and comprehensible as a toothache, one of those cavities sufficiently deep to expose the nerve endings, a cavity that feels like someone has jammed an ice pick through your eye, shrinks your world into an impenetrable bubble of agony. It hurts, and it hurts, and that, the hurt, is everything. You can't think about anything except wanting the hurt to go away.

Ideation

BUNNY PICTURES THE BATHTUB. IT'S filled with warm water; a pack of cigarettes and ashtray are on one ledge. On the other ledge of the tub is a wineglass, but it's filled with vodka, not wine. She will smoke a cigarette and drink the vodka in a measured way. That is, in neither diminutive sips nor swigging it as if she needed it to assuage a particularly bad day or to steady her nerves, as if her hands were shaking. But her hands would not be shaking, and this day would, in fact, be far better than the days preceding it. She'll smoke the cigarette, and she'll lean back in the tub and picture an end-of-summer afternoon, late August. She'll picture floating on an inner tube on a lake, squinting up at the late afternoon sun as the shadows shift and light breaks through the dark density of the fir trees. When the bathwater cools, Bunny will extend her left leg and turn the *H* faucet with her foot, prehensile in its ability to perform that particular task.

Did it ever happen, Bunny wonders. Was there ever an end-of-summer day when she floated on an inner tube on a lake surrounded by fir trees and squinted up at the sun? Not that it matters. On this last day of December, there is no end-of-summer afternoon, no inner tube, no lake. But still, her ideation is not unlike squinting up at the sun, the way the light breaks through the darkness.

One more cigarette; she'll smoke that one, too, to its very end. Alongside the ashtray is the box cutter, and not pausing for so much as a thought, she'll cut one wrist, then the other. Immediately, she'll wish she'd had one more cigarette, but it will be too late for that. She will watch her life flow from her wrists into the bathwater, and as if blood were food coloring and this, exsanguination, is like a grade school science experiment, the bathwater will turn pink and grow cold, and because she'll no longer have any control over what is happening, there will be no way for her to stop Jeffrey from pawing at the door, which he always does when Bunny is in the bathroom. He doesn't like to be left alone. Bunny sees herself well into leaving the world, or maybe she's already gone, when sweet stupid Jeffrey gets the door open, and instead of drinking from the toilet as he usually does, as if he believes himself to be a lion drinking the cold water from Lake Tanganyika, she pictures him lapping the pink bathwater.

Here is where Bunny's ideation quits. To picture Jeffrey, having no idea that she's dead, drinking the bathwater pink from her blood, that just about kills her.

Lunch

A SIGN, HAND-WRITTEN ON CARDBOARD, is taped to the door: *We will be closed from 5 P.M. 12/31 and reopen on January 2nd.* The Far Left Corner Café—referencing location, not political leanings—is a soup and sandwich place, not a New Year's Eve hotspot, but now in the afternoon, every table is taken. Albie scans the room looking for Muriel. She is seated in the back at the table next to the bathroom. As he makes his way over to her, Muriel gets up to greet him, tucking a lock of her hair behind one ear. Shoulder-length hair. Thick, glossy, ash-brown going gray at the temples. Muriel is from England, and she looks it, like a woman who has a garden that produces prizewinning gladiolas. She is tall, large-boned, and solid. The Venus de Milo but with arms. She's an attractive woman, if a touch horsey. Her skin is flawless, white and pink like the inside of a seashell. The only makeup she wears is the mascara that draws attention to the color of her eyes, the light blue of sea glass. Albie takes hold of her hands, strong hands. Almost masculine, but her fingernails are incongruously painted cherry red. Albie and Muriel kiss in greeting. A platonic kiss, although it lasts a beat longer than you might expect from a kiss between friends.

When they break apart, Muriel cocks her head like a bird, a parrot, and in a parrot-like way, a British parrot, she says, "Hello darling." It's a joke between them. A private joke, one of those jokes where you really have to be one of the players for it to be the least bit amusing. Only when they are seated does Albie remark on the slight stench wafting from the bathroom, along with the squares of trod-upon toilet paper, which lead like a trail of bread crumbs from the bathroom to just beyond their table. If anything is to be gleaned from this seating arrangement, it's Muriel's sense of proportion. As a cultural anthropologist, Muriel has seen children with their hands cut off, famine and disease running rampant, elephants slaughtered for spite, all of which keeps a table by the bathroom in perspective. When she says, "It was the only one available. Can you bear it?" Albie nearly swoons over how reasonable she is, how rational, how not crazy.

"You look good," he says, to which she says, "You don't. You look dreadful."

"Not half as bad as I feel."

"Do I dare ask?"

All Albie can do is shake his head.

"That bad?" Muriel says.

"Worse," Albie tells her. They have yet to look at the menu, but the waitress is there at their table. Her pad open and her pen poised. Albie orders what he had the last time he was here, what he orders *every* time he is here, an avocado and tomato sandwich on whole wheat toast, extra mayo. Muriel asks about the soup of the day, which turns out to be lentil soup. "My favorite," Muriel says, as if the waitress played a part in lentil being the soup of the day.

Albie adds two Dr. Brown's cherry sodas to their order, and then looks to Muriel who nods, and asks the waitress, "Can you put a shot of brandy in those?"

"We don't serve alcohol here," the waitress says, and Albie explains that Muriel was joking, and, as if further explanation were required, Albie says, "She's from England."

When the waitress is done with them and they are alone, Muriel tells Albie about her visit with her family, about mass on Christmas Eve and mass on Christmas Day at the Anglican church where her father is a bishop. "Then, of course, there was the huge dinner with my brothers and their wives and masses of little ones. It was perfectly lovely," Muriel says, "and positively stifling. And yours?" she asks.

Prompt: A Hat (300 words or less)

It's Sunday afternoon. A man and a woman, both in their late sixties, sit side by side on the cafeteria-style chairs. I watch them from a distance of two tables away. The man and the woman are husband and wife. They have been married for over forty years. The chairs are uncomfortable. So are the man and the woman. They don't want to be here. They live in Queens. They don't like to come into the city, which is what they call Manhattan, although there is nothing much Manhattan-like about this part of Manhattan. I'd never say that this couple looks younger than they are, because they don't, but they seem to be from another time, like they've been jettisoned from the 1950s or '60s to now, to the first days of 2009. It could be because of their hats. Despite the fact that it is warm, stuffy even, in this dining room, neither of them has yet to take off their coat or hat. They look as if they don't plan to stay more than a couple of minutes. The woman has unbuttoned her coat, but the man has not. His coat is the kind often referred to as a car coat, which is something between a traditional coat and a jacket. It's gray, not 100-percent wool, but a wool blend

with pile lining and knit cuffs. His hands are jammed
in the pockets and, although I can't see them, I imagine
they are balled into fists. The woman's coat is her good
coat, the one she wears on Sundays and special occasions. It's navy blue. She got it on sale at Macy's nine
years before. Folded neatly in her pocketbook is her
ivory-colored church veil, which is 100-percent poly-
ester. Her pocketbook is on her lap, and she grips the
strap with both hands. His hat a Donegal tweed flat cap,
brown and beige, with a snap brim. It came from Ire-
land and cost a pretty penny. The man never would've
spent that kind of money for a hat, but his brother,
who might or might not be into something crooked,
bought it for him at least twenty years ago. Although
he has never said this to anyone, the man loves the hat
and in the winter months, he rarely takes it off. In the
summer, he keeps it on the top of his closet in a ziplock
bag to prevent the moths from getting at it. The woman's hat is hand-crocheted, a cross between a beret and
a beanie, and the yarn is blue ombré, festooned with a
pom-pom on top. She did not crochet the hat herself.
She doesn't have a knack for that sort of thing.

They want nothing to do with their daughter, but
they felt obligated to visit because it's her birthday.
A drug addict. That's what she is. A drug addict who
twice now, twice, without repenting either time, tried
to kill herself, as if she didn't know that suicide is a

mortal sin. Oh, she knew, but she didn't give a good goddamn about anyone, not her parents, not the Church, nothing except some filthy cat. To think, she was once a nurse in this same hospital where she is now housed with drug-addicted mentally insane psychopaths and whatever else. "How the mighty have fallen," her mother says to her.

Her father refuses to speak to her, not even to say hello. He takes off his hat and examines it, flicking away a speck of lint.

"Have you made any plans for when you get out of here?" her mother asks. "If they let you out, that is."

"I'm going to get a cat," the daughter tells her parents.

Her father's face flushes a deep red, the result of a spike in his blood pressure. He stands up, puts his hat back on his head.

Her mother gets up, too. They've had enough. They're leaving. Her father tells her, "You've brought us nothing but disgrace." He adjusts the brim of his cap. His face is even redder than it was before.

She doesn't know what to say, and then she does. She says, "I hope you stroke out, you fuck."

*The truth is that this never happened. Her parents have never come to visit.

The Shape of It

EVEN THOSE YEARS WHEN BUNNY was well, or well enough, she was not above the occasional Christmas snit. And since it'd seemed as if Bunny had lost track of the days, or perhaps she was as indifferent to Christmas this year as she was to eating or bathing—whatever it was, for the sake of sanity, hers and his—Albie would forgo the pleasure of decorating a scrawny tree with candy canes and tinsel while Eartha Kitt sang "Santa Baby." He would forgo the gifts and the pancakes and let the holiday slip by. He would treat the twenty-third to the twenty-sixth of December as one long day. But on the twenty-second, Albie came home from work to find four brown cartons topped with red stick 'um bows fixed like demented hats at the intersection of the UPS tape, as if the UPS tape were ribbon, stacked by the fireplace. Theirs is not a working fireplace, but still it's a nice feature. Bunny had shopped for Christmas gifts online. She'd shopped for Christmas gifts for Albie, for Albie to have gifts to open on Christmas morning.

For last-minute holiday shoppers the pickings are slim. The air in the stores is frenetic; the panic contagious. Failure is pretty much guaranteed but Albie persevered. At Barney's, he found a simple silver bangle bracelet, the sort of thing you can't *not* like, and a pink and black square silk scarf. Had he remembered, or had he known in the first place, that Bunny does not wear square scarves, that she wears only oblong scarves, he would've kept looking because there's no arguing that his heart wasn't in the right place. His next stop was the Chelsea Market where, to get a box of the sugar cookies she likes, he braved the push and shove of the crowds and their decided lack of good cheer. Only the bookstore on Seventeenth Street allowed for a bit of leisurely browsing. Albie selected Allen Perry's new novel, which got a rave review in last week's *Times*. Allen Perry was not a friend of Bunny's, but they sometimes wound up at the same parties. Then, Albie stopped in Rite Aid for wrapping paper and six catnip-filled mice for Jeffrey.

Come Christmas morning, Albie set two mugs of coffee and four scones on a plate on the coffee table. Bunny sat up on the couch. "Merry Christmas," Albie said, and he handed her a flat, square box wrapped in paper riddled with elves, which she unwrapped with the deliberate care of someone intending to save the paper. With an edge of the scarf pinched between the tips of her thumb and forefinger, she lifted it from the box, and without a whole lot of affect—you could even say none, no affect at all—she said, "Thank you. It's very beautiful." She made no mention of the shape of the scarf. Perhaps she was being gracious, or perhaps it was square/oblong, who gives a fuck?

For Albie, Bunny had bought a black cashmere scarf and two crew neck sweaters—one dark gray, the other a lighter gray. A gray merino wool crew neck sweater is a gift that is second in line only to a three-pack of Hanes underwear when it comes to uneventful presents, but Albie was elated at the monotony of them. Sartorially speaking, Albie is practically Amish. His jackets, coats, gloves, shoes and socks are black and pose no conflict with the uniformity of his pale-blue or white oxford button-down shirts. Black, white, gray, pale blue, such is his rainbow. Except for his ties. His ties are his nod to color. Although he rarely wears a tie, he has many of them, all gifts from Bunny, and all as vibrant and spectacular as a collection of butterflies. He cares for them as if they were precious, delicate things. This Christmas she did not buy him a tie, but in addition to the scarf and the sweaters, she got him an authentic New York Yankees baseball cap, which he will never wear, but he *is* a devoted Yankees fan, and glad to have an authentic Yankees cap, and he loves Bunny all the more for buying him such a thing.

In the same methodical way that she unwrapped the scarf, she unwrapped the bracelet, and in the same flat tone, she said, "It's very beautiful. Thank you." The third gift she opened with equal care. Running her hand over the book jacket as if it had texture, she said to Albie, "It's curious how in all these years we've been married, you've never once bought me a book I wanted to read," and with some serious force behind it, Allen Perry's new novel went winging across the room. Albie got his coat. He walked along Eighth Avenue, which was desolate.

When the desire to choke his wife to death subsided, he went home.

While he was out, Bunny had unwrapped the box of sugar cookies, and she ate one before bringing her fist down hard on the box, breaking the rest of the cookies into pieces and crumbs.

"Since then," Albie tells Muriel, "if she's not sleeping or trying to sleep or pretending to be asleep, she's crying. Sometimes I worry that she'll never stop crying, like those people who get the hiccups forever. She lives on the couch. She hasn't taken a shower or even brushed her teeth all week."

"She must get up to go to the loo." Muriel's logic is thrilling.

Although he's not sure why, Albie elects not to tell Muriel how Bunny hurts herself, how she pummels her thighs with her fists or bites her lip until it bleeds, as if to reveal what seems to be, above all the rest of it, a secret, would be to betray her.

When their food arrives, Muriel waits for her soup to cool. Albie picks up his sandwich, but puts it down before taking a bite. "She hasn't left the apartment in six weeks," he says. "Maybe more. It's been close to a month since she's spoken to anyone except me. But now, she is hell-bent on going out tonight. And not just to dinner, but to that tedious after-party, too. I can't talk her out of it."

Muriel, who shares Bunny's heretofore expressed revulsion for New Year's Eve, plans to have the leftover Chinese food in her fridge for dinner, and then curl up with a good book, which just happens to be Allen Perry's new novel, about which she's heard nothing but great praise. She lets her spoon rest in the soup bowl and says to Albie, "Maybe this is the beginning of the end."

"So you think I should take it as a good sign?" Albie asks.

"I didn't say that. I said only that it could be the beginning of the end." Muriel reaches over the table and slides her hand along Albie's cheek.

Identity Theft

IN THE HALL CLOSET, BEHIND the infrequently used vacuum cleaner, a lamp that needs rewiring, a scrolled map of the world, and a collection of classic comic books in a carton, Bunny finds the paper shredder. A paper shredder for home use looks like a portable printer set on a mid-sized plastic bucket lined with a Hefty bag. A paper shredder for home use was a popular item back when shredding paper was thought to be a safeguard against identity theft. Now, it's hardly worth the effort to sift through garbage looking for old bank statements dirtied with coffee grounds and wet paper towels when you can hack into a computer instead. But fear of identity theft was not Bunny's reason for having bought a paper shredder. Her reason was Albie's penchant for xeroxing, in a minimum of triplicate—just in case, and despite being filed on his computer—copies of his papers, notes he's made for papers not yet written, far-flung correspondence and a gazillion articles of interest torn from newspapers and magazines. His file cabinets bulge like extra pounds around the middle when your pants won't zip up no matter how much you suck it in. "Just in case of what?" Bunny had asked, countless times. "Just in case of what?"

Just in case of nothing that has a sensible answer, except Albie finds peace of mind in having more than one of every-thing: three tubes of toothpaste, seven boxes of jumbo paper clips, four rolls of Scotch tape, a dozen six-packs of uni-ball pens (four black, two blue), five jars of his favorite fig jam, and it's possible they'll never again have to buy toilet paper. When he can, Albie buys in multiples, in bulk. Even crap they never use or things that have turned unusable over time, like the hun-dreds of rubber bands that dried out and broke.

Albie's response to the paper shredder was, "Haha. Very funny."

Bunny could've brought it back to Staples, exchanged it for more pens and Scotch tape, but she didn't bother. Instead, she put the paper shredder in the closet and, more or less, forgot about it.

Now, as if she were walking in her sleep, walking in a way that is at once vague and yet deliberate, a ghost on a mission, Bunny carries the paper shredder to the small room that serves as her office. A television documentary that Bunny and Albie once watched on the phenomenon of sleepwalking featured a man who woke up to a policeman rapping on his car window because he was parked in front of a fire hydrant. A fire hydrant that happened to be almost a hundred miles from his home. In a sound sleep, the man drove almost one hundred miles and parked his car. Bunny couldn't get over it. "In his *sleep*," she marveled. "The man *parallel* parked his car. While *sleeping*."

Because Albie grew up in the city and never learned to drive, he was less impressed by this feat than Bunny. He said something about the enigma of the brain, how little about it is understood, how it is the last frontier of physiology. "You're missing the point," Bunny said. "Most people can't parallel park when they're *awake*."

In terms of size, Bunny's office isn't much bigger than a refrigerator. It's a tight fit, but it accommodates her desk, a battered old schoolteacher's desk of heavy oak with a set of drawers on each side, the matching swivel chair, a four-drawer file cabinet, and a narrow bookcase. A corkboard hangs above the desk. Also similar to a refrigerator, the office has no windows. It suits her, or rather, it suit*ed* her quite well until five or six months ago when, as if a barbed-wire fence had been erected, a barbed-wire fence enhanced with an electrical current, she kept her distance from the room that was hers. Now, except for additional layers of dust, she finds her office exactly as she left it. Exactly as she left it is anarchy in a box. There *is* a desk under the tarp of paper that extends from edge to edge. Paper which includes bank statements, advertisements torn from magazines, mostly for makeup or skin cream she'd intended to buy but didn't, handwritten instructions, directions and phone numbers scribbled on the backs of envelopes, the crumpled wrapper of a Snickers bar, notes jotted down for later, thoughts, observations, conversations overheard, and daily to-do lists. In the midst of all this debris, rising up like a white whale, is her computer. The keyboard, however, is nowhere to be seen. A pair of scissors is open on the floor handy to a patent leather shoe with a four-inch heel. Also on the floor are a dirty ashtray, empty packs of cigarettes, a few wire hangers, and the dictionary, open. Four T-shirts and a bra hang over the back of the chair.

To plug in the paper shredder, she'll need to unplug either the computer or the printer. She doesn't bother to note which one she pulls from the outlet because what difference does it make? Then, the way a raffle ticket is picked from a bowl of hundreds of raffle tickets, Bunny plucks a sheet of paper from the mess on her desk. The shredder is shark-like, swift and ferocious. The bank statement is in ribbons. The same goes for a Visa bill, an invitation to a baby shower, a request for a donation to fight cancer along with the free pink ribbon to pin to your blouse, a postcard from the dentist reminding her she is due for a cleaning, a plea that includes a gift of return address labels from the Humane Society and her PEN American Center membership-renewal form.

Bunny opens the top drawer of her file cabinet, and with no hesitation or break in time she shreds copies and originals of reviews of her books, and interviews she gave that appeared, for the most part, in newspapers and magazines read by people who don't read books, and in obscure journals to which no more than eight people subscribe, albeit eight people who do read books. When the plastic bucket reaches capacity, when the shredded paper spills over the edge, Bunny goes to the kitchen for more Hefty bags. In the cabinet beneath the sink there is an open box of them, and three more boxes unopened.

Contracts she's never read, and royalty statements, incomprehensible to her except for the fact that each of them ends in a negative number, emerge as confetti, and Bunny moves on to the file labeled AUTHOR PHOTOS. In all of these photographs, Bunny is smiling widely. Photographs that span two decades and four books. Five books, if you include the last one, which Bunny does not. She feeds the eight-by-ten black-and-white headshots of herself into the shredder. It was a mistake, the smiling. She never should have smiled.

Next: two aborted novels, and stories that never took off.

Then: her college diploma, *magna cum laude*, together with her Phi Beta Kappa certificate, two documents that should have been proof—proof like the Scarecrow in *The Wizard of Oz* needed a piece of paper to prove that he had a brain—documented proof that she was *not* a dumb bunny. But the proof was tainted. The two nights, non-consecutive, with the chemistry professor cast doubt on the A; there was another one, too. Philosohpy of Religion. Phi Beta Kappa conferred on her nothing but shame; the shame that comes with winning when you know you cheated.

Letters from before there was email, and emails she'd printed out while under the delusion, obviously humiliating, that her correspondence might someday be of interest to PhD students of future generations.

A birthday card from Stella. *You put the fun in dysfunctional.*

The way she once saved ticket stubs and programs from high school football games, she later saved the note a man in a restaurant handed to her, nearly twenty years ago, passing by her table as he was leaving: *Do you believe in love at first sight?*

Matchbooks from places now gone—Trader Vic's, the Mudd Club, Nell's.

Mother's Day cards signed (by Albie) *Love, Angela*.

Three photographs of Bunny and Albie standing in front of City Hall the day they were married. Another photograph: Bunny and her two sisters, the three girls sitting on the couch. Flanked by Nicole, age sixteen, and Dawn who was ten, Bunny, in the middle, was fourteen and had recently put on weight. They are dressed up for their cousin Laura's wedding. Bunny's dress pinched at her waist. Her sisters are wearing big say-cheese smiles. Bunny had refused to say cheese.

Why, for all these years, did she keep this cheap print of a girl holding a bouquet of daisies? The girl in the print, facing left, has long blond hair. She is wearing a pink dress and a straw boater hat, a black grosgrain ribbon trailing down her back. When it hung on her bedroom wall, it was in a white frame, and Bunny had wondered if her mother had put it there as a rebuke, a daily reminder that nothing about Bunny was as it should've been, that everything about Bunny was all wrong. The girl in the pink dress probably wasn't even a real person in real life.

Postcards from Prague, Budapest, Venice—postcards in lieu of photographs—Los Angeles, Austin, Berlin, Paris, Minne-apolis—her travels—Seattle, Krakow, Florence. Now, trying to spin memory from knowledge, from a vantage point higher up, she pictures herself on the Ponte Vecchio, walking across the bridge, in the way that people who claim to have died on an operating table relate the experience of the soul rising from the body, rising up to the track of fluorescent lights overhead, where the soul—a transparent self—hovers, watching as the doctors try to bring the body of their dead self back to life, which happens because God has intervened. Bunny has her first articulate thought about all this shredding paper. She thinks, *God isn't going to save me.*

Unlike Albie, Bunny does believe in God. Not in any kind of formal or traditional way. More like concept, a theory. But in whatever guise, you might think Bunny's God doesn't much like her, either.

The picture of Bunny and Stella, on the day they graduated from college, dressed in their caps and gowns, sticking their tongues out at the camera. Shredded.

Devotion

THE SAME WAY A SCOTCH on the rocks at the end of a long day does not get you drunk, but rather relieves all the tension and stress of what came before it, that's what it is like for Albie when he is in Muriel's bed. "I should get going," Albie says, and Muriel concurs, but he makes no move in that direction.

It would be wrong to think of Muriel as Albie's mistress or anything else silly or sordid. Muriel and Albie are the best of friends who, every now and again, go to bed together because it's a good thing for the both of them. The good it does Albie should be obvious, and despite a general assumption that a single woman is a desperately needy woman who will cling to you like a koala bear to a eucalyptus tree—the same way it's thought that to be a single man over forty is to wear a sandwich board announcing that you have deeply rooted psychological problems—any pity for Muriel is pity wasted. She adores Albie, but what she wants from him is what she wants from any man she takes to bed, which amounts to, in her words, a happy romp in the hay. She *enjoys* fucking, but it doesn't *mean* anything. A drink, a fuck, it's all the same to her, which is not to say she is indiscriminate. On the contrary, she's terrifically picky because both activities require some degree of conversation, and Muriel is easily bored.

What Muriel does *not* want, what she absolutely, unequivocally, does not want is a husband or a boyfriend or a commitment or any obligation or responsibility to any man or anyone else, either. Muriel doesn't even have a cat.

If ever Bunny were to have asked, "Are you fucking Muriel?" Albie would've said, "Muriel is one of my closest friends." But before you go passing judgment on passive deceit, consider this: the truth, the whole truth, the cold truth, the hard truth, the ugly truth, the sad truth, and someone else's idea of the truth which is not necessarily your own—the truth can be a cruel and dangerous weapon; flat out not nice. The truth is not necessarily a welcome addition to a conversation.

But Bunny has never asked Albie if he is fucking Muriel, because who knows where such a question would lead. Bunny has her faults, but—and she'd be the first to say so—there is no one she dislikes more than a sanctimonious hypocrite, and she's got secrets of her own. What matters is their devotion. Big picture devotion. Should Albie ever find himself in need of something like a kidney, Bunny would, just like that, fork one over. "It's no big deal," she'd say. "I've got two of them," and then she'd say no more about it. Not ever again. For Bunny, what matters most is that Albie would never leave her, and all comfort is found in knowing that he won't ever leave her. Not even now, even though now she wishes he would leave her. More than once over these last weeks, repeated because she didn't recall having said so before, she's said, "If I were you, I'd divorce me."

Albie's response has been to laugh lightly and say, "I'll think about it." Then, just to be sure she understood that he was teasing, he'd kiss her on the top of her head and pretend not to notice when she winced.

Again, Albie says to Muriel, "I should get going."

Are You Here?

DRIVER'S LICENSE. SHREDDED.
Passport. Shredded.
All evidence of Bunny. Shredded.

Where Are You?

BUNNY PULLS THE PLUG FROM the socket and holds it as if she's not sure what to do with it or what purpose it has. The opacity of the moment is shattered when she hears Albie's key in the door, as if the sound of the door opening were the same as the clank of a gate closing behind her.

Albie slips off his coat and drapes it over the back of a chair. "Bunny," he calls. "Bunny?" When she doesn't respond, foreboding rises in him like heat. "Bunny, where are you? Bunny? Bunny, are you here?"

Of course Bunny hears Albie calling out for her, and she hears the disturbance in his voice, but she doesn't know what to say. Is she here? Here, surrounded by Hefty bags filled with the documentation of herself now destroyed; the evidence of her life shredded, and how does she answer the question, *Are you here?*

Albie's heart fibrillates madly while Jeffrey rubs against his legs. It's a cat's way of saying, "You're home! You're home! Don't ever go away again." Albie picks Jeffrey up and holds him close. Jeffrey purrs. It's a well-documented fact that physical contact with a dog or a cat calms anxiety and lowers blood pressure, but at this moment Jeffrey is having no such effect. Albie whispers into the cat's ear, "Where's your mother? Where's Bunny?" And then, as if by magic, magic the way a flock of doves gets produced from thin air, there standing in the living room is Bunny, who says, "You're home."

Albie puts Jeffrey down, and asks her, "Didn't you hear me calling you?"

"No," she lies. "I was cleaning up."

"Cleaning up? Cleaning up what?"

"My office." Bunny takes her place on the couch. She covers her legs with that itchy blanket, and she asks, "Did you have a nice time?"

Albie's heartbeat has settled into a more measured thump, but it is hardly the heartbeat of a person at rest. "Yes," he tells Bunny. "I had a nice time."

"I like Muriel," Bunny says.

Albie sits in a chair across from her, and says, "I like Muriel, too," and Bunny suggests to him, "You should marry her."

As if Bunny were being flippant, Albie says, "Muriel might think otherwise." Then he asks, "How are you feeling?"

"Okay, I guess," she says, but without conviction.

"And what about tonight? You still want to go?"

"Yes," she says. "I still want to go."

Heeding Muriel's good counsel, Albie makes no attempt to change her mind. Instead he says, "I'm going to take a nap."

"What time is it?" Bunny asks.

Albie looks at his watch. "Three fifty-two," he tells her.

"Three fifty-two," Bunny repeats. "Three fifty-two," as if she could hold on to what has, in these few seconds, already passed.

"I'll wake you in an hour, hour and a half," Albie says, even though it is he who is going to nap. Bunny won't sleep, but she will close her eyes.

She will close her eyes.

Prompt: Describe a Landscape (300 words or less)

Picture it like this: I am driving a car on a narrow and lonely mountain road. A narrow and lonely mountain road that winds like ribbon. I am above the tree line. It doesn't matter what kind of car I am driving, but it definitely is not a new car. It's an old car, a shit-can of a car. The sky grows dark, but not because it's nearing night. It's sometime between two and three in the afternoon. The sky grows dark because storm clouds are gathering, and it gets darker still. A drop of rain splats on the hood of my shit-can car. And then another drop of rain splats and then another and then more. I turn on the windshield wipers, but nothing happens. I turn the windshield wipers off and then on again, but still nothing happens. The windshield wipers don't work. The windshield wipers are broken. The rain is no longer falling in drops. The rain is falling in puddles that splash against the car windows as if pails of water were being emptied from above. There is no place to pull over. I can't see the road. I put the car in park, and turn off the ignition. I sit there and watch the rain wash over the windows. I watch the landscape, a world, without definition, and I listen to the rain drumming on the roof of the car.

People who are not easy to like, they have feelings just like nice people do.

While Albie Sleeps

IF STOCK IS TO BE put in the Hippocratic theory of the four humors as indicators of temperament, it would be safe to say Bunny was born with an extravagance of *melaina chole*, more commonly known as black bile. Pensive, withdrawn, wary, pragmatic and pessimistic, she was an unhappy child, and to see her now, you might reasonably assume there was never a time when she was happy; an assessment neither accurate nor inaccurate. There have been long stretches of something like happiness. But from the onset of puberty until the end of her first semester at college, there were six seamless years of immaculate misery. Her anguish was pure, her angst a masterwork, and her adolescent rage, like coal over time and under pressure, crystalized; a gem of flawless wretchedness that all too often manifested itself in a desire to make everyone around her wretched, as well.

One night, her father, having reached his limit, having had it "up to here," told her if she was unable to sit at the table and have a civilized conversation with her family, then perhaps she should take her plate outside and eat dinner in the yard. "Like a wild animal," he said.

"For your information," Bunny retorted, "wild animals don't eat from plates," and she picked up her plate along with her knife and fork, and went out to the backyard, where she did not eat, but she sat in the grass and pictured her family, choking on guilt and remorse, and how soon her father would come out and apologize. Maybe her mother would come with him, to give her daughter a hug, and later maybe her sisters would come to her room, just to hang out with her. When Bunny was done with this picture, she left her plate and utensils in the yard because wild animals don't put their dinnerware in the dishwasher, and she went to her room, where she sat at her desk. Her desk was part of her matching bedroom set: bed, chest of drawers and nightstand, all white with a trim of pink flowers. The bedspread and throw pillows were a pink floral print. Pink ruffled curtains, a pink rug shaped and hooked as a rose; it was a room that in no way reflected that which Bunny articulated as the darkness of her soul. Her room, *her* room, the walls and the ceilings, she argued, ought to be painted matte black.

"Not a chance," her mother had said. "Not in my house. When you have your own house, you can paint your walls whatever color want."

"For your information," Bunny said, "black isn't a color."

Bunny was big on the preface "for your information," a turn of phrase that endeared her to no one.

From her white desk drawer with the hateful pink flowered trim, Bunny took two pens and her notebook, which she opened to a fresh page. To see herself through this time that was unbearable for all concerned, Bunny wrote poems, what she called poems. Anyone who knew anything about poetry would've called them drivel, and they'd have been right. Even worse, she was prolific, some nights producing four or even five of these cringeworthy poems; sentences of lugubrious banality, the lines broken at random. Although she remembers having written reams of these things, she can't recall the specifics of any of them. Except for one, and even then, she can remember only the title, which was *Fuck You Everyone*, and at that, for the first time in a long time, Bunny laughs. Not a big laugh, it's more of a snort, but it is a genuine visceral expression of pleasure that propels her up from the couch in search of paper and a pen, which she finds in the kitchen. Without thinking, she opens the refrigerator and gets an apple.

Apple in one hand, the pen in the other, her back resting against the arm of the couch, notepad propped up on her knees, Bunny writes: *Fuck You Everyone*. Then she bites into the apple, which is perfectly crisp. *Fuck You Everyone, the revision*. But it can't be a revision when there is no trace of the original. She crosses out *the revision* and writes *the sequel*, which doesn't sound right, either. *Again? Fuck You Everyone, Again*, that works for her. She skips a line, the pen poised for words to flow. The pen poised for the words to flow, but the words don't flow. It's as if she is physically unable to transmit the impulse from one neuron to another, as if her synaptic system were clogged the way an artery can clog or the way hair and gunk will clog the bathroom sink and the water puddles around the drain with nowhere to go. The words can't, or won't, flow, from head to hand, from thought to paper. She takes another bite from the apple. On a fresh sheet of paper she writes *Fuck You Everyone, Again*. Words bottleneck at the base of her skull. She presses the point of the pen hard into the page, like pressing against an iron door, either locked or too heavy for her to open, but then she writes.

She writes: *Fuck You Everyone, Again / Stella, you had no right to die*.

Bunny lets go of the apple. It falls to the floor.

Up and Away

FRESHLY SHOWERED AND SHAVED, ALBIE'S hair is wet and he's got a towel wrapped around his waist. It appears that Bunny is sleeping. On the floor near the couch, Albie spots the apple. He reaches around the coffee table to pick it up, and Bunny's eyes open like the snap of a window shade. Where the apple has been eaten, the white flesh has turned brown. Bunny gropes for the notepad, and when she locates it safely hidden under the blanket, she rolls over to look at Albie, and she says, "I slept."

"And you ate." Albie holds the apple as if were something to contemplate, like Yorick's skull.

"What time is it?" Bunny asks.

"It's getting near six. How are you feeling?"

"I'm okay," she says. "I'm good." Then she says, "I should take a shower," and Albie dares to be hopeful. Maybe Muriel was right, maybe this is the beginning of the end.

The hot shower turns her skin pink, and it feels like a gentle massage. Bunny washes away the grime and sweat with a moisturizing liquid body soap. A facial scrub made with granules of apricot seeds exfoliates, like sandpaper, the dead skin cells on her face and neck. After she shampoos her hair, Bunny reaches for the bottle of all-natural, home-brewed hair conditioner, which was a birthday gift from her sister Nicole. Bunny had feared the conditioner contained something like placenta from farm animals or human breast milk. But now, either she doesn't care, or else she forgot about the possibility of the grossout factor, and she combs the conditioner through her wet hair. While she waits the advised two minutes before rinsing it out, she cleans her fingernails with Albie's nailbrush.

The transformation from rancid to clean, particularly after a stretch of feculence, is like being born again, minus Jesus. Praise is not for the Lord, but for the Hydroluxe showerhead.

With one towel wound around her head like a turban and another towel wrapped around her body sarong-style, Bunny roots around in the cabinet under the bathroom sink for the blow-dryer. It's possible that after using it at last, she put it away elsewhere. She knows that to continue to look is to risk frustration, and frustration is an accelerant when fire is a metaphor for rage. To quit looking for it, to let her hair dry naturally, could be read as a mentally sound decision, and it will be fine. Although, even when all was well, she rarely bothered with the blow-dryer. Her hair is glossy black and thick with a natural wave, and Bunny has always been lazy.

Albie dresses the way he eats. One bite of fish, then a forkful of mashed potatoes, a sip of wine followed by a Brussels sprout or a julienned carrot, then another bite of fish. Now, Bunny finds him sitting on the edge of the bed about to put on one sock. He'll put on the second sock after he buttons his shirt.

The top dresser drawer is where Bunny keeps her underthings. She pushes aside the pretty black lace bras, the pink chemise, the stockings that require a garter belt. She does not consider the silk panties for the same reason that, when her towel drops to the floor, Albie averts his gaze and, now that his shirt is buttoned, he busies himself with his second sock.

Thus far dressed in a no-frills beige bra and black tights, Bunny stands at her closet, deliberating. Her favorite clothes are the vintage things she's found at flea markets and thrift stores. Dresses and jackets and hats and gloves and shawls from the 1920s and '30s, eras long before she was born, when women's clothes were unmistakably feminine; clothes made of velvet and lace and silk and chiffon, clothes that move with a woman's body like liquid silver.

Albie asks Bunny, as he always does, which tie should he wear, which of his ties would go well with his suit. Bunny goes to his closet where his ties, wild with color and kaleidoscopic in patterns, hang neatly, precisely, according to some kind of crackpot Dewey decimal system he devised, on tie racks in his closet. All his ties go with his suit. Albie's suit, his only suit, is black, which can't come as a surprise. Other than the fine weave of the fabric and that it was made in Italy and not ordered from the J. Crew catalog or L.L. Bean, it is an unremarkable suit, which is why he likes it. His shoes and socks are also black. The shirt he is wearing is white. The tie Bunny selects is heavy silk; heavy silk, yellow backdrop to multitudes of cornflower blue hieroglyphic-like birds. After tying his joyful tie into a perfect half-Windsor knot, Albie goes to the living room to read while he waits for Bunny to get ready.

Bunny decides on a dress from the late 1920s, ivory-colored velvet, mid-calf and cut on a bias. The fabric shimmers and shadows like the tiny mother-of-pearl buttons adorning the cuffs of the sleeves. Her shoes are black patent-leather T-straps with French heels. From her jewelry box, she gets her pearl-drop earrings, a gift from Albie for their tenth wedding anniversary, and a strand of pearls, another gift from Albie, but she can't remember when or for what reason. The only makeup she wears is red lipstick, a matte maraschino-cherry red, and that's that.

Fully absorbed with a book, something on paleontology, Albie is unaware that Bunny is there in the living room, until she says, "What do you think?" She turns, in place, full circle, like the pink ballerina in a music box.

For the first time in many weeks, Albie looks at his wife without feeling the need to close his eyes, and like a nine-year-old boy struck by love for the first time, he says, "You look like Snow White."

"Really?" she asks. "I look okay?"

"Better than okay." Albie gets up from the chair. "You look gorgeous."

Although his tie needs no adjusting, Bunny nonetheless slides her hand over the heavy silk as if straightening it out, a decidedly wifely gesture, and then steps back to take in the full effect. "That is one handsome tie," she says. "Where'd you get it?"

"My wife bought it for me," Albie says, and Bunny says, "Your wife has good taste." Then she asks, "Did you feed Jeffrey?"

After Albie says that of course he fed Jeffrey, there's a pause that precedes the question. "You're sure you want to go?"

Getting There

YET ANOTHER TAXI PASSES THEM by, and Albie, who is hardly without dorky tendencies, croons, *Baby, it's cold outside*, just the one line and it's off-key. Bunny suggests that they walk instead. "We could be here all night before we get a cab." She gets no argument from Albie. A native Manhattanite, he always prefers to walk, and Bunny is as comfortable in high heels as she would be in a pair of those Finnish nature shoes that her sister wears.

The wind is with them; that is, at their backs, wind that periodically gusts, hurrying them along as if they were fallen leaves or candy wrappers. They blow past revelers who are hunched over pushing into the wind, their heads lowered like battering rams. Forging ahead is a cluster of five young women wearing those occasional plastic eyeglasses, 2009, coated in silver glitter. The double zeroes are centered to look like the round-rim eyeglasses worn by Harry Potter. The girls shriek as the wind musses their hair and blows their dresses tight against their thighs, and Bunny predicts that before the night is over, one of them will have barfed on the sidewalk, another will be bent over a bathroom sink in a bar on Third Avenue, and the other three will weep with pity for themselves.

"How generous of you," Albie notes, and Bunny says, "You want to bet I'm right?"

"You can't bet when the outcome is impossible to know."

"I was speaking rhetorically."

"Right," Albie says. "I knew that."

"Sure you did." Bunny taps the side of her head, and says, "You're not all there."

"Look who's talking." Albie puts his arm around Bunny and pulls her close to him.

**Prompt: Two People Having Lunch
(300 words or less)**

I'd selected the restaurant not for the food, but for
the atmosphere. My mother, I knew, would like this
place because it was what she would call charming.
"Charming" was my mother's word. "Quaint" was
another of her words that set my teeth on edge. My
mother was deeply enamored of all things charming
and quaint. Charming and quaint is often hokey and
fake. For family vacations we went to places like Wil-
liamsburg, Virginia and Stockbridge, Massachusetts,
re-creations of Colonial American towns where we saw
how candles were made and horseshoes forged. We
bore witness to reenactments of battles between red-
coats and blue coats. This restaurant, which I chose,
was decorated to look like an old-fashioned ice cream
parlor, and it specialized in quiche Lorraine. "Specialized" was yet another of my mother's words.

Even then, an adult, at least in the eyes of the law, I
was desperate for my mother's love. Later, after I was
married, Albie had said to me, "You need to quit trying
to get what will never happen."

Having arrived at the charming restaurant a few

minutes early, I sat at a window-side table where I studied the menu. When my mother got there, I stood up and kissed her on the cheek. Age had not diminished my mother's beauty. Before sitting down, she set her pocketbook on the far end of the table where it rested against the window, where it was out of the way, but decidedly there, to be seen. I stared at the bag, and my mother said, "You should've seen Janet's face when she saw it." Janet, one of her closest friends, was *comfortable*. Comfortable or very comfortable or well-off or well-to-do were her euphemisms for rich. According to my mother, only vulgar people said rich. Her ideas about the behavior and the lexicon of fine people, such as herself, were fixed. "Fine" was yet another one of her words that pained me. Janet wasn't *rich* rich, but she was *very* comfortable.

Cupping her hand around her mouth and leaning in closer to me, my mother had a secret she was anxious to share. "It's a reproduction," she said.

From two blocks away and at night, you'd spot that pocketbook as a knockoff. One of those achingly cheap knockoffs, the kind with tin hardware or crooked seams or the poop-brown leather embossed with LW instead of LV. "You'd never know it was a copy, would you?" my mother said, and she waited for me to agree.

The thing is, it's not as if my mother had been longing for a Louis Vuitton pocketbook, but what she did want, what she ached for, was to give the impression that my father's business was more successful than it was, that he was a big earner, a man much admired by his own standards of admiration, a man who could afford to buy his wife a Louis Vuitton pocketbook. Because my father believed that dignity was measured in dollars, my mother believed that her twenty-dollar knockoff Louis Vuitton pocketbook lent her husband stature on his terms, which also happened to be the terms of her friend Janet.

By this point in time, I had learned to say, "You're right. No one would ever know."

Long before this point in time, my mother was flipping through one of her magazines—*Family Circle* or *Redbook*, an issue dedicated to home decorating tips. In the section on Kitchens, she was overcome by the incomparable charm of an exposed brick wall. Even without an exposed brick wall, our kitchen was gagging on charm: yellow calico potholders trimmed with red bric-a-brac and matching dishtowels, ceramic salt and pepper shakers in the guise of Amish children, the radio fashioned as an old-time telephone, the sort with a hand-crank, and more decorative roosters than any kitchen should have to bear. Unfortunately our house had no brick wall to expose, and racing through the article for the information she was after, my mother learned that it would be prohibitively expensive to lay brick on sheetrock. However, the magazine, aware that the price tag for the incomparable charm of an exposed brick wall was steep, suggested to their readers the affordable alternative: a faux-brick veneer. Sheets of clay-red, brick-shaped molded polymer, the edges darkened as if weathered by time and smoke and soot, and it was as easy to install as it was to hang wallpaper.

All day, while my sisters and I were at school, she was at it, pausing only now and then to stretch and rub the small of her back. At ten minutes past three, when Nicole and Dawn got home, our mother was nearly done installing her faux-brick veneer. Nearly done, but not quite, and because she wanted her daughters to get the full effect that would be best appreciated when the job was completed, she called out, "Don't come in." Nicole and Dawn plopped down on the couch. A few minutes later, I arrived home—I was a dawdler—to find Nicole drawing a picture of a lake surrounded by mountains, a hawk flying overhead. Dawn, picking at the eczema on her elbow, without looking up, said, "Don't go in the kitchen."

Before I got the chance to ask why, our mother called out, "Okay, girls." Like a game show hostess calling attention to the grand prize, she extended her arm with a flourish to usher us into the kitchen.

"Ta-da," she said, and then she asked, "Doesn't it look exactly like real brick?"

Dawn nodded like a bobble-head and said, "It looks just like the fireplace where those ladies made candles," and Nicole said, "It looks *exactly* like real brick to me," and I said, "Are you blind?" I said, "It's totally fake. Not in a million years would anyone think this is real brick."

The same as after a sucker punch or the flash between an aneurysm and death, there was that split second of incomprehension followed by incredulity, and then our mother swiftly left the room. Swiftly, but not before I got a good look at the expression on her face. Dawn ran after her, calling out, "Mommy, no!" Nicole glared at me, and as if that weren't enough unhappiness for one day, she asked, "And you wonder why no one in the family likes you?"

Until then, I had wondered no such thing; until then, I'd assumed they all liked me just fine, but once Nicole put it into words, spelled it out for me, it made sense; as much sense a nine-year-old girl could fathom of *no one in the family likes you.*

Fantails

A FORCIBLE BLAST OF FRIGID wind sweeps them through the door where Albie parts a heavy red curtain, a buffer against the cold. On the other side of the curtain, Bunny looks around slowly, and like a puppet come to life, deliberately, as if the only way to take in this room is through the sum of its parts.

That the Red Monkey has managed to retain its cachet long after its Asian-fusion expiration date can be credited, in large part, to the fact that—thank you Susan Sontag—camp is forever, and the Red Monkey is up to its monkey neck in Hollywood Regency chinoiserie: glossy black wallpaper flocked eponymously with red velveteen monkeys in a variety of monkey poses, red silk lanterns hanging from the ceiling, and Art Deco wall sconces lit with brothel-red bulbs. Mirrors are framed in faux bamboo. Call it camp or call it a tribute to French colonialism aiming to evoke an air of romance for a time and place, which maybe had a certain glamour to it if you had no objection to oppression, subjugation, forced labor and the depletion of natural resources, which included people as well as rubber trees.

The young woman who checks their coats is wearing a form-fitting *áo dài* that is the same shade of poppy red as her lipstick, her nail polish and the red silk flower pinned behind her ear. Her hair is done up in a French twist. Bunny knows that her red silk tunic is called an *áo dài* because in high school she had to write a paper for geography class on Asia, and Bunny wrote about the various traditional costumes, for which she got a C, along with the teacher's explanation for the poor grade: *Frivolous*. Mild criticism, all criticisms considered.

Albie takes the coat-check chip, red on one side, black on the other, and slips it into his jacket pocket. Scanning the room, he sees Julian at the bar waving to them. Julian is aiming for nonchalance, but if you knew Julian, you'd know he's slightly hysterical because Bunny and Albie are late.

"We couldn't get a cab," Albie apologizes. "We walked," he says.

"No problem." Julian claps him on the back, and Trudy fingers the sleeve of Bunny's dress. "Vintage?" she asks. Trudy is wearing an austere black dress. She's got a closet full of these black dresses, and each one costs more than a car. Elliot is wearing his usual shaved head and black-frame eyeglasses. As a couple, Trudy and Elliot have got that whole Berlin minimalist thing down pat, although their daughter, who is seven, refuses to wear anything that isn't lavender, which they find ironic and amusing. At first glance, it looks as if Lydia shopped for her outfit in a laundry basket: a gray sweater buttoned incorrectly rendering it asymmetrical, a teal-blue tulip skirt, lemon colored tights that sag and pink ballet flats. The overall effect is of a middle-aged woman dressed like the kind of goofy twelve-year-old girl who gets overly excited about origami. But look carefully, because every four weeks she drops four hundred and fifty dollars to get her hair cut to look as if she never gets a haircut, and the sagging yellow tights and pink flats were featured in last month's *Vogue*. Her steel-frame eyeglasses, which you might reasonably assume came free with a group insurance plan, are Prada.

Now that they've finished sizing each other up, they make their way to the podium at the entrance to the dining room, where the hostess, also wearing a formfitting poppy-red *áo dài*, tells them their table is being cleared, it'll just be a moment, and where Julian instructs them to take note of the floor. Glass tiles set contiguously; thick glass tiles, scratch resistant and artificially lit, cover a nearly wall-to-wall pool where red, black and gold ornamental fish swim below and around lily pads. As if it might not be recognized for what it is, Julian says, "It's a koi pond. Isn't that too much?"

"Yes," Bunny says. "It is. It's too much."

Lydia informs them that the smaller fish are the males. "The male koi are smaller and their tails are more elaborate," she explains, "to attract the females."

"Actually, those are goldfish," Albie corrects her. "The smaller ones are goldfish. Shubunkin fantails," he says.

"Really?" Lydia's eyes go wide as if she were a child, and Albie has just plucked a quarter from her ear.

"They can grow up to a foot long, but they're still goldfish."

Bunny never could figure out how Albie does that, how he can correct ignorance and stupidity without giving offense.

Their table is ready, and the three couples follow the hostess as she leads them through the dining room. Her formfitting poppy-red *áo dài* shimmers like the fantail of a shubunkin goldfish.

Hanoi Holiday

THE CHAIRS ARE BLACK LACQUER with red damask cushions that match the red damask tablecloth. Bunny takes a seat alongside Albie, which is sort of against dinner party rules, but no one says anything about it because of how Bunny is mental. Julian sits to her left. As if to avoid her gaze, he busies himself with his napkin, shaking it free of the intricate folds of a lotus flower, or perhaps it is meant to be an artichoke. Western silverware is set alongside the napkins, and black lacquered chopsticks rest on a diagonal across white plates. Each table setting also comes with a red paper party hat, conical, and dusted with gold glitter, and one of those party favors, the kind that unfurl like a snake's tongue. Because the proximity of the paper hat disturbs Bunny, she slides it away, closer to Albie's paper hat. Lydia is at Albie's right, which he doesn't mind, really. He is fond of her, although he does wish she wouldn't try to engage him in discussions about the Oort cloud or game theory or string theory, subjects about which Albie is not particularly knowledgeable, and about which Lydia, despite being a devoted reader of the Science section of the

Times, understands nothing. Lydia is determined to be an egghead, but as Trudy has put it, "Soft-boiled, at best," as opposed to her husband, Elliot, whom Trudy considers to be a genuine genius, in a way that inspires Bunny to imagine him as a giant brain equipped with spindly arms and legs and a pair of black glasses. Something like Mr. Potato Head.

The waiter comes to the table to ask if they'd like to start with a cocktail, and Julian says, "Six Hanoi Holidays."

Trudy quips that a Hanoi Holiday sounds like it should come with a Happy Ending, to which Elliot says, "That's funny." Elliot never laughs, but when he is amused, he will say, "That's funny." His voice is permanently pitched in a dry tone, as if every word he utters is sardonic even when he means to be genuine, which is an affect Albie chalks up to a touch of Asperger's. Bunny, never as generous as Albie, chalks it up to further indication that Elliot is a fraud. Elliot *is* something of a fraud, and his fraudulence is perpetuated by other frauds in service of their own fraudulence. Elliot is, like Bunny, a writer, but unlike Bunny, Elliot is taken seriously. *Seriously* seriously. Elliot is money in Bunny's piggy bank of self-debasement.

The Hanoi Holidays come in large goblets garnished with wedges of lime, sprigs of lemongrass and a plastic monkey that dangles on the edge of each glass by its tail or an arm. There was a time when Bunny might've slipped her blue plastic monkey into her purse, but not now. Trudy raises her goblet. "To happy endings," she toasts, "and new beginnings." Glasses clink all the way around.

"And to President-Elect Barack Obama." Lydia lifts her glass in a way closer to a salute than a toast, and they pay tribute to America's first black president.

"And next time," Trudy adds, "a woman."

Stalwart liberal Democrats, Julian, Lydia, Trudy, and Elliot are passionate, at least in terms of lip service, about issues like illegal wars, global climate change, and saving the Chelsea Hotel. Bunny and Albie do not define themselves as good liberal Democrats. Albie is a far-left Democrat. Bunny refers to herself a right-of-center Marxist. Nonetheless, they, too, toast Barack Obama because they are proud that America, that *they* elected a black man for president. *They.* Even now, Albie does not know that instead of going out to vote, Bunny stayed home and cried.

The conversation at their table buzzes with talk of the Iraq War and thank God Obama is going to bring it to an end and about his vow to close Guantanamo. Albie notes Obama's promise to take on climate change, and Julian signals the busboy to clear away their empty glasses. Trudy is thrilled that the First Lady plans to tackle childhood obesity.

Julian tells the busboy to let their waiter know that they are ready to order their appetizers.

"I'd have preferred she get involved with the arts," Lydia says, "but don't get me wrong. She is amazing."

"I'm not ready to order," Elliot says. "I haven't even looked at the menu."

"Trust me." Julian assures Elliot that he will chose well and wisely.

Trudy and Elliot exchange a look.

When the waiter appears, as unobtrusively as an apparition, at their table, Julian orders: roasted aubergines, shiitake croquettes, garlic shrimp wrapped in sugarcane, confit of charred octopus. "And we'll start with a bottle of, make that two bottles of Sancerre," he says. "The Vacheron. You can bring the menus back after we're done with our appetizers."

The waiter collects their menus, and Albie, because he is a decent person, says, "Thank you," and Bunny says, "Octopus?"

It's a gesture of affection, the way Albie closes his hand over Bunny's forearm, but also it's a signal for her to stop right there, to refrain from the lecture on the intelligence of octopuses and their pronounced nerve endings. To know that an octopus experiences pain in the extreme is the sort of thing that causes Bunny pain, too. It is also the sort of thing she uses as a weapon, an arrow of reproach at the insensitivity of others.

The waiter holds the bottle of wine for Julian to read the label, and after a seamless uncorking and smooth pour of a splash in Julian's glass, he stands there like he's made of marble while Julian lifts his glass by the stem and turns it ever so slowly as if to catch light. A gentle swirl is followed by his sniffing the wine like a dog sniffing at an unidentifiable splat of something on the sidewalk. After gargling with a mouthful of Sancerre he pronounces it excellent. "Soft, zesty, yet purely structured," he says.

The incongruity of the words—soft, zesty, yet purely structured—confounds Albie. "How do you arrive at soft, zesty, yet purely structured?"

"I can see it," Elliot says. "Soft, zesty, purely structured. Sounds like Trudy."

Trudy thanks her husband for the compliment, and Lydia mentions having read recently about balsamic vinegar being served as an after-dinner drink. "They said it was unimaginably delicious," she says.

"It is," Julian weighs in, "but it's got to the very best *tradizionale*, the stuff that goes for four to five hundred bucks a pop."

Elliot wants to know if there is really *that* much difference between the *tradizionale* and a good *condimento*, and Julian asks, "Are you kidding me?"

"No," Elliot says. "I'm asking."

"Don't get me wrong," Julian says. "There are some very decent *condimentos* out there, but even the best of them can't be compared to a *tradizionale*"

"There's a lot of counterfeiting with the *condimentos*," Albie tells them. "Adding caramel to simulate the aging process. It's a problem."

Lydia asks how would you know if it's not genuine, and Julian drones on about the complexity of flavors, and how only someone who knows absolutely nothing about balsamic vinegar would be fooled, and Trudy says she uses the commercial grade when making a honey-mustard vinaigrette, and Julian says, "Oh, Trudy, how could you?" and Bunny wonders how much longer she can sit at a table with five people engaged in passionate discourse about balsamic vinegar, the answer to which turns out to be three seconds. "Excuse me," she breaks into the conversation, "but do any of you really give a shit? I mean, you're going on about balsamic vinegar like it *matters*. Does it?" Bunny realizes that she is dangerously near to tears or hysteria or both. "Does it really matter?"

The moment that follows is awkward. No one responds until, as if she were about to approach an animal who might or might not be friendly, Lydia asks, "What would you like to talk about?"

Bunny doesn't want to talk about anything in particular, but put on the spot, she says, "Olive oil," and they are relieved because it's Bunny being Bunny. Elliot says, "That's funny," and the others laugh, although Lydia's laugh skitters along the edges of anxiety and fear.

But, before any conversation about olive oil gets off the ground, their food arrives, and Albie reminds Julian, "No octopus or shrimp for Bunny." Then he adds, "I think I'll pass on the octopus, too."

"You don't like octopus? You should've said something." Julian's distress is genuine. "I just assumed everyone liked octopus. I should've asked. Let me order something else." Julian's need to please Albie, to win his admiration, is staved off by Albie's ability to deflect obsequiousness. "Julian, it's fine," Albie says. "There's more than enough food here, and it looks fantastic. It's no big deal."

Bunny begs to differ. "It's a very big deal for the octopus," she says.

It could be that she was speaking too softly to be heard, or at least it seems that way. She gets no response, but Julian says to Albie, "Okay. All the more for me then." Julian thinks that to own up to gluttony is disarming.

"You?" Trudy asks. "What about the rest of us?"

Trudy and Julian banter about the size of the portions. Lydia says, "This is way too much. I want to save my appetite for the entrée." Albie expresses ecstasy over the aubergines, and a buzz, a high-pitched persistent buzz, shimmies its way into Bunny's ear and into her head where it amplifies and spreads out in all directions. Her nerves are jangling like bangle bracelets, and she grows more and more agitated, as if she can't remember if she turned off the stove or not, as if while she and Albie are out having their lovely dinner with lovely people, Jeffery could be dying of asphyxiation. She springs up from her chair. "A cigarette," she says. "I need a cigarette."

"Do you want me to go with you?" Albie asks.

"No," Bunny says. "I just need a cigarette. I'll be right back."

"You're sure?" Albie says.

"It's a cigarette," Bunny snaps. "I'm going out to have a cigarette, okay?"

Albie takes off his jacket, and drapes it over her shoulders.

Elliot pushes back from the table and says, "Do you mind if I join you?" and Bunny says, "You don't smoke."

They watch her walk across the dining room and out the door. "She'll be okay," Albie tries to sound as if he believes this for a fact, and Trudy tells Elliot, "Go out there. Stay with her."

The Tip of a Cigarette

WITH HER THUMB GROWING SORE, Bunny keeps at it, keeps trying to light her cigarette, but the wind repeatedly extinguishes the flame before it can catch. As if the plastic Bic lighter were like a lawn mower or a clunker of a car and that giving it a rest before trying again might just do the trick, Bunny pauses to afford the lighter the same kind of rest as a tired engine, which is when Elliot shows up. He takes the lighter from her hand. "May I?" he asks, and then he plucks the cigarette from between her lips, too. With her cigarette in his mouth, he cups one hand over the lighter to block the wind, and he gets it lit on the first try. Taking a deep puff, he holds the smoke in his lungs before he passes the cigarette to Bunny. When he exhales, he says, "Damn, that's good. You never lose the taste for it." He tells her that he quit smoking almost twenty years ago, but he'd take it up again in a skinny minute, if he could.

"Why can't you?" Bunny asks.

"That's funny," Elliot says, and Bunny says, "I didn't mean it to be funny. It was a question."

"Okay. I can't start smoking again because I don't want to die before my time." Then Elliot asks Bunny when is she going to quit and she says, "Quit what?"

"Smoking. When are you going to quit smoking?"

"Never." As if it's meant to be an exclamation mark, for emphasis, she takes a long drag on her cigarette.

They stand there, shivering, and Elliot says, "I know how you feel."

"Yeah," Bunny nods. "It's freezing out here."

"Funny," Elliot says. "But you know what I mean. The depression." Elliot tells her that he, too, suffers from depression.

Bunny bites down hard on the inside of her cheek, and Elliot says, "Wellbutrin. It really helped me. Have you tried Wellbutrin?" Elliot waits for Bunny to answer his question, and when that doesn't happen, he adds, "Of course it doesn't work for everyone. It's all about trial and error with antidepressants. But if you haven't tried Wellbutrin, you might want to talk to your shrink. It's working for a lot of us." *Us?* Elliot, taciturn Elliot, suddenly doesn't know when to shut up. "I can recommend a first-rate psychopharmacologist, if you want. This guy I go to, he's good. Top-notch."

Bunny drops the remains of her cigarette onto the pavement, and Elliot snuffs it out with the heel of his shoe. "Come on," he signals Bunny to follow him inside. "It's too damn cold out here. My hands are numb."

"You go ahead," Bunny tells him. "I'm going to have a cigarette."

"But you just had . . ." Elliot stops short. "Oh," he says, "okay," and he returns to the restaurant to join his wife and his friends in the warm and satisfied glow of the Red Monkey and the comfort of his genius and his top-notch psychopharmacologist, and his literary success, and his having no idea what it's like not to be taken seriously, having no idea how it is to feel ashamed of who you are.

Wellbutrin, now *that's* funny.

Bunny takes out another cigarette but, same as before, when she tries to light it, the wind extinguishes the flame. She tries again, and again when she sees two men walking in her direction. One of them smoking, the orange glow of the tip of his cigarette is a beacon of light. Bunny steps in front of him, holding up her cigarette as if to say, "I come in peace." Rather than fiddling with a lighter, he hands her his cigarette, and she lights her cigarette the way one candle is used to light another.

"Thanks," she says, and the man says, "These things will kill you, you know."

Bunny takes a deep drag of the cigarette, and as she exhales, the smoke laces with her breath and her words. "Not soon enough," she says, and the man laughs.

Chopsticks

WHEN BUNNY GETS BACK TO the table, Albie gets up to help her off with his jacket. She twists slightly to free her left arm. Lydia says, "You must be chilled to the bone."

"No," Bunny says. "If anything, I'm a little warm. Is it warm in here?" Then she asks Albie what time it is, and he tells her, "It's nine twenty-seven."

"I hope you don't mind," Julian says, "but we ordered dinner while you were out. I got you Banh Cuon Chay."

"Mushroom ravioli," Albie translates. "With lotus root."

"That's fine," Bunny says, and it is fine. Provided that her meal did not at some point have a beating heart, she's never been a fussy eater, and now, her ability to taste, to distinguish flavors, has dulled to the point where all food is tofu. As Bunny takes her seat, her attention fixes on a patch of the glass-tiled floor where one of the fish, a big one, calico, orange dappled with white and black, is floating, belly-up dead. It bobs the way a body, tossed into the Hudson, drifts between the pylons and gently laps at the pier, as if a murder victim were a rowboat.

"He's dead," Bunny pointedly addresses Julian, as if he'd strangled the fish with his bare hands.

"Who's dead?" Trudy asks.

"One of the fish." Julian crumples his napkin, sets it beside his plate and goes off to have a word with the manager.

Doesn't this knucklehead know that it is New Year's Eve? Does he have any idea how busy they are? The manager could give a go-flying-fuck-yourself about some shit dead fish. He flashes an icy smile, assures Julian that he'll take care of it and offers a round of drinks by way of apology. Then, in Korean, the manager tells the waiter to bring six flutes of champagne, the cheap shit, to those motherfucking jerkoff assholes at table twelve.

That's how it happens when you know the chef. Julian sits tall in his chair. Prompt disposal of the dead fish and champagne on the house, and they all pretend not to notice that the champagne is plonk. But only Bunny notices that the fish has not been disposed of. Rather, it has drifted off and come to rest alongside a nearby table where two couples, wearing their red paper hats, are too busy cracking each other up with the party favors to notice a dead fish, a mere ripple in the water.

For people such as Bunny and her friends, people who believe themselves respectful of the cultural norms, except of course when it comes to cultural norms like female circumcision and then the whole Margaret Mead thing goes out the window, to forgo chopsticks in an Asian restaurant would be an admission of provincialism. Because Albie has been eating in Chinese restaurants since the time he could chew solid food, he handles his chopsticks with dexterous flourish, like a pair of batons tossed in the air at a parade, as if they'd twirl overhead as a tiger prawn falls into his open mouth. Julian, not quite as deft as Albie, is nonetheless as masterful as expected, and Trudy and Elliot know what they are doing. Albie pronounces his food to be spectacular, and asks if anyone would like a bite. Trudy says, "I would, except then I'd have to offer you a bite of mine, and I'm not sharing." Elliot says, "Not half bad," and Julian asks, "Have I ever steered you wrong?" That Lydia uses her chopsticks the way a chimp uses a twig for a tool, to bring termite-size bits of food to her mouth, is not indicative of an inability to eat with chopsticks. Rather, it's that Lydia is a person who eats raisins one at a time. Trudy asks if they've seen the Louise Bourgeois exhibit at the Guggenheim. "Not yet," Lydia says, "but we're planning on it. I've heard that it is amazing," and Elliot says he didn't think it was amazing, he thought it was okay but overrated, and he wants to know if any of them have read the Bolaño. That's how he refers to *2666*, as "the Bolaño."

Bunny is not doing well with her chopsticks. Her hands are shivering, and they twitch as she tries to catch her food. The noise level in the dining room has risen, and the pitch of the din is an indefinite treble, a noise that seems to absorb all sound. Bunny sees mouths moving but she can't hear Lydia as she goes on about some friend of hers who is expecting triplets. She sees expressions of laughter and amusement, and Trudy's exaggerated shudder when she says, "Dear God. One was plenty for me.

Triplets? I'd kill myself," which brings the conversation not to a grinding halt, but to the kind of full and immediate stop that follows a gunshot, and with that, as if she's woken up to find herself in a car more than a hundred miles away from home, Bunny finds herself on New Year's Eve at the Red Monkey at a table for six, to hear Trudy say, "Bunny, I'm sorry. It was just a figure of speech."

"What was a figure of speech?" Bunny asks, but she really doesn't care, which is why she doesn't repeat the question when Julian mentions how some food critic he knows just got back from New Orleans, and reported that it's still a disaster area. "Right," Elliot says, "heck of a job, Brownie," and, with the exception of Bunny and Elliot, they all laugh at the foolishness and insensitivity of George Bush, and Trudy says she's counting the minutes until Inauguration Day. Albie reiterates his hope that Obama will give environmental concerns greater attention, and Julian has a thing or two to say about industrial farming, and hasn't anyone noticed that strawberries are now the size of gourds. "And they don't taste like strawberries. They taste like mush with a strawberry flavored additive."

Despite her concentration, Bunny can't keep her hands steady. The chopsticks blur as if her eyesight, too, is trembling. For the first time in weeks and weeks, she is truly hungry, and desperately she wants the food that is eluding her the way words will elude her and the way the flame went out, again and again, when she tried to light her cigarette.

Lydia asks, "Have any of you read *Anathem?*"

Elliot says he heard it was schlock, but he is curious to know Lydia's opinion.

"I'm only a few hundred pages in," she tells him, "but already it's a transformative experience." Transformative experiences are big this year. Lydia tells Albie that he must, must, must read it because it deals with philosophy and mathematics. And quantum physics, too.

"I don't know," Albie says. "I don't have much of a grasp on quantum physics."

Elliot says if you really want to have a transformative experience go to YouTube and check out "hamster on piano eating popcorn."

Lydia swats him on the arm, and, hallelujah, Bunny succeeds in gripping a ravioli between her chopsticks. Trudy asks Julian what he thinks of cast-iron frying pans and is it true that you're not supposed to wash them while, with absolute concentration and care, Bunny brings the ravioli from her plate to her mouth when a nearly imperceptible sensation crawls along the back of her neck. It's nothing, nothing is there, but the extreme disturbance of this virtual nothingness makes its way down her back and through her arms to her hands, and the ravioli gets away like a frog making its escape, and Bunny tells herself: *do not scream.*

Do not scream, do not scream, do not throw the plate across the table, do not turn the table upside down. With every effort, she maintains her calm and sets the chopsticks down alongside her plate. Picking up the fork, she grips it the way a small child in a high chair grips a spoon to hack away at a bowl of Cheerios and milk. Poised and ready to spear a ravioli, she tightens her fist around the fork, as if, were she to loosen her grip, she would lose both the fork and any semblance of composure. She squeezes the fork the way you would squeeze a stress ball. Her knuckles turn white, and all she wants is for it to stop, for all of it to stop, she wants quiet, and as if she were about to pound her fist on the table, to demand it, to demand order to the chaos, to demand that everyone shut up, please just shut the fuck up, she raises her arm and in one swift move, with all her force behind it, she brings the fork down hard into the softest part of her upper thigh.

The prongs deeply embed in her flesh, the fork stands upright, as if with a flick of a finger, it would ping. Five droplets of blood weep through her dress, and then more blood comes, and it spreads like spilled wine, deep red on white velvet.

Oh, Bunny. What did you do?

What did you do?

What have you done?

PART 2

To Have and Have Not

ALLOWED AND NOT ALLOWED. **BUNNY** learns
that the difference between *Allowed* and *Not Allowed* is
the difference between a person and a crazy person. Shortly
after she is checked into this hospital, during the hours between
lunch and dinner, one of the aides leads Bunny, along with
Albie, to the dining room, which is now deserted except for the
four lunatics at a far corner table playing Parcheesi. The dining
room here is a study in institutional beige. Beige cafeteria-style
tables are met with folding chairs of a slightly darker beige surrounded by beige walls. Bunny's red suitcase, flat on top of one
of the Formica tables, looks like a surprise.

The aide is a middle-aged woman with lank blond hair and
pink lipstick. The name tag pinned to her royal blue hospital
scrubs reads: *Patricia*. Bunny takes the seat on Albie's left and
shifts her chair to be nearer to him. Patricia unzips Bunny's
suitcase and dumps the contents onto the table. Then, as if to
rid the lining of sand or lint or contraband hidden in a pocket,
Patricia gives the suitcase a vigorous shake. Nothing falls out,
but still Bunny feels like a criminal. Setting the open suitcase

on the empty chair beside her, Patricia focuses her attention on the pile of comfortable clothes and Bunny's other items for everyday use. One by one, item by item, as swiftly as if she were sorting fruit, she sorts Bunny's things into two groups: *Allowed* and *Not Allowed*. What is *Not Allowed* goes back into the red suitcase, which Albie will take home. Her cardigan sweater is *Allowed*, but her bathrobe is *Not Allowed*. The yoga-style pants get tossed into the suitcase for the same reason her bathrobe got tossed into the suitcase: what ties around the waist can tie around the neck.

T-shirts, jeans, wool skirt, bras, panties and socks are *Allowed* but her black tights are *Not Allowed*. She can keep the legal pad and three felt-tipped pens but the spiral-bound notebook and ballpoint pens are *Not Allowed*. Cigarettes are *Definitely Not Allowed*. Nicorette gum is dispensed at the nurse's station.

"I'm sorry," Bunny says. "I'm so sorry."

"Sorry about what?" Albie asks, and Bunny says, "Everything. I'm sorry about everything."

Jewelry is *Not Allowed*.

Bunny takes off her wedding band and gives it to her husband, who turns it over between his fingertips before slipping it into his shirt pocket.

"I'm so sorry," Bunny says again.

Nail polish is *Not Allowed*. Cosmetics are *Not Allowed*. Chapstick is *Allowed*, but dental floss? No way, no how.

The woman whose job this is, whose job it is to take away Bunny's gray silk scarf, her ballpoint pens, her cell phone, her house keys, her pocketbook with the shoulder strap, this woman never looks up, but she takes away Bunny's shoes.

Shoes with heels are *Not Allowed*. Sneakers are *Allowed*. Sneakers, but no shoelaces. With or without laces, Bunny doesn't own sneakers. Albie says he will buy her a pair. The *Allowed* things go into a bag that is something like a laundry bag except there is no drawstring. The aide tells Albie that he has to go now, and she says to Bunny, "You wait here."

It would seem that the aide has disdain for her, but it's not disdain. It's resentment. She's not getting paid enough to strip these sad people of their personal belongings, although it is better than her last job at the nursing home where she was expected to rat out old people for having sex.

The aide walks off with Bunny's *Allowed* bag. Albie hugs his wife and he tells her that he will see her tomorrow during visiting hours, that he loves her very much, that it's all going to be okay.

Bunny watches him leave with her red suitcase filled with her things *Not Allowed*, and she waits.

She waits *here*.

She waits here.

Catatonia

IT IS ANOTHER AIDE, NOT the one who took her shoes, who, on this first day in the insane asylum, shows Bunny to her room. This aide, who is wearing pink scrubs, points to her name tag and says, "I'm Shawna. If you need something, you ask me." Then she says, "It's going to be okay. No need for you to be crying now."

Unaware that she *is* crying, Bunny touches her face, which is, indeed, wet. Shawna takes a packet of tissues from her pocket. "Here, you blow your nose and wipe away them tears. Come on, now. Let me show you your room. It's a nice one. You got a big window facing the river."

The bag, the one with Bunny's things *Allowed* is already there, ahead of her, plopped down on her bed, in the middle of her bed; a bed that is narrow like a bed you'd expect to find in a convent or an orphanage. Bunny's bed is the one closest to the door, which is to say that Bunny's room is not exactly *her* room. On the other bed, a woman with excellent posture sits facing the window as if she were waiting, primly and patiently, on a bench in a train station. Her black hair is done up neatly in a bun. "Please," Bunny keeps her voice low. "I can't have a roommate." She doesn't want this woman to take it personally but, even growing up in her family's three-bedroom house, it was Nicole and Dawn who shared a bedroom. Bunny had a bedroom to herself.

Unless you count Albie (and if you make an exception for the brief stint with Stella when she was between apartments), the only roommate Bunny ever had before now was a college roommate in her freshman year. Bunny's college roommate was a very nice girl who arrived with plans for the following year to live in her sorority house, which was a revelation to Bunny, who had thought that, surely by now, sorority houses and sororities themselves had gone the way of those bras that turned normal breasts into breasts shaped like nuclear missiles.

It was not a happy arrangement for either roommate, but they tolerated one another well enough until the night when, after all of ten minutes of watching Bunny look for, but not find, her cigarette lighter—a disposable Bic, two for a dollar, hardly a big deal—the aspiring sorority girl said, "If you were organized you wouldn't lose things. You'd know where everything is. Frankly, I don't know how you can find anything in that mess."

"You're right," Bunny said, and she pulled open the top drawer of her desk. All the way open; open and out, and she dumped the contents of the drawer, which included a half-eaten Snickers bar and the missing Bic lighter, onto the floor. For good measure, Bunny flung the now empty drawer across the room. Although the aspiring sorority girl was not in the line of

trajectory, she nonetheless dashed for the door the way a cartoon character makes a beeline for the nearest exit. From there,
she went to the Housing Office, while Bunny calmed herself
down with a few good kicks to the wall.

Bunny was sent to Student Mental Health Services, a wish ful-
filled, and, even better, she was afforded the luxury usually reserved
for upperclassmen: a single, a room without a roommate.

Now, on the verge of a full-blown freak-out, she says to
Shawna, "I can't share a room. I have to have a room to myself."

"Does this look like a hotel?" Shawna asks. "This is a *hospital*.
No private rooms in the hospital. But don't you worry. You and
Mrs. Cortez will get along just fine. She's no bother." Shawna
raises her voice. Perhaps Mrs. Cortez is hard of hearing. "Isn't
that right, Mrs. Cortez? You're no bother. Mrs. Cortez don't
talk. She *can* talk. She just don't want to. She'll talk when she's
got something to say. Isn't that right? Mrs. Cortez, this is your
new roommate. You want to say hello?"

Every indication is that Mrs. Cortez is deaf as well as mute.
"Oh, she can hear," Shawna says. "She hears just fine when the
dinner bell rings. Isn't that right, Mrs. Cortez?"

Even Bunny has to admit—if she has to have a roommate,
she couldn't do better than Mrs. Cortez.

On her bed, along with her *Allowed* things, are a pair of blue
pajamas, a dull, monochromatic cerulean blue, and a pair of
slipper-socks in a similar, but lighter, shade of blue. The pajamas
are made of paper. Not paper like notebook paper, but paper
like those washable paper towels for wiping up kitchen spills.

On the pillow is a single sheet of regular paper, placed there to be noticed as surely as a tear-soaked note from a teenage girl explaining why she has run away from home; the sort of note from the sort of teenage girl who periodically runs away from home, but never stays away for more than a few hours because where would she go? Except this sheet of paper is a printout of a grid beneath the heading: Weekly Schedule of Activities.

"Let's get you settled in nice," Shawna says. "This here is your closet." She opens the door to a locker made of laminated particleboard that is a color that is not a color. Four plastic hangers hang from a rod below two shelves. "If you need more hangers, you just let me know," Shawna says. "And this here night table's got two drawers for your undergarments and personal effects and the like." She demonstrates how to switch the table lamp on and off, and from there they go to the bathroom, where Shawna pulls open the shower curtain. "Cold water," she taps the faucet on the right. "The other one is the hot water. But to tell you the truth, it don't get much hotter than warm." Then she directs Bunny's attention to one of two side-by-side sinks. "This one here is yours, and that's your cup." The plastic cup is cloudy from far too many rounds in the dishwasher. Shawna holds up a travel-size tube of toothpaste, and a toothbrush packaged in cellophane, which she unwraps, stuffing the cellophane into her pocket. "We like to keep things sanitary around here, but some folks are forgetful. You don't need to worry any about Mrs. Cortez though. She's not the sort of woman to use someone else's toothbrush."

Above the sink is a mirror—not a real mirror, but a sheet of aluminum or maybe it's stainless steel—and in the cabinet below are extra rolls of toilet paper.

Bunny is not up to the task of putting away her clothes, getting herself settled in or washing her face and hands, which she couldn't do even if she'd wanted to because Shawna neglected to give her soap and towels. She could, but she doesn't, brush her teeth. Instead she pushes her belongings to the foot of the bed, and sits on the edge as if she has been hard at work and now is merely taking a break. The bed, her bed, is covered with a waffle-weave cotton blanket of a color best described as sandy beige. The mattress can't be more than three inches thick and through the blanket and sheets, which you could not, in all good conscience, ever refer to as white, Bunny can feel the plastic mattress cover, a precaution against urine stains or menstrual blood stains or the sweat of fear, and who knows what other fluids leak from the deranged. The pillow is the same kind of pillow that you get on airplanes when you fly coach. As a pillow, it is useless, but Bunny hugs it anyway. It is dark outside now, and Bunny sits on the edge of her bed, as still and as quiet as Mrs. Cortez sitting on the edge of her bed; the only difference between them is posture. Bunny's shoulders sag. In this way, time passes until the dinner bell rings.

Mrs. Cortez, ramrod straight, shoulders back, head held high, walks past Bunny as if she doesn't see her, as if, on top of everything else, Mrs. Cortez has opted to be blind.

The First Supper

MEALS ARE MANDATORY, BUT UNABLE to bring herself to join the line of crazy people snaked around the dining room, Bunny keeps to the wall like a bystander. Many of the psychos, with the bovine insouciance of men who go to nice restaurants for dinner all dolled up in cargo shorts and baseball caps, are wearing their paper pajamas, which come in pale brown, as well as the blue. One man, a large man whose hair is long and gray, is wearing his underpants, white Hanes briefs, over his blue jeans. Bunny glances at his feet, curious to see if he's put his socks on over his shoes, but he isn't wearing shoes. He is wearing the slipper-socks, the blue ones, the same as Bunny's slipper-socks, and Bunny dwells on this fact, that she and Underpants Man are wearing identical footwear, and what does that say about her?

What distinguishes the cafeteria in the psycho ward from cafeterias for normal people is the silverware. In the psycho cafeteria only the spoons are metal. Knives and forks are plastic. Also, plates and cups are paper. The inmates are not allowed anywhere near glass or sharp objects or anything that could be construed as a sharp object like the ballpoint pen they took away from Bunny and her nail clippers, too.

By the time she gets her food—steam table dregs of boiled broccoli and gloppy spaghetti; meatballs are on offer, but Bunny declines, although she does take two individual packets of peanut butter—there are no vacant tables. Not many chairs are free either. She isn't frightened of the other crazy people. This isn't the sort of a mental ward that houses the criminally insane. If anything, these people look incapable of defending themselves, but she doesn't want to sit with them because she doesn't want to *be* one of them. But she has to sit somewhere. Holding her tray, she scans the room, ultimately taking the one empty seat at a four-top table where three men sit with their heads bowed, as if they've nodded off midmeal. Bunny eats a pat of peanut butter with her metal spoon.

Holy Fuck

DINNER IS FOLLOWED BY VISITING hours. The psychos who are not expecting visitors, not tonight or maybe never, exit the dining room as if they were bumper cars or ants, seemingly in all directions without a destination, but there is a destination. In the living room, a game show, *Family Feud*, is playing on the wide screen television that takes up most of one wall. On the other walls there is nothing to liven up the beige. No paintings or posters or prints. Three rows of couches, two couches per row, line up to face the television. Two of the couches are upholstered in grayish-brown vinyl. The other four are a listless shade of sepia with a nubby weave that is best described as larval.

Behind the rows of couches, chairs are arranged haphazardly. The people sitting in those chairs are socializing. Bunny doesn't want to watch *Family Feud*. Adrift in the sea of beige, tan, liverwurst, slate, sickly mint green, and wenge, Bunny keeps to the hallway where she is alone, except for Underpants Man who has planted himself by the pay phone on the wall, as if he were expecting an important call.

It feels like breathing, but, in fact, Bunny is speaking out loud. "Please," she says, "help me. Someone help me," although she is not asking, not really, for help. It is more like a figure of speech. Nonetheless, some insane woman shows up and puts her arms around Bunny, patting her back, short and rapid pitter-patter pats the way you'd pat a wailing baby, telling her not to cry, telling her not to worry, which serves only to exacerbate Bunny's despair, when one of the nurses happens by. The nurse stops and says, "Come on, Jeanette. You know there's no touching."

Jeanette, whoever Jeanette is, lets go of Bunny and says, "But she's crying."

The nurse, *Lisa Kendall, R.N.*—her black name tag pinned at the V of her white scrubs—is wearing pink ballet flats like Bunny's friend Lydia wore on New Year's Eve, except Lydia's pink ballet flats were Clergerie and Nurse Kendall got hers from Payless.

When Jeanette breaks away, Bunny gets a look at her face, which is a mess of a face, like maybe it was reconstructed after a hideous accident, the kind of accident where she went face-first through the windshield of a car, or it could be that she went overboard on the cosmetic surgery. Because the people here are not right in the head, you can't rule out the possibility that this was the face she wanted, like that woman whose picture was plastered on the front page of the *New York Post* after undergoing extensive plastic surgery to look like a lion. Lions are beautiful creatures, but a lion's face did not look good on a person. Also, there was the woman who turned herself into a Barbie doll. If Jeanette was after that kind of transformation, Bunny has no idea who or what she was aiming to be.

Nurse Kendall takes a packet of tissues from her pocket. The people who work here carry around packets of tissues the same way some people always have a safety pin with them, or change for a dollar. Nurse Kendall leads Bunny away from Jeanette and says, "Maybe you want to go to sleep now? You've had a rough day." The nurse walks Bunny to her room where Mrs. Cortez, sitting on her bed, facing the window, says nothing and Bunny returns the courtesy.

Without taking the trouble to undress or brush her teeth, Bunny gets into bed. A beacon of light comes through the open six inches between the door and the jamb. A rod affixed to the top of the door prevents it from closing all the way. Not even in their sleep is privacy allowed. Bunny closes her eyes, and a voice in the void, someone, a man, calls out, "Holy fuck." A few seconds go by, and again he calls out, "Holy fuck. Holy fuck." Intermittently, he calls out, "Holy fuck." Anyone who knows anything about experimental psychology or the fundamentals of torture will tell you that noises at irregular intervals are one of the surest ways to break a person.

"Holy fuck."

Side Effects

A**T SEVEN IN THE MORNING,** an aide rouses Bunny from her bed, the same as all the crazy people are roused from their drug-induced sleep. The aides, like border collies, herd the loons as if they were sheep into the living room, and the truth is, the loons are like sheep; sheep on their way to slaughter for all they care. Slumped in their seats, they wait passively for their wellness check. "Wellness" is one of those words, along with words like "parenting," "inappropriate," and "chakra," that drive Bunny crazy, even before she *was* crazy. One of the nurses takes her temperature and blood pressure—neither of which, Bunny notes, gets written down.

At both ends of the living room are carts stocked with bars of mini-soap—wretched, cheap soap redolent of motel rooms from the 1950s; towels devoid of color and fluff; fresh paper pajamas and slipper-socks. After they all replenish their supplies, they go back to their rooms to shower and get dressed, or not.

Bunny does not take a shower, but now that she has soap and a towel, she does wash her hands and face, and she brushes her teeth, which is something, and she strips off the clothes she'd slept in. From the bag of her things *Allowed*, she chooses a black T-shirt and a pair of jeans; a fresh set of clothes, which she puts on over her dirty underwear.

At breakfast, the vast majority of the psychos are pajama-clad.

Bunny sets her tray down on an outlying table where only one of the four chairs is occupied. An obese young woman, a girl really, all of seventeen, is eating peanut butter, Skippy Creamy, with a plastic knife from a plastic jar. Bunny stirs her cornflakes and milk with her spoon the way you'd stir coffee and cream, and she asks the girl, "Where did you get a jar of peanut butter?"

"My parents brought it for me," and in a preemptive strike against what she fears might come next, she tells Bunny, in no uncertain terms, "I don't share my food." Then she says, "You don't have to cry about it. Your parents can bring you food. Or your friends, if you have any."

While Bunny wipes her eyes with a napkin, the girl outlines the procedures and policies as they apply to food coming in from the outside. "And don't put stuff that can rot in the cabinets," the girl warns. "Last week they found a slice of moldy pizza in there stashed behind a box of Saltines." Then she adds, "People are disgusting."

Arts and Crafts

TO OCCUPY YOUR TIME HERE with hobbies and social engagement is not exactly mandatory but it is encouraged, *highly* encouraged, as if to play a game of charades or to sit around a table making paper swans from squares of cut-up newspaper with a bunch of other mental patients is a pathway to sanity. Bunny is not one for hobbies or games, and she has always placed great importance, perhaps a disproportionate importance, on solitude but, during the day, unless you're catatonic, the bedrooms are off-limits.

The catatonics are *Allowed* to stay in their rooms during the day, although it is possible that the catatonics are *Not Allowed* to stay in their rooms during the day, but try arguing with a person who, for all intents and purposes, is oblivious to the existence of you and everybody else. Really, as far as the catatonics are concerned, it doesn't matter where they are because wherever they are, they are alone.

In the living room, in the hopes that no one will notice her there, Bunny curls up in chair with a legal pad and a felt-tipped pen and wonders if she could feign catatonia, and for how long, until one of the aides, Antoine, spots her. "Hey," he says, "why are you sitting here all by your lonesome self? Don't you want to go to an Activity?"

"No," she says, but Antoine insists they find something she'd like to do. "Come on, now." The diamond stud in his ear sparkles like a smile. "Let's have a look at the Board."

Beauty, Yoga, Watercoloring, Arts and Crafts, Creative Writing, Music, Dog Therapy, and Board Games. Also Group Therapy. Group Therapy (MDD); Group Therapy (BPD); Group Therapy (OCD); Group Therapy (Eating Disorders); Group Therapy (Phobias).

"What's Dog Therapy?" Bunny asks, and Antoine explains, "You hang out with a dog. Pet him and stuff." The dog is a dog that's been certified as consistently trusting and friendly but not nuts the way some friendly dogs will go wild from the happiness of a pat on the head. Social-worker dogs have been trained not to bark, growl, snap or hump.

"Okay," Bunny says. "I'll go to Dog Therapy."

"That's good. He's a nice dog." Antoine gestures to the bench against the wall across from the board. "Have a seat. They'll be bringing him along any minute now."

Bunny watches the clock. One minute. Four minutes. Ten minutes. She's been waiting there for almost twenty minutes before Antoine comes back. "Hey," he says. "I just got word. The dog isn't coming today. How about you give Arts and Crafts a whirl?" Then Antoine reaches into his pocket and pulls out a tissue. "Here," he says. "Wipe your eyes. They're running. Now, come on. I'll walk you over there."

Seated around the Arts and Crafts table, nine lunatics are gluing things to other things. Bunny sits next to the girl with the private peanut butter stash. The teacher, who isn't really a teacher but a social worker who took a class in art therapy, sets a square piece of plywood in front of Bunny along with a bowl filled with small mosaic tiles: white, speckled beige, black, a couple of reds and there is a teal-blue one in the mix, too. "Have you ever done anything like this before?" she asks.

In the third grade, in arts and crafts class, on three consecutive Friday mornings between the hours of ten and noon, Bunny, along with her classmates, glued small mosaic tiles to their allotted squares of plywood. On the fourth Friday, when the grout between the tiles had dried, they could take their projects home.

Bunny took the long route back to her house. When she got to where Allen Street met Nelson Road, she stopped. Scouting around in all directions, confident that there was no one who could see her, she squatted over the water sewer. As if disposing of evidence of a crime or something shameful, she slid her square of wood with the glued-on tiles through the wide iron slat. It made a satisfying kerplunk when it hit the dark sewer water where it floated among the rotting leaves of late autumn.

After that, in third grade arts and crafts class, they made pencil cups from empty soup cans.

Devoid of enthusiasm or inspiration, rather than pick

through the tiles with a scheme in mind, Bunny takes a fistful from the bowl as if the tiles were almonds at a party. Similarly, with no thought to a pattern, not bothering so much as to line them up adjacently, she glues the tiles to the wood. There is no indication that she has any intention to see her Arts and Crafts project to completion. The inability to complete simple tasks is, of course, a common symptom of depression, but it could be a symptom of other things, too, such as the value of the task itself.

The obese girl is staring at Bunny's tile-on-wood. "That's really cool," she says. Can I have it?"

What the girl sees, what she thinks is cool, what Bunny does not see, is that Bunny's tiles are arranged as if the tiles were letters grouped together as if they were words, and the words were arranged as if they were a poem on a page.

<pre>
          xxxx xxx

          xxxxx

          xxx   xxxx

               xxx
</pre>

A poem along the lines of *Fuck You, Everyone*.

Prompt: A Blessing (300 words or less)

It's a bad year no matter who you are. Acne, black-heads, facial hair, chest hair, pubic hair, underarm hair, breasts on parade, testicles dropping—dropping? dropping how?—and the dank smell of it all. Sniff your underarms, take a whiff of your panties, socks, jock-straps, and if you bleed through your tampon, stray dogs will follow you home. No one loves you, no one understands you. You have no friends. It's a wonder you don't kill yourself.

And, as if adolescence weren't already enough of a shit-storm of frogs, it was then, the year I turned thirteen, that inexplicably and practically overnight, I packed on the pounds. A roly-poly, jelly-belly, tub of lard, five-by-five, avoirdupois, fat, fat, fat, I was an anomaly in my ectomorphic clan.

Back then, on Sunday nights there was a popular TV show, a family favorite, documents of real-life stories, human-interest stories with an Oliver Twist-ian sensibility—heartwarming, puke-inducing treacle. That week's episode was about a piglet who was rejected by the sow, but adopted by a border collie with a litter of her own. Basically, this was the same storyline as the movie *Babe*, although *Babe*—the movie and the book which preceded it—didn't come out until years later. This is not to accuse anyone of ripping off anyone else's story. It's a common enough occurrence that great discoveries—and lousy ones, too—happen independently of each other. Like how Isaac Newton and Gottfried Leibniz both formulated calculus, and a few years back two novels based on the Siamese twins Chang and Eng were released in the same season, and I once had a boyfriend, a musician, who thought he'd invented a new kind of music when he distilled the complexity of European classical music with the simplicity of the four-quarter beat of the Beatles. Then, someone told him about Charles Ives. It happens.

This pre-*Babe* story we were watching took place on a farm in Scotland. The camera homed in on the piglet nursing along with the collie's four puppies, two on either side. Piggy in the middle. My sisters shared a sidelong glance and a smirk, and our mother said, "Aren't dogs just the sweetest animals?" The film then cut to the puppies and piglet at play, all of them delirious with joy, happiness unrestrained, happiness that can come only with being new to the world. That the piglet was oblivious to his inability to keep up with the puppies—pigs can't dart and weave or crouch, paws down and ass in the air—rendered his efforts all the more adorable. It was too cute for words.

What I wanted most then was to be invisible, but to get up and bolt from the room would be to call attention to myself. To cry in front of them, in and of itself, was not at issue. Not when twice weekly at a minimum I went practically berserk with crying. What's one snivel more? What *was* at issue was the likelihood that sudden departure would be misinterpreted as fat-related: pigs are fat; I am fat; ergo, I am a pig. Except that wasn't it, but I knew that any attempt to explain myself would've only widened the divide. If I had said, "It's not the pig, per se. The pig as a pig is irrelevant. It could've been a goat or a squirrel or whatever the fuck," and our mother, after admonishing me for using the f-word, would've said, "So, what then *are* you crying about?" and, at that, I would've said something like, "Go oink yourself." *Go oink yourself,* a retort for self-delight; *I* would've thought it funny as all get-out, and I would've been alone there, too. What I did was this: I bit down on my lower lip to keep it from quivering, and like that, biting down hard on my lower lip, hard enough to draw blood, I sat out the minutes until the end of the show about the piglet, unwittingly Chaplin-esque, who thought he was a dog right up until that very moment just before slaughter. At that same moment, border collies were on a grassy hill darting and weaving, herding the sheep, to bring them home.*

In the eighteen months that followed, the weight I'd gained fell away. Snap, poof, just like that, with no explanation despite the girls at school insisting that there had to be an explanation: Grapefruit? Juice fast? Atkins? Laxatives? Amphetamines? Did I barf it up? As if there had to be an explanation for everything. Whatever it was, the pounds were lost for good, and in that way I was again the same as everyone else in my metabolically blessed family.

*That last bit about the pig going to slaughter while the dogs herded sheep, that wasn't part of television show, but that's what really happened.

The Round-Headed Nurse

AFTER ARTS AND CRAFTS IS lunch, and after lunch, on her way out of the dining room, Bunny is waylaid by a very tall and gangly nurse whose head is perfectly round. Perfectly round like a basketball, or the head of a cartoon character, a character from *Peanuts*, but Bunny can't remember which one of the *Peanuts* characters had the round head.

"Hon," the nurse says, "Dr. Fitzgerald wants to see you." She says "hon" but Bunny hears "bun," and she says, "It's Bunny."

"Bunny," the nurse says, "I'm Ella."

Bunny follows Ella down a long corridor. At the end of the hallway, they turn left, and at the second door on the right, Ella stops and says, "Here you go, hon."

Standardized Testing

DR. FITZGERALD'S OFFICE IS LIKE an office you'd expect to find at the Department of Motor Vehicles. Without windows, fluorescent track lighting overhead, and industrial metal file cabinets line one wall. The doctor, sitting on a swivel chair at a laminated particleboard desk, leans in as if she were about to stand up. Instead, she tells Bunny to take a seat in one of two of the matching particleboard chairs on the opposite side of her desk. The chairs are without arms.

Bunny imagines Dr. Fitzgerald is wearing navy-blue leather shoes with one-inch block heels. Expensive and boring. Her chin-length hair, tucked behind her ears, reveals the safest choice in earrings: small gold studs. Her engagement ring, a one-carat diamond solitaire, is big enough not to require explanation like how they're saving their money for a house, but not so big as to raise eyebrows. Everything about Dr. Fitzgerald is better than Bunny, and not just because Bunny is wearing slipper-socks or because a gob of snot that looks like a jellyfish is bubbling from her nose, but simply because Dr. Fitzgerald *is* better. She slides a box of tissues across her desk, a desk with no clutter.

Bunny takes a tissue but makes no move to dry her eyes or wipe her nose. Rather, with sweaty hands she fiddles with it as if the tissue were a strand of worry beads. Damp bits break off, falling onto her lap, and Dr. Fitzgerald asks, "How long have you felt this way?"

"What way?" Bunny says.

A string of questions follow: Has she ever been depressed before? How often do the episodes occur? When was the last one and for how long did it last? Are you sleeping? Have you gained weight? Lost weight? How much? How is your personal hygiene?

Bunny claims to be washing her hair weekly and brushing her teeth once a day, which doesn't exactly qualify as good hygiene, but it is better hygiene than the truth. Dr. Fitzgerald gives her the fish eye, but she lets the lie stand.

The questions that come next seem to be some sort of standardized test, something for which Bunny, idiosyncratically, has always had a knack. Contrary to all expectations, and indeed met with incredulity, her SAT scores were in the top one percentile. But unlike the SATs, these questions don't aim to gauge a scope of knowledge or an ability to solve problems of logic. Rather, these questions require Bunny to give a numerical distribution to darkness, defeat, panic, anxiety and grief. As if infinity could be rated on a scale of one to ten, Dr. Fitzgerald asks her, "On a scale of one to ten, how would you rate your depression?"

Bunny remembers what Dr. Lowenstein had said about the far ends of the spectrum, that to be understood, to be normal, was to be in the middle, and she says, "Five."

"And on a scale of one to ten, how would you rate your clarity of thinking?"

"Five."

"Your productivity?"

"Five."

Yet, despite five being the middle ground, average, the norm, *normal*, somehow, five accumulates in an exponential decrease, adding up like negative numbers.

Protocol

WHILE DR. FITZGERALD IS BUSY with her computer, entering notes or data or maybe she is catching up on her email, Bunny is brushing the bits of wet tissue from her lap to the floor. After a few minutes, or maybe closer to fifty-five minutes, the doctor asks Bunny, "What medications are you currently taking?"

"Wellbutrin," Bunny says, which is not a lie insofar as it is the medication she took most recently. Most recently is near enough to currently to be more or less true.

"Would you say it's been effective?"

To keep herself from saying what she wants to say, which is, "What the fuck kind of stupid question is that? Would I be here if it were effective?" Bunny keeps her jaw clenched and shakes her head.

The doctor asks about other medication. "Other than Wellbutrin?"

Bunny neglects to mention the Lexapro; perhaps she's forgotten about it, as it, too, obviously, hasn't done her any good, and it's been who knows how long since she quit bothering with it. However, she does own up to the Ambien, although not the Lunesta.

"And prior to Wellbutrin," Dr. Fitzgerald asks, "which antidepressants have you tried?"

"All of them," Bunny says.

"All of them?" Dr. Fitzgerald is skeptical. "Which ones exactly?"

"I don't remember, but all of them."

"Do you drink?" the doctor asks.

Bunny takes a fresh tissue from the box. "Not much. Wine with dinner. A drink at a party." And although Dr. Fitzgerald doesn't ask, Bunny volunteers, "I smoke."

"You know you can get Nicorette at the nurse's station? But this might be a good time to quit, don't you think?"

No. No, Bunny doesn't think this is a good time to quit. If anything, this is the worst time imaginable to quit, and even that is to assume Bunny *wants* to quit smoking, which she most definitely does not.

Dr. Fitzgerald's plan of action, the road map to a sound mind, begins with first weaning Bunny off Wellbutrin. "We'll cut your dose in half for two days, then halve that for two days more. Then," Dr. Fitzgerald says, "I want to put you on a course of paroxetine with an adjunctive treatment of aripiprazole."

Paroxetine? Aripiprazole? A doctor who speaks to you in a language they know you don't understand is not unlike a snooty waiter who recites the dinner specials in French, except Bunny is fluent in French whereas she is not fluent in the vehicular language of medicine. However, she does have a working knowledge of psychopharmacologic terminology. Paroxetine is generic for Paxil. Bunny's time with Paxil was interminable, four months that dragged on into an eternity of lethargy, but aripiprazole she did not know. "What is that?" she asks.

Dr. Fitzgerald fiddles with the gold earring on her left ear, and says, "It's an atypical antipsychotic."

Delusional melancholia can't be ruled out when it comes to major depressive disorder, but psychotic? "I'm psychotic?" Bunny asks.

Bunny is not psychotic, but this classification of antipsychotics has been proven very effective in treating depression. Dr. Fitzgerald tells her that Abilify augmented with Paxil has yielded excellent results.

Aripiprazole might've been new to her, but when she learns the brand name, Abilify, Bunny says, "No." Abilify is legendary.

"No?" Dr. Fitzgerald sounds as if that—no—was a word she's never heard before. "No? What do you mean?"

"I mean no. No Abilify," Bunny says. "And no Paxil, either."

Dr. Fitzgerald asks, "Why not?"

Why not? Dr. Fitzgerald has got to know why not, but nonetheless Bunny tells her, "Because of the side effects."

"Every drug has side effects." For a psychiatrist, Dr. Fitzgerald is short on patience and slim on insight.

Yes, every drug has side effects, but side effects such as dry mouth or the possibility of an erection that lasts for more than four hours is not the same as a side effect that can result in death or hair loss. The side effects that Bunny experienced with Paxil—lethargy that bordered on narcolepsy, and a loss of libido that left her with the sexual desire of a desk lamp—were identical to symptoms that ail her now, and Abilify? Abilify is a drug that brings on significant weight gain, along with uncontrollable twitching and chances are you'll turn into a bed-wetter, too. How is that a cure for a person afflicted with depression? No one in their right mind, or even someone not in their right mind, would call that a better life.

"Not everyone experiences all the side effects," Dr. Fitzgerald says. "And some people experience none."

Bunny continues to shake her head well beyond a single no.

"You need to listen to me," Dr. Fitzgerald says. "I'm trying to help you."

For the duration of an instant, Bunny goes blind. Everything is black, tar-black and deep purple, which is then followed by a ring of light, a crisp and sharply edged light framed by fire, and the glow bores through the darkness. This is how Bunny sees rage. Slow and measured, she says, "No, you need to listen to me."

Show Me the Way

BUNNY LEAVES DR. FUCKHERSELF'S OFFICE to find Activities in full swing. The dining room is busy with severely depressed people putting together a jigsaw puzzle, which could raise the question about the chicken or the egg. At another table, three of them are playing Go Fish with a deck with forty-seven cards, a painfully obvious metaphor. But all Bunny can think about is the pressing urgency for solitude, the way it is pressing when you need to find a bathroom fast, or else. Bunny needs a place to cry, to hear herself cry without some woman with a messed-up face telling her it's going to be okay, without some nurse giving her a tissue to wipe her eyes and blow her nose. She hurries past the living room where a handful of crazy people doing their daily exercises try to touch their toes.

Yet, she stops and pauses outside the Music Room. A social worker is playing the piano while seven or eight loonies sing about someone or other who's a singular sensation. Bunny knows it is a song from an old Broadway musical, but she is unable recall which one. If she were to hear more of the song, perhaps she'd be able to identify it, and because all her efforts of concentration are focused on that, on listening to the song, she is unaware that someone else is there, standing alongside her until, in a voice that is neither quite speaking nor quite singing, but with a hint of a tune, he says, *"Show me the way to the next whiskey bar, Oh, don't ask why."*

Bertolt Brecht, Bunny knows, and she brightens at the recollection. Bertolt Brecht, but is it a song from *Threepenny Opera* or *Mother Courage*, and then she is unable to remember if *Mother Courage* is a musical, at which point she is certain that "musical" is the wrong word. Unable to locate the right word, panic sets in, which must show on her face because the man, who is clearly one of the loons—it takes one to know one—says, "I'm sorry." Tall and lanky, his hair is dark brown, and his countenance is heavy with sorrow so deep as to seem ancient, which makes it difficult to determine his age. Wearing a faded Yale T-shirt tucked into gray sweatpants with a thick elastic waistband, he is dressed for the basketball court, for a game of one-on-one, except that his black Converse high-tops are without laces.

Bunny ignores his apology and she says only, "I know that I know, but I can't remember. Is it *Threepenny Opera?*"

He tells her that he, too, doesn't remember, that he can remember only the lyrics, and even then, only the first three lines. If either of them were capable of laughing, they would laugh. But they are not, and so they don't.

The Early Bird Special

AS IF HE HAS NEVER before encountered a baked potato, Bunny's tablemate is staring at his plate of food as if it might do something like jump up and squirt water in his eye. On Bunny's plate is white rice mixed with canned peas and carrots. She is not hungry, and she interrupts his meditation on the potato to ask, "Why do they serve dinner at five in the afternoon?"

"I don't know," the man says, "why do they serve dinner at five in the afternoon?"

"It's not a riddle," Bunny says. "It's a question."

The man says that he is sorry, and Bunny lets it go at that.

After Dinner

VISITING HOURS START AT 6 P.M. and end
at 9 P.M. except on Sundays when they run from noon
until 5.

Albie glances at his watch. "How are you doing with the
smoking?" he asks.

Today is not Sunday. Maybe it's Wednesday. Or Tuesday.

"They give me Nicorette gum."

"You're okay with that?"

"No," Bunny says. "I'm not okay with that. I met with one
of the psychiatrists today. She wants to put me on Paxil and
Abilify. I said no."

Albie remembers the Paxil days all too well. "So, now what?"
he asks.

"Now nothing."

"Nothing?"

"Nothing."

"What about talk therapy?"

"I *said* nothing. Nothing is nothing."

Albie is about to say how that's not possible, that they must have something planned, after all, this *is* a hospital, but instead, he asks, "What did you have for dinner?"

"Rice with canned vegetables."

"How was it?"

"Are you for real?" Then she tells him, "You're allowed to bring me food, as long as it's not in a glass jar."

Because she can't think of anything in particular she wants, Albie suggests she make a list. "You can give it to me tomorrow."

Then, as if this were something like exchanging gifts, she says, "I made something for you in Arts and Crafts, but one of the fruitcakes stole it."

Albie suggests that perhaps she ought not to refer to the others as loons, fruitcakes, nut jobs or the mentally defective, that perhaps it's not nice to call them squirrels and psychos, but Bunny disagrees. "*You* can't call them squirrels and psychos, but it's okay if I do it, because I'm one of them."

Throughout the years of their marriage, Albie's feelings toward his wife have crisscrossed the emotional range: love, deep affection, joy, anger, delight, frustration, irritation, passion, fear, sorrow, but never pity. Until now; and Albie wonders if to feel pity is something from which you can recover. "Maybe you'll feel better if you take a shower," he suggests, as if somehow she would be less pitiful if she were clean.

Again, Albie glances at his watch, and Bunny asks, "Is today Wednesday?"

Something Like Leprosy

WATCHING TELEVISION ISN'T MANDATORY. BUNNY is free to go to her room, which requires she walk past Underpants Man as he stands guard over the phone mounted on the wall. Although the phone is a pay phone, it doesn't accept coins because money is *Not Allowed*. To make calls, the lunatics use prepaid phone cards. However, they can receive calls free of charge. Underpants Man, the self-designated phone monitor, is there to enforce the ten-minute rule, although keeping phone calls to ten minutes might not even *be* a rule other than one imposed by Underpants Man. Ever vigilant, with one eye on the clock and the other eye on a woman who is talking on the phone, presumably to someone on the other end, Underpants Man squawks, "Two minutes. You've got two minutes." Bunny waits to see what will happen next. "One minute, forty seconds," he says. "One minute, twenty seconds. Sixty seconds. Fifty-nine seconds. Fifty-eight seconds."

When he gets down to thirty-four seconds, Bunny loses interest.

The way it's said that an atheist who prays every day will come to believe in God, perhaps if she goes through the motions of normalcy, she'll be normal. To take a shower is normal. In the bathroom, Bunny pulls her T-shirt up over her head, recoiling from the stench of herself. Back when she took showers as a matter of course, she liked the water to be hot enough to fog the mirror and turn her skin pink, but Shawna was right. Warm is as hot as it gets here. Bunny unwraps the bar of motel soap, which is a sickly shade of white, white that has yellowed from age.

The shower isn't draining properly, if at all. Standing in a puddle that is two inches deep, Bunny wonders if this is how people get tapeworms or parasites or trichinosis. She remembers the word "trichinosis," and she has a vague notion of an association between it and some disgusting disease like leprosy, which might or might not be an accurate association. Try as she does, she is unable to recall what trichinosis is. Soap scum settles around her feet, but figuring she's come this far, she stays in the shower long enough to wash her hair, too.

After patting herself dry, she puts on the fresh pair of paper pajamas.

She does not feel better.

In bed, with her legal pad propped up on her knees, her pen is poised to write down what it is she'd wanted to ask Albie. Something about the water in the shower, but what? What about the water in the shower? She tries to remember but she cannot, and fury goes off like a bottle rocket. She flings the notepad to the floor.

And all the while, Mrs. Cortez sits on her bed, facing the window, as if she's been there forever frozen, a regal monument of the will not to live.

Cats at Home

BUNNY SNEAKS BACK TO HER room for her legal pad and a felt-tipped pen. On the top page are her notes for Albie, things she doesn't want to forget. Thus far, she has written: 1) peanut butter; 2) what's that disease you get from standing in dirty water; 3) books; 4) pizza (maybe); 5) did you find out . . . What? What did she want him to find out? Beneath that page are the pages she wrote last night.

In the living room, the television is on. Mrs. Cortez and an older man wearing a yarmulke sit on opposite sides of the front-row couch watching an infomercial for a vacuum cleaner. The Bertolt Brecht guy is sitting in one of the armchairs that are arranged in every which way. He waves and motions for Bunny to join him. She hesitates. She was banking on time to herself, but she doesn't know how to refuse the gesture. With him is a woman sitting sideways, her back resting against one arm of her chair and, as if the armchair were an inner tube and she were drifting on a lake, her legs dangle over the other side.

Resting on the woman's lap, unopened, is a tattered copy of *Martha Stewart Living*. The cover features Martha standing in a pumpkin patch wearing a plaid jacket and a jack-o'-lantern grin. "It's not even from this past year," the woman says. "It's from, like, two Halloweens ago." Her fingernails are painted bright red. She might be the same age as Bunny, although she looks, not older exactly, but worn thin and color-faded like the cover of the Martha Stewart magazine. Her name is Andrea, and she introduces the Bertolt Brecht guy as Josh.

A point in their favor, neither of them comment on her name, and Bunny asks her, "They let you have nail polish?"

"Fat chance," she says. "Nail polish is like a controlled sub-stance in here. Like we might drink it. For the formaldehyde. Yeah, right. Though," she concedes, "if you sniff enough of it, you can get a little buzz going." She splays her fingers, and tells Bunny, "Twice a week Beauty is an Activity. That's where you can get your fingernails painted and your eyebrows tweezed. You can get your hair done there, too. Curled, with rollers," she adds.

Grooming for the men is scheduled for every day except Sunday, but it's all about shaving. "Because unsupervised we might slit our throats with the electric Norelco," Josh says.

Andrea is, was, a nurse, in the gastrointestinal unit of this same hospital. Now, she's a patient in the psych ward because, at home in her kitchen, she put her head in the oven. "My neighbor couldn't mind her own business," Andrea says. Her neighbor smelled the gas and called the fire department. "I explained to them it was because my cat had died. I keep telling them that when they let me out, I'll get a kitten and then I'll have something to live for."

"Don't they believe you?" Bunny asks.

Andrea shrugs. "Maybe. But they're all freaked out about the codeine, too. I was addicted to codeine. They're acting like it's a big deal. Yeah, right. Codeine. Codeine is nothing."

Although the mental ward is not unlike a prison, the inmates don't much discuss what they're in for. They don't have to ask. Depression, obsessive-compulsive disorder, anorexia—it's right there in plain sight. What they are interested in is the cure, which is why Andrea asks Bunny what medication she's on.

"None," Bunny says, and Andrea concludes, "You're an ECT-ite."

"A what?" Bunny doesn't understand.

"An ECT-ite. The people who are getting ECT are the ECT-ites. ECT," she clarifies, "you know. Electroconvulsive therapy." When Andrea says, "Josh is an ECT-ite," she sounds like a mother bragging, as if ECT were something like a PhD.

Electroconvulsive therapy gets bad press, and really, how could it not? The vocabulary alone—electroconvulsive, electroshock, brain seizures, convulsions, electrodes, fits—is enough to scare away any sane person. We've all seen the movies, the black-and-white photographs of broken people with blank faces wearing soiled hospital gowns, we've heard the stories about how it zaps away who you were, leaving behind an empty shell, like a conch shell, and only the dim sound of a faraway ocean remains.

Bunny tries not to stare at Josh. "No, no," she says. "It's just that I refused Paxil and Abilify. But they'll put me on some other drug."

With the authority accorded to her profession, or maybe it is the authority of someone who's been in and out of the nuthouse more than once or twice, Andrea warns her against Trazodone and Seroquel. Josh says they put him on lithium the last time he was here, and he has nothing good to say about it. Andrea is now on Lamictal, but she can't tell if it's working or not, and Bunny says, "I have a cat. At home. Jeffrey."

Andrea brightens considerably and asks, "Do you have a picture of him?"

"No, but I'll ask my husband to bring one." On the top page of her legal pad, Bunny writes: 6) picture of Jeffery.

Andrea peeks at Bunny's list and asks, "How about chocolate? Chocolate is like gold here."

Bunny adds to the list 7) chocolate; and then, as if she is on to something; 8) legal pads; 9) pens.

"How about some magazines?" Andrea says. "*People* or *Glamour*. We have no idea here what's going on in . . . I'm sorry," she says. "I don't get a lot of visitors."

"I don't mind," Bunny says. "*People* and *Glamour*." Then she asks Josh, "What about you?"

As if he's just woken up, or as if time stood still for a minute or two, Josh says, "Me? I had a dog when I was a kid. He got hit by a car, and the guy who hit him didn't even stop."

It is all too apparent: wounds never heal, but rather, in a torpid state deep inside the medial temporal lobe of the brain, grief waits for fresh release.

Prompt: A Business Meeting (300 words or less)

On a frigid day, a late morning in mid-January on Sixth
Avenue near Fourteenth Street, Stella paused at the
SeXXX shop where, in the window, three blow-up dolls
wearing white fishnet stockings and red Santa hats
were positioned around a pink tinsel tree decorated
with nipple clamps and topped off with a vibrator in
lieu of a star. Stella could not linger, however. Late for
a meeting, she had to rush, practically run, which was
why she didn't notice the wide crack in the pavement
where one of her four-inch spiked heels got caught, and
fell flat on her face.

"Talk about lousy luck," she told me. "A bump on
my forehead and a scraped knee. Not even the lowest
bottom-feeding lawyer would take this case. One
broken finger, was that too much to ask?"

I commiserated with her misfortune. It was a
dream of hers, to sue to the city. Then I asked if she
got to her meeting on time.

"Yeah, I did. But John sent me home. He didn't
want me there looking like a wreck," she said. "My
stockings were torn up. My hair was a mess." Then
she yawned. "Must be the excitement wearing me out.

I'm going to take a nap. I'll call you later. Maybe we can grab dinner."

"I can't tonight," I told her. "How's tomorrow?"

"Sounds good," Stella said.

While Stella napped, the small bump on her forehead bled backward, into her brain, and she died.

I was listed as next of kin. When the doctor called, I said, "No." I said "no" in a way in which you would have expected a polite "thank you" to follow.

I said no, and then I said nothing.

Homecoming Queen

THE WAY IT CAN HAPPEN to the new girl at school, to be appropriated by the popular kids claiming her as one of their own, Josh and Andrea steer Bunny to their table. Although she has yet to figure out if this is something to worry about or not, it's clear that Bunny is in with the in-crowd. With the authority of a queen bee Andrea introduces her to Evan and Jeanette. Evan is a sweet, tubby guy with thinning red hair and the red-rimmed eyes of someone with bad allergies on a day when the pollen count is through the roof. Also, people who cry a lot have the same kind of red-rimmed eyes. To sit at the cool kids table is something of a step up for Evan, even if it's the cool table in the loony bin. In real life, Evan is a junior high school math teacher, and who wouldn't go crazy with that job? The fact that Evan is a teacher sticks with Bunny in a way that his name does not. *Teacher*, she remembers. Jeanette is the same Jeanette with the fucked-up face. The man with a two-day stubble and sculpted biceps is Chaz. Chaz is a member of the New York City Police Department; he's a beat cop in Inwood. "They're all ECT-ites," Andrea says.

It would seem that here in the psycho ward, ECT is like a fraternity. Epsilon, Something or Other, Tau. And, in direct opposition to sanity, it has much to do with what distinguishes the cool kids from the not-cool kids. Never mind that they are as batty as an old attic, their dining room table the equivalent of the high school cafeteria table commandeered by the football team and the mean girls. Andrea is not on the ECT list, but she watches over Josh, protecting him as if he were a kitten, although even without that bond, Andrea would've had a seat at the ECT table because Andrea has had a seat at every cool kids' table since kindergarten.

Bunny's roommate Mrs. Cortez is also on the ECT list, but Mrs. Cortez isn't popular for obvious reasons.

This morning, Chaz and Jeanette underwent a round of ECT, which they refer to as "treatment." Although the ECT-ites identify as such, they don't speak about treatment in specifics, as if what goes on there needs to be kept under wraps. It could be it's too horrible to recount, or perhaps like the secret rituals of the Freemasons or Scroll and Key, it is knowledge you're forbidden to share with the uninitiated.

For lunch, the choices are chicken potpie or macaroni and cheese, the kind that comes in a box with a packet of orange cheese-flavored flakes, which stimulates Bunny's appetite no more than would a bowl of lint. Bunny is spreading the always-on-offer single-serving-size cup of peanut butter onto a slice of white bread when a man wearing a bright white golf shirt with the collar flipped up and red pull-up pants, a white stripe running along the outer side of each leg, sets his tray down on their table. Because there are no available chairs, he takes one from another table and wedges it in between Teacher's chair and Jeanette's.

Josh digs his spoon into his potpie and hits ice.

Once seated, the golf-shirt guy rubs his hands together as if to herald a fine feast. Something has to be very wrong with this man. He exudes pep.

"No one invited you to sit here," Andrea says, and he laughs—*laughs*—as if she were teasing him. "Good one," he says.

"No," Andrea says. "Not a good one. Really, we don't want you here."

He laughs again, although this time there is an edge of nervousness to it, more armor than mirth. "You won't say that when you see what I've got for later. Pam brought me two boxes of Whitman's samplers, a Pepperidge Farm assortment, nacho chips. Other stuff, too."

It's not an introduction, exactly, but Andrea tells Bunny, "That's Howie. He's a hemorrhoid."

Josh is picking around the chunk of peas and carrots frozen in the center of his potpie, and Howie, leaning in to confide in her, says to Bunny, "I was going to kill myself. Pam, my girlfriend, saved my life."

"Oh, no." Teacher says. "Not this again."

"If it wasn't for Pam," Howie blinks, like he's trying to hold back tears, "I'd be dead."

"That's nice," Bunny says.

Great Expectations

IT'S SUNDAY AFTERNOON AND THE dining room bustles with visitors unpacking shopping bags, mostly of food but other gifts, too: fresh T-shirts, magazines, and flowers to brighten the soul-crushing color scheme of this place. Flowers are *Allowed* provided the vase is plastic and the stems are without thorns. The obese girl's parents come with a big, pink teddy bear for their daughter who, it seems, doesn't appreciate the thought because she throws it in the trash while they watch. After having heard, by now, several renditions of Howie's tale of his attempted suicide and Pam's heroic role in preventing it, Bunny had imagined Pam as Wonder Woman, but Pam the person is five feet tall, built like a fire hydrant, frizzy brown hair streaked with wiry gray strands in a ponytail held together with a pink scrunchie. She sets down her grocery bags as if they contain the weight of the world. Mrs. Cortez pays no attention to her two adult children as they try to make small talk with her. The woman visiting Teacher looks to be his sister, maybe even a twin sister. Chaz's mother has brought a Tupperware tub of lasagna for his lunch, and she fusses over him as she would if this were Sunday dinner at home, while his father sits there seemingly as broken as his son. Chaz's father might also be a cop in Inwood because he is wearing shoes that Bunny associates with policemen.

Thus far, in Bunny's time here, Andrea has never had a visitor. The same goes for Underpants Man, and Jeanette.

Bunny takes careful note of Josh's friends, three of them, sitting around the table with him like college buddies shooting the shit over a pitcher of beer. Or, maybe they were childhood friends, a group of four boys who made a pact—blood brothers—to be friends forever, no matter what happens. *Friends forever*, Stella, hits Bunny hard.

Albie rushes to her and hurriedly puts the shopping bag down on an empty chair. "The trains were a mess." He sits and slides his chair close to Bunny's chair. Their knees touch, and her weeping subsides into a whimper. When Bunny dries her eyes with the palms of her hands, Albie is struck by how innocent she seems, and as if he were speaking to a child, he asks, "Do you want to see what I brought you?"

From the shopping bag, he retrieves four Cadbury bars—two with almonds, two without—and sets them on the table, along with a box of crackers and a jar of Peter Pan Creamy peanut butter because all-natural peanut butter comes only in glass jars to be recycled. Bunny says, "I'm sorry."

"Sorry?" Albie asks. "Sorry about what?"

"I mean thank you," Bunny says. "Thank you."

From the same bag, Albie next takes out a packet of three

legal pads and six black felt-tipped pens. Uneasy, but cautiously optimistic, Albie asks, "Are you writing?"

"Not really," Bunny says.

"You're making paper airplanes?"

Bunny rewards Albie's question with a smile. "I'm just writing stuff down. Stuff I don't want to forget."

In another shopping bag are books from home. "I just grabbed whatever off the shelf," he says. But Albie did not just *grab* whatever off the shelf. He selected the books with great care, eschewing contemporary novels lest she use them as a measure of her own failure. For obvious reasons, he rejected Jean Rhys and Ernest Hemingway; and Virginia Woolf—don't even think about it.

Bunny will re-read books she loves, three or even four times, but, although it is one of the rare opinions she's kept to herself, *Pride and Prejudice* and *The Pickwick Papers* are not books she loves, or even likes. The third book in the stack, Darwin's *Voyage of the Beagle*, pleases her far more.

"I seem to recall your saying you wanted to read that," Albie says, "or am I misremembering?"

"How would I know?" Bunny asks. She places *Voyage of the Beagle* on top of the legal pads and pushes the other books away as if they were a meal with which she was done. "You can throw those out on your way home," she says.

Later, when Albie leaves, Bunny puts the chocolate, the peanut butter, and the box of crackers in a brown paper bag, on which she writes her name with the black marker there for that purpose. Then, she stashes the bag in the cabinet over the kitchen sink. The cabinet handles are grimy, tacky to the touch.

Out on the street, one block away from the hospital, Albie drops *Pride and Prejudice* and *The Pickwick Papers* in a trash can. Then he calls Muriel and asks her, "Do you feel like a drink?"

"Why? Do I look like a drink?" Well aware that her joke, such as it is a joke, is lame, Muriel doesn't wait for a laugh. "Sure," she says. "How about Crow's in a half hour?"

Halfway to the subway, Albie changes his mind. The trains are spectacularly unreliable on Sundays. Instead, he hails a cab.

Things Learned

ALSO, THERE IS SLICED TURKEY and salad—lettuce, a few bits of shaved carrot and a cherry tomato—served in a small, beige plastic cup like the salad that comes with the meal served on a plane. Dessert is vanilla pudding, which no one eats. Bunny offers her tablemates chocolate, but when she retrieves the bag from the cabinet, the bag with her name on it, the bag she stashed there only a few hours before, she discovers that her chocolate bars are missing.

"I'm sorry," Andrea says. "I should've warned you. You can't keep chocolate in the cabinets. Some of these whackjobs are like junkies. They'd steal the chocolate out from under your pillow, if they could." They can't steal the chocolate out from under your pillow because food is *Not Allowed* in the bedrooms, but Chaz advises her on how to beat the system. "Chocolate bars are flat," he says. "All you do is tuck one in your waistband under your shirt or inside a magazine."

"And in your room, the best place to hide it is in your laundry bag," Andrea adds. "That way, if someone finds it, they'll have to explain why they were rummaging through your dirty panties."

Teacher blushes, presumably at the word "panties," and he twists to look at the table behind them. "The rabbi has chocolate cake," he notes.

The rabbi is the voice in the dark, the voice that, night after night, calls out, "Holy fuck." It's not known, and frankly no one gives a fuck—holy or not—if the rabbi is really a rabbi or just some guy wearing a yarmulke. It's his kosher meals that are the source of speculation, and envy too. Even for a person such as Bunny, a person hardly nymphomaniacal in pursuit of the palatal orgasm, the food here is, in a word, repulsive; a formula for failure as far as the Anorexics are concerned, and you can be sure that when the maraschino cherry turns out to be a pale-green grape dyed red and bleeding out over your vanilla pudding, it's not doing the Depressives any good, either.

More Waiting

AGAIN, BUNNY WAITS FOR THE dog. This time it is Ella, the tall, gangly nurse with the round head, who tells her that the dog isn't coming today. "Hon," she says. "I don't think the dog is coming today. How about Arts and Crafts?" Bunny doesn't want to go to Arts and Crafts. The other Activities scheduled are Jigsaw Puzzles and Creative Writing. Jigsaw Puzzles? Bunny is depressed enough without Jigsaw Puzzles, and Creative Writing—you've got to be kidding me.

Antipsychotic

BUNNY DOESN'T RECOGNIZE THE NURSE who escorts her beyond the Group Therapy rooms to the conference room, which is at the far, far end of the hallway. There, Dr. Fitzgerald is seated at an oval table made of the same laminated particleboard as the desk in her office, but these chairs have armrests and padded seat cushions, like chairs in a restaurant; and like a basket of bread, there is a box of tissues on the table. Sitting next to her is a bald man, bald except for the monk-like fringe of hair semi-circled around the back of his head. It is impressively nuanced, the way Dr. Fitzgerald introduces the man as Dr. Grossman, the head of psychiatric medicine, if to say, yes, he is the head of psychiatric medicine, but he's not really up to the job, as if she, Dr. Fitzgerald, should be the head of psychiatric medicine. But she is not the head of psychiatric medicine, and she has to defer to the chain of command, no matter how unjust.

Dr. Grossman speaks first. "I understand that you're not comfortable with the advised drug protocol," he says. "Is that right?"

"Bunny is concerned about the side effects," Dr. Fitzgerald butts in. "Please explain to her that whatever the side effects are, when compared with . . ." Dr. Fitzgerald doesn't finish her sentence because Dr. Grossman cuts her off with a look that says, *Have you considered urology?*

As if he and Bunny are now co-conspirators, as if he were deliberately shutting out his colleague, Dr. Grossman leans in and says, "You're right. The side effects are not insignificant. Some people can tolerate them. Others can't."

Bunny decides she doesn't hate Dr. Grossman.

Dr. Fitzgerald interjects, "We could try lithium carbonate." Does she think that Bunny does not know perfectly well that lithium carbonate is plain old lithium?

"How about we table drug protocol, at least for now," Dr. Grossman suggests. "Let's take a look at the other options."

Option one is to do nothing. Over time, the episode could potentially subside on its own. Potentially means that it might subside on its own, but it might not. "And," Dr. Grossman points out, "you do run the risk of the depression worsening."

Cognitive Behavior Therapy, which is the preferred form of Group Therapy (MDD) here is a goal-oriented form of therapy that seeks to modify distorted cognitions and change destructive patterns of behavior, is option two.

As Bunny hears it, Cognitive Behavior Therapy could be effective if she were a moron.

"That's it?" Bunny asks. "There's nothing else?"

With his fingertips pressed together—*here is the church, here is the steeple*—Dr. Grossman asks what does she know about electroconvulsive therapy. E-C-T. Because she doesn't respond, the doctor goes on to explain what it is and how it works, debunking the myths, relating the new methods and greater understanding, and chronicling the efficacy of electroconvulsive therapy; all the while, Bunny is turning the letters E-C-T around and around in her head. E-C-T; T-E-C; E-T-C; C-E-T.

"The anecdotal evidence for recovery is very strong." Dr. Grossman tells Bunny the truth as he knows it. "However," he admits, "there is no way to achieve a scientific standard of proof."

Bunny can't find a word to be made from these letters. T-E-C. T-C-E.

Despair can't be monitored like blood pressure or measured in centimeters like a tumor.

T-E-C

DR. GROSSMAN URGES BUNNY TO talk it over with her husband. "All we want is for you to get well," he says. "And you want to get well, don't you?"

But Bunny can't say for sure if she wants to get well. To get well will take effort, so much effort, and she is weary. And what if she does try, tries her very best, and fails nonetheless? To try and to fail is all too familiar to her. All her life, she has tried and tried, and now she is tired, dog-tired, of trying.

Capital Punishment

THAT NIGHT, WHEN ALBIE ASKS Bunny how she is feeling, she says, "They want to electrocute me."

Bored Games

THE MONOPOLY BOARD IS OPEN on the table. Pink, blue, yellow, and green money is divided up more or less equally between Josh, Andrea, Chaz, and Bunny who are not, and have no intention of, playing Monopoly. But to sit around an open game board gives the appearance of Activity engagement, which is enough to keep the aides, nurses, and occasional doctor hurrying by from hounding them about Activities. Josh has been worrying the dice in his hand for about twenty minutes. Andrea is picking off bits of the red polish on her fingernails, and Chaz says, "Someone is watching us."

Bunny twists around to look in the direction of Chaz's line of vision. A young girl is there; eleven years old, maybe twelve, decidedly prepubescent, and Andrea perks up. "Nina," she says. "I knew she'd be back." Andrea knows Nina from before. Andrea says that the mental ward is like a minimum-security prison for repeat offenders of non-violent crimes. "It's a revolving door," she says.

Nina resembles nothing more than a newly hatched sparrow; prominent veins protruding through translucent skin covering bones so light as to seem hollow, short downy hair on her head. Bunny imagines her craning her neck, her mouth open improbably wide like the beak of a baby bird ready to be fed a worm, although if Nina were to open her mouth wide like that, it wouldn't be for food; rather, it would be to emit a primal scream, an endless scream with the intent to purge herself of herself.

"Do you believe she is twenty-six, at least twenty-six?" Andrea says. "She might even be twenty-seven by now." Nina is anorexic, but not your run-of-the-mill anorexic. She is also bipolar and not your run-of-the-mill bipolar either. Sometimes, she cycles in a matter of minutes, and even worse, the cycles sometimes overlap, so that her depression *is* manic, a depression on speed. "She's a mess," Andrea says. "The last time we were here together, she spent half her days banging her head against the wall. She really wanted out."

"Who doesn't want out? No one *wants* to be here," Bunny says, but Josh disagrees. "Howie wants to be here," Josh says. "He loves this place," and not for the first time Bunny gets the idea, although she'd be hard-pressed to explain where she got such an idea, that Josh is someone who would go ice-skating for the fun that comes with falling down; he would've done such a thing.

"I didn't mean *here*," Andrea says. "I mean that she wanted out of life. She doesn't want to be alive."

Bunny and Josh, both, make a point to look away from the other.

It is true what Josh said about Howie. Howie *does* want to
be here, here in life and here in the hospital, which, you could
say, makes him the most mental of them all. Twice already, the
doctors agreed that Howie was ready for discharge. Pam was
here to pick him up, take him back to New Jersey. All he needed
to do was answer one last question, sign on the dotted line, and
he'd be home in less than thirty minutes, assuming that traffic
on the George Washington Bridge wasn't at a standstill. But
Howie—he sat in the conference room across from the doctors
and lowered his gaze. "Not to others," he said. "I'd never hurt
anyone else. But myself, I think about it. I had my gun out, and I
was ready to do it, but my girlfriend stopped me. If it wasn't for
her, I'd be dead. But I still think about it. About doing it. A lot."

Although Howie and Pam had been together for almost
seven years, and he is now forty-four and she is thirty-nine—
neither of them spring chickens—he wasn't willing to marry
her. Tired of waiting around, Pam signed up with Match.com,
which was when Howie called her and said, "I've got a gun, and
I'm going to kill myself."

Howie's gun might well have been a toy gun, the kind that
looks authentic but shoots foam rubber pellets or bits of raw
potatoes. Howie was never going to kill himself for real. Not
then, not now, not ever. Howie is mental, but his mental ill-
nesses—decidedly nuts and a wicked case of mindblindness—are
not among the entries in the *Diagnostic and Statistical Manual of
Mental Disorders*. He is a different species of crazy, entirely.

Regardless Pam raced as fast as her short legs could carry

her to his house, hustled him into his car, and drove across the bridge to the best hospital with a psycho ward in the tri-state area. Pam now atones for having signed up with Match.com by bringing him bags of food and doing his laundry. Never again will she press him to marry her.

Howie, meanwhile, is having the time of his life here. He goes about his days as if the loony bin were a Carnival Cruise ship, and he is the Activities Director full of vim and vigor and in charge of games like charades and Simon Says. All he needs is the whistle hanging from a lanyard around his neck, which, of course, he can't have. Lanyards are *Not Allowed*.

"I'll bet that when he was a kid, he got the living shit kicked out of him every day," Andrea says. "Because you know he's the kind of guy who never learns."

"He thinks we're his friends," Josh says.

"Shit." Chaz tears off the corner of a blue Monopoly bill. "That's so fucked up."

"Yeah, it is," Josh agrees. "But he's lonely. He's a lonely guy."

"Maybe," Andrea says. "Maybe that's it, but he's got Pam. I don't know. Maybe," and then she says, "In three days, it's my birthday."

Help

BUNNY SITS IN THE CHAIR across from Dr. Fitzgerald's desk, and tells her, "I want to go home."

"Good," Dr. Fitzgerald says. "We can start you on the Paxil and Abilify tomorrow and, if all goes well, you'll be home before you know it."

Bunny closes her eyes, and she shakes her head, which the psychiatrist interprets as a different decision made, that Bunny has decided on electroconvulsive therapy. "If that's what you want to do," she says, "I'll set up an appointment with Dr. Grossman."

"No," Bunny clarifies, "I want to go home now."

"Bunny, that's not possible," Dr. Fitzgerald tells her. "You can't simply check out. The staff has to agree that you are ready to be discharged." She explains that, unlike every other unit in the hospital where you can get up and walk out even if the doctor has advised against it, the rules are different in the psycho ward, although Dr. Fitzgerald does not use the word "psycho." She says "psych ward," because the doctors aren't allowed to say "psycho." Or, at least not in front of the psychos themselves.

Bunny tries to comprehend the unfathomable. "You mean you could keep me here forever?"

"It's for your own good," Dr. Fitzgerald says. "And it's the law."

Bunny can't sign herself out of the loony bin because, by virtue of her being here, she is not of sound mind. Nor is it possible for Albie to sign her out even though he *is* of perfectly sound mind because now that she's here, the hospital is legally responsible for her safety.

With more compassion than she has heretofore exhibited toward Bunny, Dr. Fitzgerald tells her, "You can petition the courts, but it can take a long time to get a hearing."

Bunny blows her nose into a tissue, and then blots her eyes with the same tissue, and she repeats, "I want to go home now."

"And we *want* you to go home. We want you to go home as soon as possible. But you're not doing anything to help yourself." Dr. Fitzgerald picks up her pen and twirls it between her fingers. She is anxious to get back to her paperwork. "You're refusing drug treatment, you haven't gone even once to therapy, and you're not partaking in Activities, either."

"I went to Arts and Crafts, " Bunny says, "and I go to Creative Writing."

"You went to Arts and Crafts one time, and Creative Writing meets for one hour three times a week. What are you doing with the rest of your days?"

"I've been waiting for the dog," Bunny tells her. "And I've been writing. Creatively," she adds.

"Alone? By yourself?" Dr. Fitzgerald makes a bird noise. "How can you expect to get better when you are off in some corner all alone? Bunny," Dr. Fitzgerald says, "writing is not the answer."

Prompt: A Pair (300 words or less)

The Delman twins were new to my school. They had extremely chubby cheeks, and short brown hair. Identical twins were deliriously remarkable in and of themselves, but these twins were all the more remarkable because of the resemblance they bore to my hamster. I was anxious to introduce them to my hamster, whose name was My Darling. When the Delman twins got to my house, I showed them to my mother and said, "Don't they look just like My Darling?" It was the chubby cheeks. When My Darling shoveled sunflower seeds in her mouth, storing them in her pouch, her cheeks got fat. Also, their hair was the same shade of brown. My observation, in my opinion, was a huge compliment because My Darling was the cutest thing I'd ever seen. My mother, however, flatly contradicted me in a way meant to convey that I'd said something I shouldn't have said, which was something that happened all too often for my mother's liking, and mine, too.

That year, at my birthday party, after I blew out the candles on the cake, which my mother cut into ten slices to put on paper plates, I opened my gifts.

From past birthday party experience, I knew that
most of the gifts would be things I didn't want, but I
was schooled to pretend otherwise, which was why
I pretended that the Skipper doll was exactly what I
wanted more than anything in the world. But when I
opened the second doll, I didn't have to pretend. Two
Skipper dolls were nothing like one Skipper doll.
Two Skipper dolls were twins. Twins like the Delman
twins.

Two days after my birthday, My Darling eviscer-
ated herself on a sharp edge of her hamster wheel.

Prior to the start of summer when the Delman
twins went away to sleepaway camp, they held the top
two spots on my list of best friends, which I wrote as
1a) and 1b) because how could I choose between them.
Up until the latter half of my first year in college, my
list of best friends was a fluid list, which could alter
dramatically within minutes.

Sometimes you don't know something is missing
until it's there. The way someone born blind in one
eye might wake up some morning to find both eyes
working at 20/20, I didn't know that I was only half
of a person. I didn't know there was any other way
to be until I met Stella. When I met Stella, I became
a full person. To be complete is to see the world with
two good eyes. Twin eyes. I don't know how else to
explain it. There was nothing that I could not tell

her because it was as if she already knew. It was like sharing myself with myself, the only difference being that Stella didn't pass judgment on me, nor I on her. Instead, all things that had been shameful, painful, hurtful and humiliating whipped seamlessly into hilarity.

If I wasn't an easy person to like, Stella was near to impossible to like, although my husband loved her, which made sense because he loved me, too. Despite that she was the most brilliant person I ever knew, her sole ambition was to get rich, get rich quick. To that end, she came up with all kinds of schemes, but she had very little follow-through. Also, she made poor choices; married, and divorced, three times. All her husbands drank too much, and for reasons we could never figure out, each of them got fired from his job soon after she married him. Except for the one who didn't have a job to begin with. That marriage lasted longer than the others, just shy of three years.

Stella and I looked nothing alike. She was tall with strawberry blond hair and small, pretty features. She was an only child from Mississippi who never lost her accent, but still, she said to me, "In our last lives we were sisters. Twin sisters."

Twin sisters.

Like the Delman twins, minus the resemblance to the hamster.

Another Way to Get There

BUNNY AND ANDREA MEET UP on the lunch line where Andrea recounts her morning session with Dr. Fitzgerald. "I'm a changed woman." Andrea laughs. Then, she elbows Bunny to look at Nina as she cuts across the dining room to where Antoine is leaning up against the far wall. Nina's pink sweater, cropped short, skims the waistband of her red skirt; a waistband that has been folded over four or five times, the way, Andrea remembers, at the end of the day, she, like all the Catholic school girls, would roll up the waistbands of their plaid, pleated skirts. Nina's hemline lands mid-to-upper thigh. Her legs are bare and on her feet are black flats with the kind of pointed toes that generally complement stiletto heels. Nina got the shoes on eBay where, she'd told Bunny, she buys all of her clothes, which are, for the most part, vintage. Circa 1960s. Early 1960s. Mod, not hippie, and she does, somewhat, resemble the iconic model of that era, except Twiggy was fatter than Nina is. Sometimes, Nina and Bunny talk about clothing and fashion.

"Ten to one," Andrea says, "she's not wearing panties."

After high school, instead of getting a job or traveling

cross-country to find herself or going to a normal college, Nina went to Bible college because her mother is one of those whack-a-doodle Born Agains who rely on prayer to fix everything, and if only Nina would ask Jesus for help, she'd be fixed, too. "Like that time with my car," her mother repeated the story ad nauseam, about how one night her car broke down on a lonely stretch of road, how the battery on her cell phone had run dry, but she wasn't afraid. She knew exactly what to do. She prayed. She prayed to Jesus to fix her car, and apparently she caught Jesus at a moment when He wasn't particularly busy answering the prayers of people who were starving or dying or suffering in any of the multitude of ways that genuine suffering exists, because, on the next try, the post-prayer turn of the key in the ignition, her car started up, the motor purring like a cat.

Nina makes no secret of her attraction to Antoine. It's likely that most women here would be attracted to Antoine except for the fact that most of the women here no longer have a libido. Antoine is from Haiti. Port-au-Prince, a place that sounds as if it suits him because his bearing is regal; tall, muscular, a raised tilt to his jaw. Looking up at him, Nina twists a lock of hair around her finger, and Andrea says to Bunny, "He'd split her open like a melon."

For the record: because it's impossible for a cat to have a personal relationship with Jesus, cats are barred entry to the Kingdom of Heaven. This is true of all animals except horses. There are horses in heaven because horses are needed to pull the chariots.

You Scream, I Scream

COGNITIVE BEHAVIOR THERAPY (MDD) IS underway when Bunny slips in and takes the chair nearest to the door. Two identical couches—fudge-brown fabric dotted with nubs of mustard brown for pizazz—and three profoundly faded orange plastic chairs are arranged in an approximation of a semicircle. The woman leading the group is positioned like a kindergarten teacher reading a story to the children. She is wearing a white lab coat. The doctors on the psych ward all wear white lab coats, and stethoscopes hang from their necks like loosely draped scarves. They never *use* the stethoscopes, but they wear them with their white lab coats the way the Pope wears the robe and the ring. This woman does not have a stethoscope. The clipboard on her lap looks official, except the paper is not for taking important notes or checking off appropriate boxes. Rather, it is a cheat-sheet of questions and prompts for discussion. Even for the uninitiated, she is obviously a freshly minted social worker. Her smile is huge. Her shoes are from Talbots. She is scared shitless.

"Welcome to our group." She lifts her arms to make an

all-encompassing circle, like she is singing *He's got the whole wide world in his hands.* "And you are . . . ?" she asks.

"Bunny."

"Bunny?" her voice lilts. "Is that your real name?" The social worker, lacking the iota of perception necessary to read Bunny's expression, goes on, "Or is it a pet name from childhood, you know, like you were *cute as a bunny?*"

When you're in the mental ward, to get up and kick your chair across the room as if it were a football is not a wise move. Bunny clenches her fists, her fingernails bite into the palms of her hands, and she gnaws on her tongue as if her teeth were small and sharp. The physical pain generated by the self-inflicted trauma subsumes the madness. Bunny does not run amok.

"Okay, then. My name is Carolyn. It's great to meet you." Carolyn is putting out that Higher Power kind of vibe, which is worrisome. "Everyone, let's go around the room and introduce ourselves to Bunny."

"She already knows us," Chaz says.

"Maybe she doesn't know all of you."

Chaz allows for no doubt. "She knows all of us."

"Okay, then." Carolyn adjusts her posture to sit taller in her chair. "Before we pick up where we left off last time, does anyone have any questions?"

Bunny has a question; a string of questions, all related: What is the intent of the counter-intuition in this place? Why do they serve slop instead of food? And what gives with the color scheme? Why is everything—the walls, the furniture, the carpet, the curtains—in a spectrum of colors that, in the crayon box, would have names like: Listless, Hopeless, Sour Milk? Why is it that the one pop of color is the blue of the loony-socks, and even then, the bulk of the loony-socks, as they are distributed, are the same brown as sand? When our surroundings are over-whelmingly depressing, how can we be anything but depressed? But the question "Does anyone have any questions?" turns out not to be a question, but a transition in the form of a question. "Okay, then. Good. Let's pick up where we left off last time. Edward was talking about his children, and how he is going to get reacquainted with them in a positive way."

Edward was one of the three men at Bunny's table on her first night here. He seems more alert now, but that's about it.

"Alicia is only five. Eric is two." Edward sounds like he is pleading for his children's safety, as if they were being held hostage or something like that. "He's a baby. They haven't seen me in almost three months. Two years old, he doesn't remember what happened yesterday." Edward's voice cracks. "He won't know who I am. Alicia will be afraid of me." Edward hunches over, head in hands. Jeanette pats his back, even though to pat his back requires touching him. Carolyn is either unaware that touching is *Not Allowed*, or else she is too scared to tell Jeanette to cut it out. Edward cries harder. Jeanette continues to pat his back, which, from Bunny's vantage point, looks like she is rubbing up against him, although Edward seems not to notice. Carolyn tells him that his fears are groundless. "Of course your son is going to remember you. And your daughter is going to be so happy that you're home. It's going to be wonderful, I promise."

"Whoa, Carolyn," Chaz intervenes. "That's messed up. You don't go around making promises when who the fuck knows what's going to happen." Perhaps he is speaking from experience as a policeman, or maybe he was always aware of the danger of heightened expectations and trust broken. "Right now," he tells Edward, "all you can do is cross your fingers and hope for the best."

For himself, Chaz has no hope for the best because when he gets out of here, he'll be doing desk duty until the day he retires.

Carolyn consults her clipboard, flipping pages for help. "Okay, then," she says. "Let's talk about the first happy thing we are going to do when we get home. Something really nice. A special treat."

Jeanette says the first thing she wants to do is get a pedicure. At Beauty, they don't do pedicures, although they will clip your toenails.

Edward wipes his eyes and says, "My children. All I want is to hug my children."

The obese girl looks forward to time with her Xbox.

First thing when he gets home, Howie is going to take Pam out for a lobster dinner. "Pam is my girlfriend. She saved my life," he tells Carolyn. "If it wasn't for her, I wouldn't be here." All of them in Cognitive Behavior Therapy (MDD), including Carolyn, have heard the story of Howie and Pam, and more than once, too. It's not even a good story, at least not the way

Howie tells it. Whatever emotional depth it could have clings to the surface like pond scum, the characters are flat, and any humor it generates is unintentional. Only Bunny who, to date, has heard it at least nine times, wants to hear it again. What she likes are the variations that come with revision; how the story changes with each retelling. Yeah, yeah, everyone's heard about how Pam raced to his house to keep him from killing himself, but in this latest iteration, Howie adds a new detail. "With nothing but flip-flops on her feet," he says. "In the freezing cold, she ran all the way to my house with nothing but flip-flops on her feet." Bunny likes the flip-flops; she'll use the flip-flops.

Another girl who, like the obese girl, also attends Group Therapy for Eating Disorders, although this girl is skeletal, says the first happy thing she wants to do when she gets home is to treat herself to a colon cleanse.

"Good," Carolyn says. "That's good."

How is it, Bunny wonders, that Carolyn doesn't know that, no, an anorexic looking forward to a colon cleanse is not good, not good at all. She also wonders if Carolyn's face aches from the isometric exercise it takes to hold that huge, insipid grin of hers in place.

"And what about you, Bunny? What's the first happy thing you want to do when you get home?"

"I don't know," Bunny says.

"Come on," Carolyn cajoles. "You can think of something."

"No. Really, I can't think of anything."

"There has to be something. At home, what's your favorite thing to do?"

"Read," Bunny says.

"No, no. I mean something really, really fun," Carolyn urges. "Like going to the beach or on a picnic."

Bunny doesn't mention her aversion to sand, but she does ask, "Isn't it still January?"

Carolyn explains that she didn't mean literally go to the beach or on a picnic, but something along those lines. "Do you ski? Or like Howie, do you look forward to going out for a delicious dinner with friends?"

"A delicious dinner with friends is how I got here," Bunny tells her. "I want to go home where it's quiet. Where I can be alone and read."

"Yes, but what do you *really* look forward to?"

To put an end to this, Bunny does something like sign a confession to a crime she did not commit. She says, "I want to eat ice cream."

"Good, good. That's really good," Carolyn jiggles, jiggles for real, in her seat. "Now, what kind of ice cream do you want to eat? What flavor?"

"Strawberry," Bunny says, and Carolyn claps her hands.

Party Planning

THE PLAN IS TO THROW Andrea a surprise party for her birthday. Bunny is taking notes, not notes for the party planning, but notes for herself that have nothing to do with the party. Teacher volunteers to make decorations and hats. "Hats?" Bunny looks up. "Do we really want hats?" Josh will ask one of his friends to pick up a pizza, and Chaz has a Pepperidge Farm angel food cake, untouched, in a brown bag in the refrigerator. No one messes with Chaz's food. "I guess there's no point to bothering with candles," Jeanette says, and Josh says, "Not if you're thinking about lighting them." Nina offers to donate a small box of almonds coated in pastel colored sugar. "They look pretty," she says, "but I'll never eat them," and Chaz points out, "You never eat anything."

Something to Do With Cats

WATCHING BUNNY PEEL AN ORANGE, one of the six he brought for her, Albie mentions, "It looks like your appetite's come back."

"No. It's just that there's nothing else to do here." She breaks the orange apart and gives him one half. Nothing else to do, unless you count Activities, which Bunny doesn't because a) still no dog, and b) although Bunny no longer actively thinks of herself as a writer, she cannot and will not accept the notion that Creative Writing is an Activity the way Decoupage is an Activity. Bunny writes as a way to kill time between meals. There is a lot of time between meals.

If they'd let her sleep all day, she probably wouldn't be writing. If they'd let her sleep, that's how she'd kill away the day. But they don't let her sleep, and already, she has filled almost four legal pads with sentences and paragraphs.

"What else can I bring for you?" Albie asks. "More chocolate? Or some pears?"

His question prompts Bunny to remember. "A T-shirt with

a picture of a cat on it," she says. "Or a book about cats. Something to do with cats. And a card. With a cat on it. It's Andrea's birthday."

"Andrea?" Albie asks. "Is she one of your friends here?"

Bunny squeezes the half of the orange still in her hand. The juice spurts. "I don't have friends here," she says. "I don't have friends anywhere."

Albie pries open her fingers to get the desiccated orange, which he sets on a napkin to take to the trash. Bunny wipes her hand on her paper pajama top. Albie takes his wife's other hand, the one not sticky from the orange, and brings it to his lips. "You're a good person, Bunny," he says. "You really are." And Bunny says, "Wrapping paper, too."

A Breath of Fresh Air

BUNNY ISN'T ELIGIBLE FOR GROUP Walk. Group Walk, which is a regular walk except you're walking with a gaggle of loons escorted by three social workers taking a spin around a relatively grim part of the city, is not, for Bunny, a dream that must be deferred. With more than half her fellow campers out for this morning stroll, the living room is deserted, and that is the best scenario here, as far as she can imagine it. She turns one of the armchairs to face the window with a view of a parking lot and a row of dumpsters and, sitting with her feet resting on the windowsill as if it were a coffee table, she opens her legal pad to the page where she last left off. Bunny reads over the sentences, and then looks up to think of what comes next.

Because this window, like all the windows here, is made of plexiglass that is scratched and dull and liberally speckled with dollops of pigeon shit in various degrees of decomposition, there's no way to know if the sun is shining or is the sky cloud-covered or is it raining, perhaps a light drizzle? Needless to say, the windows are sealed shut. Not so much as the idea of a draft can get through. If she didn't know that it is January, she'd have no idea what the season was. There are no people in the parking lot with their gloves tucked into the pockets of coats unbuttoned to convey to Bunny that the day might be a balmy one, whereas if it were really cold, hats would be pulled down low and there would be women wearing Ugg boots. She tries to recall the smell of fresh winter air; cold, crisp air promising snow, but she fails. Because it would only frustrate her to push herself further, to attempt to conjure a memory which she can't bring to mind, and because to keep at it would not end well, she aims to divert her attention. She puts her pen to the paper, and she writes. She writes. More than three pages without so much as a pause. Only when she senses someone standing behind her, looking over her shoulder, does she stop, and she flips the pad so that the blank cardboard back is faceup, and Howie comes around to sit on the windowsill where he blocks her view, such as it is a view. Then, as if responding to a question, except no question has been asked, Howie says, "I was at Group Therapy. OCD."

"OCD," Bunny says, "is that new?"

"Not really," Howie tells her.

Not for a skinny minute does Bunny believe that Howie is OCD, but curious to learn what he will say, she asks him how these obsessive compulsions of his manifest. He mulls over the possibilities, trying to determine which of them gleaned from his hour in Group Therapy (OCD) might seem credible:

hand-washing; pattern-counting; removing seeds, one at a time, from cucumbers. "At home, I'm kind of a neat freak," he says. "I can't let dishes pile up in the sink. I pin my socks together before putting them in the washing machine. That sort of thing. There's more, but the therapist is still figuring them out." Then he asks, "What are you writing?"

"I'm not writing," Bunny says, and Howie tells her, "I'm thinking about writing a novel. About this place. Everyone here would be a character in it."

"Yeah, well, good luck with that." Holding fast to her legal pad and pen, Bunny gets up from her chair, leaving Howie scanning the room for someone else to bother.

No one is using the telephone, but still, Underpants Man is there at his post. Mrs. Cortez sits on the bench across from the Activities board. Alongside her sits another catatonic. Bunny pauses to write: *Needless to say, they are not engaged in conversation.*

Early Returns

AT THE NURSE'S STATION, NURSE Kendall and Antoine are flirting up a whirl, which is just another way to pass the time. From his pocket, Antoine retrieves a roll of peppermint Life Savers. He peels one off the top, pops it in his mouth, and then offers one to Nurse Kendall, and one to Bunny, too. Bunny does not want a peppermint Life Saver. She's here for a piece of Nicorette gum. "You already got one this morning." Nurse Kendall rations the Nicorette as if nicotine were an opiate.

"Come on. Have a heart." Antoine cajoles Nurse Kendall on Bunny's behalf. "Give the woman a damn piece of Nicorette gum."

Because the crazy people are *Not Allowed* to touch anything remotely related to medication, not so much as a vitamin, with their own hands, Nurse Kendall peels away the backing on the Nicorette wrapper, and Bunny receives the piece of gum on her tongue as if it were a Communion wafer.

"You need anything else?" Antoine asks.

"Yeah," Bunny says. "Could you tell me the weather? Outside. Is it cold?"

"You bet it's cold. It's damn cold."

"Is it overcast? Or is the sun out?"

"It was sunny when I got here," Antoine says. "But now, who knows. They'll be back from the walk pretty soon. One of them can tell you better."

Pretty soon turns out to be all of two minutes, when snap! just like that, the corridor is swarming with crazies taking off their coats and then wandering off in every which direction, while the social workers, like kindergarten teachers on a class outing, try to keep order. Group Walk was cut short because of Josh, because he bummed a cigarette from a construction worker. Josh doesn't smoke. He bummed the cigarette to give to Andrea, but no one cares why he did it. It's *Not Allowed*, and there is nothing more to be said.

In the living room, Andrea spreads her coat over her legs. She is still shivering, and Josh says, "I'm sorry."

"Sorry? Forget what those fucks said. You did us all a favor." She turns to Bunny and says, "You would not believe how fucking freezing it is out there." Then, in perfect imitation of one of the social workers, the one who is very petite except for her breasts, which are the size of Volkswagens, Andrea mimics, "One rotten apple, that's all it takes. One rotten apple," she repeats, and Josh looks like he is about to laugh, and Bunny realizes that she is holding her breath in anticipation of what isn't going to happen.

A Disturbance

AT MEALTIMES, THE EATING DISORDERS are supervised. Under the watchful eye of an aide, they are required to eat, and then for two hours after the meal, neither the Anorexics nor the Bulimics can go to the bathroom unaccompanied, although the night before Bunny saw Nina sneak into the Arts and Crafts room where she vomited into a trash can.

Now, Bunny hears Nina before she sees her. A yowling into the telephone, a lachrymosity as cacophonous as a car crash, and all the more remarkable coming from this waif with matchstick arms and legs. To add to the disturbance, Underpants Man, like a low-level buffoon with a bullhorn, orders her to get off the phone. "Time's up," he points to his wrist as if he were wearing a watch. "Time's up."

The fact that Underpants Man wears his underpants as outer pants does nothing to temper Bunny's dislike for him, but even if he wore his underpants as they are intended to be worn— *under* his pants—Bunny would still loathe him. Underpants Man, the telephone Stasi.

"Time's up." Underpants Man jabs again and again at his imaginary wristwatch. "Time's up."

Time's up for what? No one is waiting to use the phone; Underpants Man, least of all. He calls no one and no one calls him. Under different circumstances Bunny might've felt compassion for him, but the circumstances are what they are: Underpants Man is relentlessly badgering Nina to get off the phone while she blows snot bubbles from her nose.

Cats Are Love

THE T-SHIRT IS YELLOW AND embossed with a kitten; a blue-eyed kitten of an indeterminate breed. "There wasn't much of a selection," Albie explains. "And I wasn't sure about the size, so I got a large. Better too big, right?" From a different bag, Albie takes out the fresh three-pack of legal pads, more pens, a birthday card—a cartoon of cats in a chorus line—and purple tissue paper. "The guard confiscated the ribbon and the Scotch tape," he says.

"Scotch tape?" Bunny ponders. "I suppose you could tape your mouth and nose shut and suffocate yourself."

"It was the metal teeth on the dispenser," Albie tells her, and Bunny asks, "Dispenser? Is that the right word?"

"Yeah. It's the right word."

"It doesn't sound like the right word."

"I got this, too." Albie sets a cat calendar on the table. "I thought maybe you'd want to give her two gifts."

Albie's kindness overwhelms her, and she says, "You deserve better than me."

Each month on the calendar features a different breed of cat.

Bunny turns the page from January's Maine Coon to February's Russian Blue. June's cat is a white Persian, and then comes July. A Siamese. All Siamese cats do not look alike, far from it, but July's Siamese bears an uncanny and unsettling resemblance to their Angela, right down to the one crossed eye.

Bunny loves Jeffrey because he's Jeffrey, and there is room for new love, but new love does not replace what was lost. It does not mend the tear or fill the hole or heal the wound. To replace lost love, the way you can replace your broken computer with a new one or replace the battery in your watch, is not an option.

Folding her into his arms, Albie rubs her back. "I'm sorry. I should've looked."

When Bunny is done crying, Albie brushes at the sizable wet spot on his shirt. Because salt is a nonvolatile substance, tears evaporate at a slower rate than water. It was an experiment Albie did as a boy: to put a cup of salt water alongside a cup of fresh water and measure the rates of evaporation. Curiously, it was a question Bunny had once asked him; something to do with something she was writing, and it was not dissimilar to the question she asks now: "For how long can you cry before you've cried yourself dry?"

Albie cups her face in his hands. He kisses one eye and then the other. Her eyelashes are wet. He tastes the salt. One more kiss, this one to her forehead, and then he says, "I'm pretty sure a person can go for seven weeks, four days and three hours before dry-eye syndrome sets in."

What Albie knows, but will not say, is that, excepting when

we are asleep, the lachrymal glands never cease secreting protein-rich and antibacterial fluid, tears, which keep the eyeball lubricated. In other words, with sleep and death as the only respites, we cry forever.

Intuition

BETWEEN THE HOURS OF BREAKFAST and lunch, Bunny wanders the halls, thinking, where do I go from here? When she is done with that, with thinking, when her thoughts are sorted out, she can get back to it, uninterrupted at least for a while. Josh is at his biweekly meeting with Dr. Grossman. Teacher is at Origami making paper hats for Andrea's party. Howie is at Group Therapy; which disorder is up for grabs. Chaz went to Calisthenics, and, having decided to go wild in celebration of her birthday, Andrea is at Beauty where she is deliberating between green nail polish on one hand and blue on the other, or perhaps pink and orange, which Jeanette prefers. With any luck, Bunny will have the living room to herself. With any luck, she will have time alone.

Except there is no luck. Instead, there's Nina, curled up, partially hidden, in an armchair turned to the far wall. Bunny cannot see Nina's face, but she can see her wrap a section of her hair around her index finger, which she twirls, as if her finger were a curling iron. Hair as thin as Nina's hair can't hold a curl. When released, the coil will droop.

Bunny deliberates whether or not to sit with her. Nina looks lost and lonely in the chair that is too big for her, but Bunny senses that she wants to be left alone. On the grounds that *it takes one to know one*, the psychos intuit things like this about each other, although they don't always respect it. Their own needs tend to take precedence. Satisfied that Nina, too, wishes to be alone, Bunny turns around and walks away, which is why she isn't there to see Nina's finger twirl her hair tighter and tighter until her finger is resting flush to her head. Then, the way a Band-Aid is pulled off, hard and fast, Nina yanks the hank of hair from her scalp.

Jelly Beans

ANDREA IS LATE COMING TO lunch, which allows the others to go over the arrangements for her party. Bunny passes around the birthday card for them all to sign. Teacher announces that he has made eight paper hats.

"I'm not wearing a paper hat," Bunny says, and Chaz says, "Me neither."

Teacher's eyes fill up fast and his chin quivers, but he recovers when Chaz says, "Okay, okay. I'll wear a hat."

Any good that is done here is the good they do for each other, and Bunny wishes that she, too, could acquiesce about the hat. But it isn't possible.

Howie worries that one pizza won't be enough. "Eight people, eight slices. Suppose someone wants more than one slice?"

Teacher points out that it's highly unlikely, really no chance at all, that Nina will eat a slice of pizza. "So someone can have two," he says, and with that, all talk of the party stops because Andrea is there, holding out her hands, fingers splayed, for everyone to admire. Unable to settle on any one pairing of colors, each fingernail is painted a different color. "Like a bowl of jelly beans," Teacher effuses, and then inexplicably, he begins to cry. Not that anyone here needs a reason for crying, but it could also be that he is still distraught about the hats, and his crying now is merely crying delayed.

Bunny tells Andrea that her fingernails look fabulous, which is not what she really thinks.

"I wanted to do something happy," she says. The corners of her mouth twitch, and she quickly covers her face with her hands. It would not be unusual to have more than one person per table crying, but none of them, not even Josh, has ever seen Andrea cry. Then her hands fall away and, like magic, her eyes are dry, her smile is back, but it is not as if it never happened.

"They got hamburgers for lunch," Chaz says. "With fries."

Something Happened

TWO NURSES CUT THROUGH THE dining room as if a tornado or maybe Bigfoot were not far behind. Anxiety gathers in their wake. Heads swivel, but no one moves until one of the aides, a big guy heavily tattooed, calls for attention. "Listen up. Nice and easy now, we're heading on over to the Therapy rooms."

Underpants Man calls out, "We haven't had dessert yet." Only Underpants Man is bothered about missing a fruit cup.

To prevent chaos, to see to it that no one goes rogue, two aides are posted at each corner of the dining room.

Bunny, Josh, and Andrea are corralled into the Music Room. Andrea asks Patricia if they can switch rooms. Patricia is the aide who took Bunny's shoes. Andrea cocks her thumb at Underpants Man and says, "I can't be locked up in here with him. I'll go crazy," to which Patricia says, "You already are crazy."

Andrea threatens to report her and Patricia says, "Go ahead. Who are they going to believe? You or me?"

It's one of the many disadvantages to being mentally ill. You are automatically in the wrong because you *are* wrong. Everyone knows that crazy people have no sense of proportion and often they are delusional and paranoid. Andrea mutters "Fuck you," and backs down.

There are not enough chairs to go around. Bunny, Andrea, and Josh sit on the floor, and Josh says, "Let's hope no one is claustrophobic. I once got trapped in an elevator with a claustrophobic. I think it's how I wound up here."

"Good one," Bunny says, and she thinks of Elliot, how he always says, "That's funny," instead of laughing. It occurs to her that maybe it's not an affect on Elliot's part; maybe he can't laugh, the way she can't laugh and Josh can't laugh, either. Then all attention turns to the door as it opens wide enough only to allow the Music Therapist to slip through. "No way am I singing-along," Bunny says. But the Music Therapist does not go to the piano. She, too, sits on the floor, her back against the wall. She could easily be mistaken for one of the psychos, the way she wraps her arms around her legs, her chin on her knees, rocking like a cradle. The obese girl who, that morning, poured maple syrup on her cornflakes, stands up and says, "I demand to know what is going on."

A month or so before, although Bunny wasn't here to witness it, she'd heard that they were herded into the Therapy rooms when Edward took off his clothes and went racing naked through the halls. It took nearly an hour before they got hold of him long enough to inject a sedative.

Time passes. Some of them fall asleep. Andrea nibbles at her thumbnail, the one painted orange. The other thumbnail is a ghastly shade of lime green, and Bunny tells her, "You're messing up your manicure." Andrea takes her hand away from her mouth, assesses the damage done, and then resumes nibbling. Josh is talking to himself but not so loud that Bunny can hear him. The Music Therapist has recovered well enough to ask if they would like to have a sing-along, but no one says yes, and then Ella opens the door, and tells them, although not in these same exact words, that the coast is clear. Activities will go on as scheduled.

Andrea stops at the door to ask Ella what happened, and Ella says, "There's nothing to worry about, hon."

Holding up her hands to show Ella her jelly bean fingernails, Andrea says, "It's my birthday."

Countdown

THEY HAVE TWO HOURS TO kill before dinner. Two hours here can feel like three days. Chaz convinces Josh to go to Group Exercise where they'll do jumping jacks, push-ups, and run in place. Howie says he'll go with them. Josh says "Okay" at the precise moment that Chaz says "No." Then Chaz shrugs and says, "Yeah. Whatever," and Howie trots along beside them like he is a dachshund or a corgi, some kind of dog with short legs. Jeanette goes looking for Nina, and Teacher has an appointment with his psychiatrist, an elderly woman whom he speaks of with high regard. Bunny can't remember her name, but wonders if they'll let her swap Dr. Fitzgerald for the elderly woman.

Andrea tells Bunny that before dinner, she's going to take a shower. "Wash my hair. Put on real clothes." She is wearing a pair of jeans and a paper pajama top. "I even have shoes here. A cute pair of flats that I can wear."

"For your birthday," Bunny notes, and Andrea drifts into talk about birthday parties she had as a child. "Every year, I got a new puffy dress. I didn't have brothers or sisters, so my mother would go hog wild with balloons, streamers, party hats, and an ice cream cake from Carvel. I was a happy kid," she says. "I don't know what happened."

"You liked the paper hats?" Bunny asks, and Andrea says, "Don't all kids like paper hats?"

Birds Without Feathers

ONE BY ONE, AROUND THE table, they all get the fish eye. Andrea suspects something is up. "What?" Josh asks. "Are you waiting for us to sing Happy Birthday to you?"

"Yeah, right," Andrea snorts. "That's just what I want." Then, as if that might actually happen, she looks hard at Howie and warns him, "Don't you dare." Howie is the only one of them capable of singing Happy Birthday.

When they finish eating, Josh announces that he has a friend coming and goes to wait for him by the door. Chaz goes to the refrigerator to get the Pepperidge Farm cake. Bunny excuses herself to go to the bathroom, and Teacher says that he has to make a phone call. "But stay here, okay?" he tells Andrea. "Don't go anywhere," and Andrea asks, "Where would I go?"

Howie, seated directly across from her, is grinning like an imbecile.

"Do me a favor," Andrea says. "Lose the smile."

"But it's your birthday."

"Exactly."

From the four corners of the dining room, Bunny, Josh, Chaz

and Teacher converge around the table. With varying degrees of enthusiasm and volume, they all wish Andrea happy birthday, and Andrea says, "I don't believe this."

Josh says that denial, refusing to believe, is the first stage of grief.

"But she's not grieving." Howie is confused. "She's happy."

"Howie," Josh says, "do you know where you are?"

As if he were dealing cards, Josh distributes the paper plates, and Jeanette asks, "Has anyone seen Nina?" Chaz slices the Pepperidge Farm with a plastic knife, taking care not to get crumbs on the gifts wrapped in paper without tape or the origami hats, which are folded in the same way as hats made from newspaper, except these hats are made from wrapping paper, yellow with red polka dots. The bold colors are almost too much amid the drab shades of beige.

Howie tells Andrea that Evan made the paper hats, and Bunny wants to know, "Who's Evan?"

Teacher raises his hand.

Andrea is about to open her birthday card when Nina arrives. Instead, without taking her eyes off Nina, Andrea puts the card down on the table. Except for the many bits of dried blood on her head that glisten beneath the thick coat of an antibacterial ointment, Nina is bald.

"Oh, baby," Jeanette wails. "What have you done?"

As if Jeanette's question were not rhetorical, as if it weren't all too obvious what she's done, Nina says, "I yanked out my hair." And as if yanking out her hair were an excellent reason to be inordinately proud, she adds, "All of it. Every last strand."

"But *why*?" Jeanette asks. "*Why* would you do such a thing?"

Why? Because the impulses of mania fly like bats at night, that's why.

Nina takes no notice of the pizza or the cake, but she zeros in on the paper hats. "Party hats! I love party hats." Nina takes a paper hat for herself. The antibacterial ointment that coats her head oozes through the yellow and red paper, and Bunny flees the table.

Who to Blame?

IT TAKES TWO CUPS OF water and a fat wad of tissues before Bunny can tell Ella that she is sorry. "I'm sorry. I'm sorry," she says. "I'm so sorry."

"Sorry about what, hon?" Ella asks, which is all it takes for Bunny to fall apart again. Ella fills the Dixie cup for the third time, and she waits for Bunny to pull herself together well enough to articulate the reason for her apology. If there is a reason, which isn't a given. Ella is all too familiar with the Depressives apologizing for what boils down to being alive.

Between sips of water and gasps for air, Bunny explains how she'd seen Nina hiding in the big armchair, how she watched Nina twirl her hair around her finger, how she did nothing but walk away. "I thought she wanted to be alone," Bunny says. "It's my fault."

"Hon, you mustn't think like that. You're not the least bit responsible."

"Yes, I am, because I just lied to you. I didn't care if she wanted to be alone or not. *I* wanted to be alone."

"Come on, hon. Do you really believe that if you'd sat with her she wouldn't have done what she did?"

Bunny knows that had she not left Nina alone this morning, Nina would not have yanked out every hair on her head. If Bunny had gone and sat with her, Nina would've had to wait until after lunch to yank out every hair on her head. But what you know and what you believe don't always squarely align, and Bunny believes it is her fault; a belief revealed in a sound Bunny emits; not loud, but unholy, and with her back to the wall, she slides to the floor where she sits like a rag doll. "Please," she pleads. "I want to go home. Please. I don't want to be here." She pounds her fist on her thigh. "Please."

Ella kneels down and takes hold of Bunny's hand. "Come on, hon," and in slow motion, she rises, easing Bunny up alongside her. Then, Ella puts the box of tissues in front of Bunny. Sick to death of being told to blow her nose, Bunny wipes her nose on the sleeve of her sweater, while Ella taps a pill from a vial into the cup of her hand. "Here you go, hon," she says. "This will help you sleep. You need to sleep."

"I don't want to sleep," Bunny tells her.

"Yes, you do."

"You don't know what I want."

"Tell me, then." Ella is kind, her voice caring. "What do you want?"

Bunny's eyes narrow in anger. "What I want," she snaps, "I want you to erase Dog Therapy from that fucking Activities Board. There is no fucking dog."

The Gift of a Sandwich

BUNNY'S HEAD IS TOO HEAVY and it hurts.

"Trazodone," Andrea says. "That Trazodone knocked the crap out of you. That shit is no good. I keep telling them. Trazodone is no good."

"I don't know," Teacher disagrees. "I do okay with Trazodone. But forget Seroquel. Seroquel turns me into a zombie."

"If Trazodone works better for you than Seroquel, then you are the exception. But for everyone else, Trazodone is the worst. I keep telling them. No matter what, I *am* a nurse. They shouldn't blow off what I tell them, but do they listen?"

"No," Josh says. "They don't listen. No one listens," and Bunny lets her head drop to rest on the tabletop. Drifting from consciousness, she hears Andrea say, "They hand that shit out like gumdrops, but they give me grief over codeine. Codeine. Big fucking deal."

"Aren't you forgetting something?" Chaz asks.

"Big fucking deal to that, too. Who hasn't tried suicide?"

"I tried," Howie says. "I almost did it. I would've done it."

"We know. Pam saved your life," Andrea says. "You can shut the fuck up now."

No matter that Bunny cannot stay awake. To go to her room to sleep is *Not Allowed*. Like a boxer in the ring having taken one punch too many to the head, she wobbles and weaves her way to the living room, where she drops into the big armchair. Too tired to notice the strands of Nina's hair that cling to the nubby upholstery, Bunny falls into a deep and troubled sleep. She dreams of harsh fragments of light stabbing the soft darkness, and that her brain is a steel ball rolling loose in her skull; the visual depictions of a violent headache.

Who knows for how long she slept, but she wakes to find Josh sitting in the chair across from her. He is reading *The Atlantic* from fourteen months ago. "You missed lunch," he says.

Bunny sits upright and wants to know, "What time is it?"

"I don't know," he says. "I saved you a sandwich. Peanut butter." He holds out the gift of a sandwich for Bunny to take, and he apologizes that the bread is going stale.

She puts the sandwich on the seat of the chair next to hers. "You're a good person," she tells Josh. "You don't deserve this."

"None of us deserve this," Josh says, but Bunny disagrees. "I do. I don't know what I did, but I must've done something terrible. People don't like me."

"I like you," Josh says, not in a coy or flirtatious way, just as a simple matter of fact, which fills her with gratitude; gratitude which escapes without warning, without so much as a catch in her voice, in a rush of tears spilling over, as if Bunny were a fountain and the flow were perpetual. He aches to touch her, to comfort her, as he aches, as all of them ache, to be comforted, but even if it were *Allowed*, he'd be afraid. He imagines that to hug her would be like what happens when a man dying of starvation eats, when he eats too much and his stomach explodes. Still, to die from too much food is far nicer than to die from no food, not so much as a bite of a plum. He watches Bunny cry. He wishes she would eat the peanut butter sandwich.

It's often genetic, this disposition of melancholy. In the winter months, Josh would come home from basketball practice after school to find his mother sitting in the living room, in the dark. He'd turn on a lamp. One lamp in a dark room casts the saddest glow, and Josh would kiss his mother on the cheek. Always, she was listless. Always, she said, "You're a good boy." Always, he made supper. Supper, she called it. Not dinner. Supper. Canned soup with crackers and cheese; spaghetti; scrambled eggs, and together they ate the supper that he prepared. After supper, he would go to his room and cry. The dog he had as a boy used to lick his face dry. If there were a dog here, the dog would lick Bunny's face dry, too. Then, the dog would eat the peanut butter sandwich that is sitting on the chair.

But, *there is no dog.*

"Andrea is right about the Trazodone," Josh says. "You should tell Ella not to give you Trazodone again."

Bunny nods, and then she asks, "Does it scare you?"

Josh isn't sure what Bunny means by "it," which "it" scares

him, but whichever it is, it doesn't make much difference. "Yes," he says.

He picks up the peanut butter sandwich and holds it out to Bunny. "You have to eat something."

Bunny accepts the sandwich, but instead of taking a bite, she tears off a piece of crust, which she studies like she suspects there is something off with it. Mold or poison. When she is more or less satisfied that it is safe to eat, she pushes the crust of bread into her mouth, as if her mouth were already full.

Things Worth Knowing

THEY ARE LATE TO DINNER, but they are in no hurry to get there. Bunny is glad that she can't see Josh's face because they are walking side by side, and because of how tall he is. She doesn't want to see his face when she says, "Before, when I asked if you were scared, I was talking about ECT. Are you scared something might go wrong?"

Josh admits that initially he was scared. "For the first few rounds," he says. "But not anymore. Why?" he asks. "Are you thinking about it?"

"No," Bunny tells him. "No. I'm trying to think about nothing."

When they get to their table, Andrea stands up to show off her new yellow T-shirt. Running her hands down the front of it, as if stroking the embossed cat, she says, "You guys are too much."

Teacher says, "Yeah, it was a big night."

The quiet that follows is the unspoken "elephant in the room," although to associate Nina with an elephant, regardless of context, is always going to be wildly inaccurate.

"The worst part was how happy she was," Chaz notes, and then after a pause, he says, "Or maybe that was the best part." Nina was elated by her self-desecration. While it wasn't quite doing away with herself, it was doing away with a part of herself. With each success comes confidence.

Jeanette pushes away her plate. "I can't eat," she says. "They took her. My baby." Jeanette wipes her nose with a napkin. "My Nina. They took her to a hospital in Boston. To some specialist."

"McLean's," Josh says, and then, as if he thinks an explanation is warranted, he adds, "I went to law school near there."

Josh is a lawyer? How odd. Not odd that he *is* a lawyer, but odd that, until this minute, Bunny knew no such thing about him. At a party, you could clock it: from the moment of introduction to the moment of having heard all of it—that he is a lawyer, what kind of law he practices, where he went to law school, and if he graduated in the top of his class—would come in at under forty seconds. Yet, how is it that, after how many weeks of being something like bunkmates going through loony-tunes boot camp together, she knows next to nothing of the practical matters of Josh's life beyond what happens here? How did it never occur to her that he *has* a life beyond here, just as he knows next to nothing of her life beyond the dark despair of it? Why don't they engage in polite cocktail party conversation? Perhaps uncover shared interests or friends in common? Could it be because, what difference could any of it make? Could it be that *this*, only this, that they are here, is all anyone needs to know about any of them?

Prompt: The Fruits of Labor (300 words or less)

It was summer, night, and there was a ripe cantaloupe in the refrigerator. I was sprawled on the couch, probably watching television because, as if there were lead and not blood in my veins, I was too tired to hold open a book. Too tired for no reason other than seasonal sloth. The couch, although shabby, was not yet in shreds because the cat we had then, Angela, our little angel, used her scratching post unlike Jeffery, the cat we have now—no genius, he—who uses the couch to sharpen his claws, which is why the couch is in tatters. Why Jeffrey thinks it necessary to sharpen his claws is beyond me. It's not as if he uses them for anything, although now that I think of it, Angela's claws served her no purpose either.

Because I couldn't rally so much as to get myself up from the couch, I asked Albie if he would cut the cantaloupe, would he bring me a slice. "On a plate," I had to say. He said, "Sure," and to my surprise, just like that, he got up from the chair and went to the kitchen. My surprise stemmed from the fact that he did not say, "Sure. Give me a minute." Because it is something like a near-death experience for Albie to

put aside whatever is engaging him, as if so much
as a moment's interruption would be the point of no
return, you could be pretty sure that "a minute" would
be well longer than sixty seconds. Moreover, Albie is a
master procrastinator. For example, when we moved
into our first apartment together, the bedroom was in
dire need of a fresh coat of paint, but Albie told me not
to bother hiring someone. "I'll do it," he said.

"When?" I asked, and Albie said, "Soon."

Need I mention that when we moved out of that apartment, nearly three years later, the bedroom had yet
to be painted? But most emblematic of Albie's gift for
putting off what can be done now until forever and his
impenetrable focus on the task at hand was when I had
the flu, what might've been, according to me, the most
extreme case of the flu in recorded flu history. My head
clanged, my bones chattered like teeth, and my nasal
cavity, now hermetically sealed, allowed for not so much
as a molecule of air in or out. Dragging myself from my
sickbed, where I'd been listening to the cold November
rain drumming at the window, I found Albie at the
kitchen table preparing transparencies for a lecture on
the evolutionary adaptations of marine mammals that
regularly inhabit the Arctic Ocean, about which he'd
have been more than happy to answer any questions,
but I had, at that moment, only one question: Would he
go to the store to get me some NyQuil.

"Sure," he said. "Give me a minute."

Ten minutes later, I asked again, and again he said, "Sure. In a minute," and it went on this way until it was all too clear that "in a minute" was all too likely to be sometime tomorrow.

It took tremendous effort, but I got myself dressed, and when I passed by the kitchen on my way out, Albie looked up and asked, "Where are you going?"

"To Rite Aid," I told him, "to get NyQuil."

He nodded, as if this were all news to him, and then he asked if I would pick up a quart of milk. "I think we're about out," which should suffice to explain the shock of it when, on that summer night, right then, as soon as I'd asked, he got up and went off to the kitchen to slice the cantaloupe.

Some minutes went by, too many minutes given the task at hand. I went to investigate. Albie was standing at the kitchen counter with the cantaloupe, which he had not cut in half and then half again. Rather, he had pared the rind from the melon the way you would pare an apple or peel a grape. Like a grape stripped of its skin, the flesh of the melon without its rind was wet and slippery, but a grape you pop into your mouth whole and that's that. Not so with a cantaloupe. With one finger pressed firmly at the top, as if it were a globe set to spin, Albie kept the cantaloupe still, in place, while he contemplated how to remove the seeds from the core of a vulnerable melon.

Preferred Words

DR. GROSSMAN'S HANDS REST ON Bunny's file folder, and he says, "I'd like us all to go over everything together." At the conference table, he and Dr. Fitzgerald are sitting directly opposite Bunny and Albie. "Bunny," he asks, "are you comfortable having this discussion?"

In a whisper that is bracketed with whimpering, Bunny says, "I'm okay."

Sounding exactly like a high school principal informing a parent that their fuck-up kid got busted smoking weed in the bathroom, Dr. Fitzgerald tells Albie, "You're aware that your wife has refused medication."

"Medication is off the table for now," Dr. Grossman says.

Dr. Fitzgerald says she is well aware that medication is off the table for now, which could lead you to wonder why she brought it up in the first place.

"For now," Dr. Grossman says, "Bunny has agreed to electroconvulsive therapy," and Dr. Fitzgerald echoes, "Electroshock therapy," which is not a precise echo, but it amounts to the same thing. Convulsive is the preferred word. Preferred words are not necessarily better words. If anything, the preferred word, however synonymous, can obfuscate rather than clarify. It's the same truth swaddled in cotton, like how the preferred term for manic-depressive disorder is now bipolar disorder, which sounds like an Arctic expedition as opposed to someone gleefully pulling her hair out of her head. Although why electro*convulsive* is preferred to electro*shock* is anyone's guess. Both bring to mind images of mad doctors and the industrial revolution; the next step in medical science after bloodletting. But Dr. Grossman explains electroconvulsive therapy in a way appropriate to the twenty-first century. "Think of it like rebooting a computer. We perform the procedure under general anesthesia. The patient feels no discomfort."

In response to Albie's question about the side effects, Dr. Grossman concedes that some patients experience temporary short-term memory loss, but memory loss resulting from ECT does not compound the memory loss resulting from her depression. Memory loss resulting from depression is depression dependent. It's more like forgetfulness that results from preoccupation, the depression being the preoccupation. All studies indicate that within six months, short-term memory loss is statistically nil. But Dr. Grossman does have to admit that the rate of success isn't precise, in part because it can't be quantified like blood pressure or tumor size. "But in cases of depressive melancholia with acute suicidal ideation," he says, "my experience is that there is a dramatic improvement with the treatment."

The way an echo reverberates from a distance, Albie repeats

the doctor's words, "Acute suicidal ideation?" It is unclear if Albie wants to console his wife, or is he expecting her to console him. Either way, Bunny just sits there, as if she were no more alive than an icicle before a thaw.

"Bunny," Dr. Grossman's voice has the effect of a hypnotist's snap of the fingers. "Bunny, you have to pay attention, okay?"

Dr. Fitzgerald, however, seems not to be paying attention. She is doodling, three-dimensional cubes and stick figures and flowers that might be tulips, in the margins of her notepad.

Dr. Grossman is skeptical of reports claiming full recovery after a single treatment. "Twelve treatments is the usual course, three times a week for four weeks, but sometimes more are needed. Up to thirty-six."

Before treatment can begin, should treatment begin, Bunny will need to undergo a thorough physical examination. Then, she'll have to wait until there is an opening in the schedule. "A few days at most," Dr. Grossman says, and from the breast pocket of his white coat he takes a ballpoint pen, which he clicks open before passing it to Bunny along with the consent form.

Despite that a person locked up in the psycho ward can't leave until discharged by the doctors, that same person, apparently, is sufficiently *compos mentis* to agree to electroconvulsive therapy, in writing.

"Are you sure this is what you want do?" Albie asks, and Bunny asks, "What choice do I have?"

"Abilify," Dr. Fitzgerald pipes in. "Abilify and Paxil," and Bunny considers the possibility that Dr. Fitzgerald *is* concerned for her welfare; perhaps she knows that ECT is neither as effective nor as benign as Dr. Grossman contends. Wouldn't that be something? It would be something, but it's not. The expression on Dr. Fitzgerald's face says it all: she has no respect for people like Bunny; the emotionally fragile, the psychically damaged—they might as well be fat, sexless, and dull.

And Bunny asks, "What's the date today?"

The Idea Stage

IN THE HOURS BEFORE CREATIVE Writing is
set to begin, Bunny sits on the bench across from the Activities Board, where she pretends she is there to plan out her week,
to commit her plans to paper. Her legal pad is open to where
she'd left off last night. In the margin, she'd made a note: *more
Stella*, which now she crosses out. She manages to write most of
a paragraph before Howie interrupts her. "Mind if I join you?"
he asks.

"Would it matter if I said yes? Yes, I do mind?"

"Good one," Howie says.

Bunny begrudgingly admires Howie's masterful deflection of
rejection, his imperviousness to insults. A survival skill, he's like
that animal—Bunny can't remember which one, but she can
vaguely picture it—the one that plays dead to fool carnivores
who prefer to kill their dinner themselves.

"I've been working on my novel a lot," he tells Bunny.

"How's that going?" Bunny asks, as if she didn't know.

Other than Group Therapy sessions, which Howie attends
with the regularity and solemnity of novitiate, he never skips

Group Sing-along or Creative Writing. Howie hasn't actually done any writing, but in Creative Writing, he talks a lot about his novel, the one set in "a place like this." Howie's novel is still in the "idea stage." He is incapable of transferring his thoughts to paper, which is why he whines to Bunny about how the Creative Writing prompts do exactly the opposite of what they are supposed to do. According to the Creative Writing social worker, who isn't really a social worker, but an MFA student from NYU, the prompts are designed to stimulate the creative process, but Howie claims that the prompts are too vague. "A shoebox. Who could be inspired by a shoebox? A shoebox isn't creative. Who thinks a shoebox is creative?"

"Depends what's in it," Bunny says, which seems to stun Howie, as if he'd been slapped for no reason. He sits there sulking until he can no longer bear the quiet between them. "I'm still thinking it through," he says. "A novel takes time."

"So I've heard," Bunny says. Then, she suggests to Howie that he write about Pam. "About your fateful night. That'd be a good story."

As if inspiration has propelled him to his feet, Howie pops up and asks, "Can I borrow some paper? Just a couple of pages."

Bunny tears away eight or ten sheets of paper from the back of the pad, which she gives to Howie along with her pen. He takes off for the living room. Bunny, yet again, finds herself staring up at the Activities Board when that new nurse, the one with a small tattoo of a butterfly on her neck, happens down the corridor. She stops and says to Bunny, "How about Yoga?"

Her Foot Jumps

BUNNY IS ON HER SECOND cup of coffee when that aide who took her shoes comes to escort her downstairs.

"Downstairs where?" Bunny asks, "For what?"

Patricia—Bunny remembers her name—Patricia folds her arms and taps her foot. Because she is wearing sneakers for shoes, the tapping makes more of a patting sound; aggression that whispers forces Bunny to strain to take it in.

The ninth floor, the psych ward, has its own private elevator, which is, metaphorically speaking, no different than hiding the crazy people in the attic.

There is no gift shop on the ninth floor.

The elevator stops on the seventh floor, where Bunny follows Patricia out and then through a frosted glass door, which opens onto a deserted waiting room. Patricia points to one of the avocado-green pleather armchairs and tells Bunny to sit down. "Don't move," she says, and in the lackadaisical way that people walk when they have no destination in mind, Patricia moseys on over to the reception desk.

Bunny takes a magazine from the coffee table. *People* magazine; not a current issue, but a recent one. She doesn't read the magazine. She doesn't even glance at the pictures, but she turns the pages by rote, as if turning the pages were muscle memory, something she does, although she doesn't know why. When she gets to the end of the magazine, she starts again at the beginning, but she doesn't get very far into it before Patricia is back. "We got to wait." Patricia drops into a chair seemingly exhausted, as if she could not mosey one more step.

"Wait for what?" Bunny asks, but Patricia doesn't bother to answer.

What Bunny wants, right now, wants more than anything, is to keep from crying. A box of tissues is nowhere in sight, and unlike everyone else who works on the psych ward, Patricia does not carry a packet of tissues in her pocket. Bunny tears a page from the *People* magazine and blows her nose into Jennifer Aniston's hair. Because a trash can is nowhere in sight, she crumples the glossy page into a ball and holds it in her fist.

After about a half hour, Bunny's name is called, and Patricia says, "You make sure you come back here when you're done."

Bunny lets go of the crumpled magazine page of snot, and it falls at Patricia's feet.

The first stop is a closet-sized room where a technician ties a tourniquet around Bunny's arm. "You'll feel a pinch," she says, "but that's all."

As Bunny watches her blood run through the tubing and into the vial, she ideates: the bathtub, the warm water, and the vodka and cigarettes and the box-cutter and her blood draining out and her skin growing pale and how safe it seems until Jeffery comes in and ruins everything, which is the same moment when the technician says, "All done," and she puts a Band-Aid over the puncture wound.

The examining room is unremarkable. There's the black padded examining table covered with a fresh sheet of white paper, a black and steel scale for measuring weight and height, and a stainless steel sink. Only the medicine cabinet is dissimilar. Contrary to the medicine cabinets otherwise found in doctor's offices, this medicine cabinet is without scissors, syringes, and stockpiled free samples from pharmaceutical salesmen. Other than a dusty box of gauze pads and a roll of adhesive tape, this cabinet is empty.

Presumably, this doctor is an intern or a resident. He's too young to deliver bad news. However, the computer on his desk is old, very old, pre-wireless. The cables are twisted and tangled, and the keyboard has yellowed. "Please, have a seat." He gestures to the chair set perpendicular to his chair. It is a friendly arrangement. He tells Bunny his name, which she promptly forgets. Then, he asks how she is feeling. Because his smile is kind, and surely he didn't mean to ask a stupid question, Bunny says, "Okay, I guess. You know, considering."

"Right, considering." Then, as if he were asking her to do something like dance, he says, "Let's step on the scale, shall we?"

He fiddles with the weights until the scale balances. "You could stand to put on a few pounds," the boy doctor says. "If I prescribed a daily protein shake, would you drink it?"

"I don't know," Bunny says. "What does it taste like?"

"Chalk." He's honest. "It tastes like chalk. Forget I mentioned it."

Bunny is five feet and four and a half inches tall. Only in this way, has she not diminished.

With her legs dangling over the side of the examination table, Bunny shifts to get comfortable. The white paper crinkles. The doctor wraps the blood pressure cuff around her arm, and Bunny says, "They did this already this morning. My temperature, too."

He nods. He knows. He says, "They don't tell me anything," and he squeezes the pump. The cuff inflates. "One-ten over seventy," he says. "Gorgeous. Your pressure is gorgeous," and almost demurely Bunny says, "Thank you," as if to be complimented on her blood pressure were the same as being complimented on her eyelashes. Next, he listens to her heart and her lungs. With a flashlight specifically designed for the purpose, he looks in her ears. He asks her to follow his finger with her eyes to the limit of her peripheral vision. Then, he taps her knee with a rubber hammer, and her foot jumps.

"Other than being shy of your ideal weight, you'll be happy to know that you're in excellent health," the doctor says, and Bunny says, "Not really."

Thirst

WITH A KEEN EYE FIXED on the door where the guard is posted, Bunny waits for Josh to get back from Treatment. She massages her fingers and her left foot jiggles on its own accord. Teacher, too, is at Treatment. Andrea and Jeanette are at Beauty getting their hair curled. Jeanette is getting her eyebrows tweezed, as well. Of all the people here, Josh is the only one whom Bunny could imagine having as a friend in normal life. But she knows that the people here are like the people you meet on vacation, people you meet when your life, your life as you know it, is on hold. They are people for whom there is no place in your life once you get home. They simply don't fit.

When the door opens, she stands on her tiptoes, like she is about to wave. Except she doesn't wave because it is Teacher who comes in. Not Josh, and her letdown goes as deep as if Josh were never coming back.

In his mad dash to the kitchen sink, Teacher doesn't notice Bunny standing near to him. He fills a cup with water, and he guzzles it. Then another, and then one more. Bunny has observed that everyone returns from ECT hysterically thirsty, as if they were as desiccated as a resurrection plant, one like rose of Jericho or liverwort. It's not the electro-treatment that causes dry mouth. It's the dry flow of oxygen administered by the anesthesiologist that does it. Plus nothing to eat or drink after midnight the night before. Now that he is sufficiently hydrated, Teacher asks Bunny if she wants to hang out until lunch.

In the living room, three Anorexics are fixated on the television where a man wearing a chef's hat is teaching Kathie Lee Gifford how to poach salmon.

One thing Bunny appreciates about her fellow campers is they rarely tell you to stop crying. They know that if you could stop crying, you *would* stop crying. The point is—you can't. Teacher waits, and soon enough Bunny stops, and what would appear to be out of nowhere, she says, "Electroshock." As if the word has no meaning, she says, "Electroshock," as if instead of "electroshock," she'd said "mailbox."

"Convulsive," Teacher corrects her. Then he says, "I don't like salmon. I like other fish. But not salmon."

"I start tomorrow," Bunny tells him, and he asks, "Start what?"

But before she can respond Andrea and Jeanette are back from Beauty. Andrea flips her hair to show how it bounces like hair in a shampoo commercial, which it does, but without the healthy shine. Jeanette looks like she is wearing a bathing cap of tight curls. They both hold their hands out, bent at the wrists the way a dog holds its paws when begging for a biscuit. Jeanette's fingernails are painted pearly pink. Andrea's are fuchsia. They chide Bunny for not going to Beauty. But for Bunny, vanity has gone the way of dignity, and there is no dignity to be had in the psycho ward.

No vanity, no dignity; only something like unquenchable thirst.

Today is Monday, Maybe

IF THE DAYS ARE DELINEATED by breakfast, lunch and dinner, what's to distinguish one day from another? Is today Wednesday or Thursday? Is it the twenty-third of January? Or the twelfth? Or the seventeenth? Who knows? Who cares?

Except today, Bunny knows, is January twenty-first, and she's been here for nineteen days. Dinner on January twenty-first is roast chicken, mashed potatoes, string beans or a peanut butter and jelly sandwich, which, for reasons unexplored, Josh, as of late, has been referring to as a jelly and peanut butter sandwich. Bunny uses a spoon to fold the string beans into the mashed potatoes, which is the only way to make the string beans palatable. Then she puts down her spoon and asks Josh, "Does it hurt?" Because she realizes that *everything* hurts, she clarifies, "The ECT. Does it hurt?"

Josh says no, that you're under anesthesia, you don't feel a thing, but Howie says, "Yeah? And what about that guy who woke up in the middle of it? I heard you could hear him screaming from three blocks away."

"That never happened," Chaz says. "That's just one of those

stories. Like the one about the people who took a little dog home from Mexico, and it turned out to be a rat."

Although she'd rather be telling only Josh, she nonetheless announces, "I start tomorrow. January twenty-second."

"Today is the twenty-second?" Jeanette asks.

"No," Bunny says. "The twenty-second is tomorrow," and, although it makes not a lick of difference to her either way, Jeanette says, "That's a relief."

"Start what?" Howie wants to know. "Start what?" he persists.

"ECT," Bunny snaps. "I start ECT. Are you happy now?"

Howie raises his paper cup of apple juice to make a toast, and Andrea says, "Put that down. She's going for ECT. She's not getting married."

"Did they tell you which doctor you're getting?" Jeanette asks.

It's *Not Allowed*, but no one other than Bunny knows that Josh has his hand on her knee, and he gives it a squeeze.

"I'd kill for ECT," Andrea says. "General anesthesia is so fucking nice. If I could figure out how to put myself under, that'd be my drug of choice."

Bunny nods. "Dr. Tilden."

Dr. Tilden is Josh's ECT doctor, too. Josh tells her that Dr. Tilden is very peculiar, which is something significant considering where they are.

"Peculiar?" Andrea says. "The guy's a freak. But," she adds, "he is the big-deal expert, the one who trains the residents."

Teacher and Jeanette have Dr. Futterman. Chaz says, "I got the black guy. He's okay. You should ask for the black guy."

"Tilden's like those space aliens," Andrea says, "from that movie, the one where the aliens look human, but something's off."

Howie wants to know which movie that is. Chaz remembers the movie but not the name of it, and Teacher, having given up on the plastic knife and fork, picks up the chicken breast with his hands, and eats it as if it were corn on the cob.

Sins of Omission

ALBIE DOESN'T LIKE TO COME to her empty-handed. He needs her to know that he loves her, and puts a pack of two legal pads on the table. Instead of the usual yellow, this paper is pink. Also, he's brought her six chocolate bars and another box of pens. Pens have a way of disappearing no matter where you are. The jar of Nutella, he tells her, is from Jeffrey. "Jeffrey misses you," Albie says. "We all miss you."

"I miss you and Jeffrey, too," Bunny says, and without a pause, nothing to indicate so much as the start of a new sentence, never mind a new thought, she adds, "Tomorrow."

"What about tomorrow?" he asks.

"Tomorrow," she starts to tell Albie that tomorrow morning, before breakfast, she will undergo her first round of ECT. And then, just like that, she decides not to tell him.

To assume that she doesn't want to worry him is a possible explanation, the generous interpretation, but it's also possible that she fears, not that he will no longer love her, but that he will no longer love her as he once did, that he will forever see only the fault line where she cracked, now held together with Krazy Glue. Instead, she says, "I know."

"You know?" Albie's voice is light, almost teasing. "What do you know?"

And Bunny says, "I know about Muriel."

Albie has never flat-out lied to her before, never bold-face lied to her, and he isn't about to bold-face lie to her now. He needs to explain to her that, counterintuitive as it might sound, when he is fed up and tired and at his wit's end, a respite with cool, no-nonsense Muriel releases his frustration and refuels his patience. Muriel reminds him why he loves Bunny; Bunny with all her surprises of unpredictable intensity and cuckoo rationality. "I'm sorry," he says. "I love you. I really love you." But before he can say any more about it, Bunny says, "It's okay. I understand. I really do," which serves as further proof that as fond of Muriel as he is, and Albie *is* fond of her, very fond, he could never love Muriel the way he loves Bunny, and Muriel could never love him the way Bunny does. "I don't want to talk about it," she says.

Bunny and Albie both know that confession isn't necessarily the truth, and omission, opting not to tell, isn't necessarily a lie. *Why* Albie doesn't tell Bunny that, when visiting hours are over, he is going to see Muriel, to have a drink, maybe or maybe not take her to bed, should be obvious. *Why* Bunny chooses not to tell Albie that, first thing in the morning, she'll be undergoing her first electroconvulsive therapy treatment, *that* could've done with a few words of explanation, but she says only, "I'm tired."

She closes her eyes as if her eyelids were too heavy to keep open, and Albie kisses one, and then the other. "Go to sleep," he says. "I'll see you tomorrow. If you want, we can talk more then."

"Maybe," Bunny says, "I'll see you tomorrow. Maybe."

Snacking

INSTEAD OF A GAME SHOW, everyone is watching a repeat of *Law and Order* except for Chaz who has turned his chair around, his back to the screen. Lennie Briscoe and Ray, the handsome Hispanic detective, parked in their unmarked cop car, are drinking coffee when their suspect emerges from a building. If it were a different night, Bunny would've sat down and watched *Law and Order*. But it isn't a different night. It is this night, and this night will be followed by tomorrow, and Bunny is scared.

The dining room is empty except for two aides setting out the evening snack. Orange cheese sandwiches on plastic trays along with bunches of pale green grapes. Bunny sits at the table partially eclipsed by a column where she tries to focus on what *has* happened to her, but not what *will* happen to her. But, as we all know, it's impossible *not* to think about something you're thinking about. Relief is found only in distraction, and distraction, relief, comes in the form of Josh. He pulls out a chair, but before he sits down, he asks, "It is okay? If I join you?" The same as always, Josh is dressed in gray sweat pants and another worn-thin Yale T-shirt—this one sports a bulldog, faded over time and many washings. Without shoelaces, the tongues of his black Converse high-tops flop out, like the tongue of the bulldog on his T-shirt, panting. Perhaps Josh was on the basketball team in college. He is narrow and tall enough for that. He takes one of the sandwiches from the tray, and Bunny says, "You want to hear something funny?"

Josh lifts the top slice of bread as if he were expecting to find something other than the orange cheese inside. Maybe a slice of pickle, and Bunny tells him about the note she got from the Creative Writing therapist in response to her last prompt. *You are not without talent*, he wrote. *You should think about becoming a writer.*

It could be the disappointment, the hope for the pickle slice dashed, or simply a lack of appetite; whichever, Josh returns the sandwich to the tray and says, "The guy's not a therapist. He's an MFA student from NYU."

"I know, but still, it's funny." As a therapist, the MFA student from NYU has pretty much the same credentials as a do-gooder dog, although the MFA student is, if nothing else, reliable, whereas the dog has yet to show up. Still, Bunny is certain that the dog would possess the greater sensitivity of the two. "Because I used to be a writer," Bunny says.

Josh nods his head, and he tells her, "I know. I'm a fan. Of your books." Then, as if to cover his tracks, as if to deny the fact that the sandwich has been touched, he adjusts its position among the other sandwiches. "I'm sorry. Fan probably isn't the right word." Already, Josh has had twelve treatments of ECT, but still he droops as if he were a wax candle, a taper, melting.

"Can I ask you a question?" Bunny says. "About ECT? A personal question? Do you think it's helping? Is it doing you any good?" she asks. "Do you feel better?"

Josh pauses to consider his answer, and then he says, "Not that I can tell. No. I'd have to say no. I'd have to say no, it hasn't done a fucking thing," and Bunny eats a grape.

Rise and Shine

ALL DOLLED UP IN PRISTINE paper pajamas and a fresh pair of slipper-socks, Bunny is accompanied by an aide who leads her through a maze of hallways, where, at the end, she is handed over, like a baton in a relay race, to the nurse who is waiting for her. This nurse introduces herself. "Sondra," she says. "With an o." Sondra is short and has the body of snowman, including no neck; all o's, and Bunny thinks about how Ella, the other nurse whom she also likes, the one on the ward, is gangly thin. Not that she makes anything of it. It just is.

Bunny has no fever. Her heartbeat is strong. Her blood pressure remains gorgeous. Her pulse is a little rapid, but that's to be expected when you're nervous.

Sondra takes her hand. "There's nothing to be afraid of," Sondra tries to reassure her. "Dr. Tilden is the best there is. I've been at his side for hundreds, maybe even thousands of procedures," Sondra says. "Nothing has ever gone wrong. I wouldn't lie to you."

Sondra sounds sincere, but still Bunny says, "Everyone lies."

In a far-off kind of way, as if she's drifted into the past, and not referring to Sondra, she repeats, "Everyone lies."

As a seasoned professional as well as a sensible woman who has raised three children and survived their adolescences, Sondra knows when and when not to engage. With her clipboard in hand, she runs through the checklist: Breakfast? No. Liquids after midnight? No. Hearing aid? No. Pacemaker? No. Prosthetic devices? No. Dentures? Contact lenses? No. No. Jewelry? *Not Allowed.* "You're going to be fine," Sondra says.

"Isn't it pretty to think so?" Bunny says.

"Pretty?" she asks.

That Sondra does not recognize one of the most famous lines in all of American literature does not lessen Bunny's opinion of her. Nonetheless, she pegs Sondra as illiterate, the word coming to mind as *il-lit-er-ate*, almost like *Lo-li-ta*; almost, but nowhere near as good. Nowhere near as good is never good enough.

Sondra then sends Bunny to an adjacent bathroom to empty her bladder, an instruction that, for no reason other than that not all of her faculties are intact, Bunny cannot make sense of until Sondra clarifies, "Urinate. Pee."

What We'll Do to Get Attention

THE TREATMENT ROOM—TREATMENT, ONE more word Bunny now puts in air quotes, "treatment"— is dimly-lit, although it could be it seems dimly lit only by way of comparison to the ward where the rows of fluorescent lights cast a relentless and ghastly-yellow overglow, rendering everything, and everyone, ugly. This light is softer on the eyes, calming even, but the association Bunny makes with it is sinister, an association magnified by the contraption on the far side of what she's thinking of as the operating table, which is in fact a gurney and no different than an examining table except it's longer, wider, on wheels, and an examining table doesn't usually come with restraining cuffs. Wires, black wires like adaptor cords, dangle from the equipment. The dials look like knobs on an oven.

It's only natural that *Frankenstein* would come to mind, but Bunny, being Bunny, instead is reminded of the Milgram experiments, way more creepy and they really happened. But this isn't some gothic horror insane asylum. It's not even Bellevue, where Bunny ushered in the New Year strapped to a gurney and injected with a sedative. It's one of the top hospitals in the tri-state area with a world-renowned cardiac unit.

Bunny sits sideways on the edge of the gurney as if she were about to jump off. Sondra tells her that Dr. Tilden and Dr. Kim will be here any minute. "Dr. Kim is the anesthesiologist," Sondra explains. Then she tells Bunny to lie back. "Feet up. Rest your head here." She pats the pillow, which is no more of a pillow than the pillow on her hospital bed is a pillow, and she reiterates that there's nothing to be afraid of, that everything will be fine, and Bunny thinks, *There's everything to be afraid of.*

This thought is followed by another thought, a far more alarming thought: she is no different than Howie. A perfectly normal person pretending to be mental. Pretending to be mental to get attention. That she would undergo electroconvulsive therapy just to get attention is not necessarily something to put past her.

The need for attention can be like the need for air: *Pay Attention to Me.*

Dead center in the living room, gripping a butter knife, the tip poised at her heart, while her mother, who did not indulge nonsense, vacuumed around her feet. If she broke her leg on the high-school weekend ski trip, everyone would sign her cast. Even a broken arm would've been good, but that didn't happen, either. First love hit its high point with its end, when her friends gathered around to console her, to tell her she was too good for him. Her friends were a claque of dimwits; a thought she kept to herself because she wanted to be popular.

Like the broken coil she is, Bunny springs up on the table, and she tells Sondra, "I'm faking. I'm doing this just to get attention."

Sondra places her hand on Bunny's shoulder and gently eases her back into a prone position. It goes without saying: anyone who would go to such lengths just to get attention, that person would have to be seriously sick in the head.

If It Quacks Like a Duck

ALTHOUGH *NEW YORK MAGAZINE* DOES not include this particular specialization in their annual round-up of the "10 Best Doctors in New York," Dr. Tilden *is* tops in the field of electroconvulsive therapy which, granted, is not a crowded field, but what matters here is that as far as the psychiatric community is concerned, he is the gold standard.

Then again, the Nobel Prize was awarded to the quack who thought up the lobotomy as a quick fix.

No matter the forewarnings about Dr. Tilden, Bunny is not prepared for the man's plaid pants. Gray, navy blue, yellow plaid with a thread of lime green running through like the plaid upholstery of a couch at the Salvation Army selling for $18.99. Bunny worries that the plaid pants are bell-bottoms. Dr. Tilden's lab coat is buttoned all the way to the top button, as if it were a white shirt to be worn with a tie. A lock of chest hair peeps out like a pin curl. Bunny goes rigid at the thought that beneath his lab coat he is not wearing a shirt, and she thinks, "This quack is about to mess with my brain."

Dr. Tilden fusses with the equipment, checking that plugs are plugged in and cables are connected. He is attentive to details. That Dr. Tilden acknowledges Bunny no more than he would greet the plastic Visible Woman from Anatomy 101 is not something she should take personally. He appears equally oblivious to Sondra and Dr. Kim, who is the anesthesiologist. He's definitely got some kind of Asperger-y thing going on.

"We are now going to perform bilateral electroconvulsive therapy," he announces, as if he were addressing an imaginary group of medical students gathered around the gurney to observe the master. "Stimulating electrodes will be pasted, bilaterally, on the scalp."

For the second time in twenty minutes, Sondra slaps a blood pressure cuff around Bunny's upper arm.

Dr. Kim seems like a normal person.

Dr. Tilden says that electrode paste prevents burning. If his horizontal voice were calibrated and recorded like a heart on a monitor, he'd be pronounced dead.

Sondra rolls up the bottom of Bunny's pajama leg, and she wraps another blood pressure cuff midway between her knee and her ankle, followed by two self-adhesive electrodes she tapes to Bunny's foot, all to monitor her gorgeous blood pressure while she is under sedation.

Dr. Kim inserts a catheter, an IV line to administer the muscle relaxant and the sedative, into a prominent vein on Bunny's right hand, and she dots Bunny's breastbone with a few electrodes of her own. "And this," she says, "will monitor your blood-oxygen tension." She clips the oximeter like a clothespin to Bunny's index finger.

After planting two more electrodes, one square in the middle of her forehead and another one on her collarbone, Dr. Tilden turns to the machine and again fiddles with the dials.

Dr. Kim puts an oxygen mask over Bunny's mouth and nose.

"I want you to start at one hundred," Dr. Kim instructs, "and count backwards."

If Albie were here, Bunny would ask him, "What the fuck is blood-oxygen tension?" If Albie were here, she wouldn't be alone. But Albie isn't here, and for that she has only herself to blame.

She can't remember what comes after ninety-seven.

Bunny is sorry.

Bunny tells herself that this is not real, this can't be real.

Ninety-four, ninety-three.

Prompt: Describe a Landscape (300 words or less)

Picture it like this: you are driving your car on a narrow and lonely mountain road. A narrow and lonely mountain road that winds like ribbon. You are above the tree line. It doesn't matter what kind of car you are driving, but it definitely is not a new car. It's an old car, a shit-can of a car. The sky grows dark, but not because it's nearing the night. It's sometime between two and three in the afternoon. The sky grows dark because storm clouds are gathering, and it gets darker still. A drop of rain splats on the hood of your shit-can car. And then another drop of rain splats and then another and then more. You turn on the windshield wipers, but nothing happens. You turn the windshield wipers off and then on again, but still nothing happens. The windshield wipers don't work. The windshield wipers are broken. The rain is no longer falling in drops. The rain is falling in puddles that splash against the car windows as if pails of water are being emptied from above. There is no place to pull over. You can't see the fucking road. You put the car in park and turn off the ignition. You sit there and

watch the rain wash over the windows. You watch the
landscape, a world without definition. You listen to the
rain drumming on the roof of the car, and you think,
*People who are not easy to like, they have feelings
just like nice people do.*

A Possible Conclusion

WHEN BUNNY WAKES UP IN the recovery room, Sondra is there, standing over her. Bunny sees her as if she's in a downpour: a series of blurry o's that shimmer from lack of definition; opaque without determined features.

In all her years working as an ECT nurse, never before has Sondra had a patient wake in this way. Even more disconcerting, this copious weeping started up well before the anesthesia had begun to wear off, and creepier still, her expression was deadpan, flat, and there was no sound, and still there is no sound as she continues to weep the way blood flows from an open artery.

Later, Sondra will share this information with Dr. Tilden only because her respect for him as a skilled practitioner is absolute, and her sense of professional responsibility is firm. Otherwise, to engage in conversation with Dr. Tilden is to invite the feeling that comes when trapped in an elevator, when panic has set in but you're not quite ready to hyperventilate. She knows it's the Asperger's, but still, he gives her the willies.

Now that Bunny is conscious and able to talk, Sondra pulls up a chair alongside the gurney, and she sits in the chair as if she's not expecting to get up again any time soon. "Do you want to tell me about it?" Sondra asks.

Bunny wants to say no, but she fears that, were she to open her mouth to speak, words would not come out; instead, she would spew dark gray and black matter, something like a wet pellet of undigested rodent fur and teeth and bones. She imagines that there is nothing inside her other than the remains of a barn owl's last meal. She shakes her head, and one sob escapes. Then more.

It was Albie, of course, who had told her about owl pellets, and he had described the barn owl as a ghostly creature. Bunny has never seen a barn owl, but feels as if she, too, is a ghostly thing.

"Are you dizzy?" Sondra asks. "Or queasy? It's not unusual to come out of anesthesia feeling dizzy or slightly sick to your stomach."

Again, Bunny shakes her head.

"Are you sure you don't want to talk?" Sondra gives it another go. "You might feel better if you talk."

Bunny rolls over. Her back is to Sondra who sits in the chair by the side of the gurney where she stays until Bunny's weeping comes to a close.

Inarticulation

ALTHOUGH IT'S NOT YET TIME for lunch, Josh and Andrea, along with a smattering of the others who blew off Activities or walked out in the middle of Group Therapy, are in the dining room. They, the others, are focused on Bunny, searching for signs of well-being, for signs of life as they once knew it. Despite prior evidence to the contrary, these people cling to the hope of immediate and dramatic results, like those promised in the *before* and *after* photos for a miracle diet. Irrational expectations are not limited to mental patients.

Bunny looks like crap.

At the same moment that she takes a seat at the table, Josh, like a partner on a seesaw, stands up.

From the kitchen cabinet he retrieves the two single-serving containers of orange juice that he'd secreted away after breakfast and stashed behind the jar of Coffee-Mate. He knew that Bunny would be thirsty.

Josh apologizes because the juice isn't cold.

The glop of the electrode paste, like drying paint, is tacky to the touch and it clumps and dulls Bunny's hair. Her eyes are wept-puffy and pink, and there's a rank smell about her. Bunny doesn't care if the orange juice is cold or not. In two long gulps, she drinks all of it, which really isn't much. Those individual-size servings are individual-size for children. Rather than quench thirst, they tease it.

Josh asks if she wants a glass of water, and when he goes off to get it for her, Andrea says, "You know, you've got more than a half hour before lunch. Maybe you want to take a shower. Wash your hair." She does not add, "It'll make you feel better," because they both know it won't make her feel better. Bunny downs the glass of water that Josh has brought back for her. Then, she goes to her room.

In the bathroom, she grips the sink with both hands to hold herself steady, and she catches sight of her reflection in the aluminum rectangle fixed to the wall. The reflection that aluminum casts is hazy and inarticulate. "Inarticulate," Bunny says. Out loud, as if speaking to the image in the aluminum mirror, she says, "I am inarticulate."

To be inarticulate is to be incapable of giving effective expression to thoughts and feelings. To be inarticulate is to be incapable of pointing to where it hurts.

Bunny turns away and peels the slipper-socks from her feet. Her paper pajamas are dank from sweat and fear. She takes them off and drops them in the trash can. Then, she steps into the shower. The water is cool, but tolerable. Bunny arches her neck and lets the spray wash over her face the same as if she were looking into the rain, and again she reminds herself, *This is not a true story.*

This is fiction.

Acknowledgments

Infinite thanks: to Mark Doten—first reader, best reader and every writer's dream editor; to Joy Harris, blessed agent who had faith even when I had nothing; to everyone at Soho Press (in alphabetical order because there is no other way)— Janine Agro, Juliet Grames, Bronwen Hruska, Rachel Kowal, Paul Oliver, Steven Tran, and Alexa Wejko—who have made this the best publishing experience I ever could've hoped for; to my dear and treasured friends (in no particular order)— Lauren, Johanna, Deborah, Timothy, Nalini, Elissa, Mike, Wally, Alicia, Claire, Barbara; to William Wadsworth for seeing me through it all; and to Babs Kirshenbaum and Barry Luke Brock-Broido for being cats.